Desolation Point

By the Author

Snowbound

Desolation Point

Desolation Point

by

Cari Hunter

2013

DESOLATION POINT

ISBN 10: 1-60282-865-2
ISBN 13: 978-1-60282-865-0

This Trade Paperback Original Is Published By
Bold Strokes Books, Inc.
P.O. Box 249
Valley Falls, NY 12185

First Edition: April 2013

Credits
Editor: Cindy Cresap
Production Design: Susan Ramundo
Cover Design By Sheri (graphicartist2020@hotmail.com)

Acknowledgments

Huge thanks to Cindy for editing this one into shape. To Sheri for a beautiful cover. To Rad and BSB for encouragement and support. To Kelly (the Work Wife) for listening to my ramblings, playing Jelly Bean Roulette, and keeping me laughing at stupid o'clock. To Sue C for fielding random questions about American terminology. To all those who took a chance on a newbie and read *Snowbound*. To everyone who sent feedback and friendship requests and mittens and snax. And to Cat, for being such a bloody fantastic beta, but mainly just for putting up with me.

Dedication

For Cat

We're a matched pair, sweetheart.

CHAPTER ONE

Los Angeles

Glass crunched beneath Alex Pascal's boots as she took hesitant steps down the alley. The stink of garbage dumped and left to rot in the midsummer heat hit the back of her throat, and she clamped her mouth shut, sucking in breaths through her nose as if that made a difference.

"Jack? Anything?" She kept her question taut, too focused on her immediate surroundings to engage fully in conversation. Her radio crackled into life as her partner responded.

"No, all clear. I'm gonna double back, meet you halfway."

"Copy that."

Sweat trickled down her forehead. When she lifted her hand to wipe it away, her flashlight's beam swung crazily across the brick walls and doorways that hemmed her in and provided so many shadows for a potential ambush. She had been driving back to the station at the end of an uneventful shift when Jack spotted the twins on the opposite side of the road, brothers who were wanted for the rape and violent assault of a fifteen-year-old girl. Their victim was still in the hospital, having needed more than fifty sutures to repair the wounds inflicted upon her.

Alex brought her hands back into position, balancing one wrist on top of the other to ensure her flashlight and her gun were aimed in the same direction. She approached and then peered warily up the ladder of a rusted fire escape, but nothing moved in the darkness and no one jumped down on her. Multiple sirens wailed in the distance, closing in at speed but not quickly enough to be of any comfort to her. With her heart thumping against her breastbone, she set off walking again.

A metal can skipped out from beneath her boot and clattered across the alley. She gasped, whirling around as the unexpected noise sent rats skittering for shelter.

"Shit." She smiled ruefully and took a deep breath to try to slow her racing pulse. A second light at the far end of the alley caught her eye: Jack making his own tentative progress. She straightened her back, drawing confidence from the gun in her hand and the knowledge that she wasn't completely alone.

Determined to complete her fair share of the sweep, she angled her flashlight toward a door that hung from a broken hinge. She frowned, pushing the door with her foot. It opened too easily, the trash that had been collecting in front of it newly cleared aside. Goose bumps prickling at the nape of her neck, she reached for her radio, but a sudden swish of air made her hesitate. She turned toward the sound, barely catching a glimpse of the two-by-four before it splintered across her upper back, the force throwing her to the ground. Too stunned to cry out, she landed heavily, her gun flying from her hand, its momentum carrying it beyond her outstretched fingers and out of sight. She saw a figure move past her, grimy sneakers with frayed laces looming in her vision before disappearing just as quickly. One of the sneakers struck out to connect hard with her gut; she moaned low in her throat, pulling up her knees to protect her chest even as a hand grabbed her by her collar and dragged her through the ruined door.

"Don't—" The word left her in a rush as she was propelled forward, with no time to do anything but try to break her fall.

"Cops're fucking everywhere, Manny." The voice was that of a young male, breathless with fear but strangely laced with excitement. She could hear his feet tapping as he circled her restlessly. "We goin' down in style, then, yeah?"

"Fuckin' A, bro." The exchange gave Alex her positive identification: Manny and Tomas Alvarez, the brothers for whom the APB had been issued.

Tomas's hand patted her shirt. He pulled her radio free and launched it against the wall, where it shattered into pieces. She lay motionless, counting his steps and attempting to gauge his location. Then she twisted sharply, whipping her legs out to lock around his. She heard his startled yelp and felt his legs waver as he lost his balance. When he fell, he fell awkwardly, and landed in a crumpled heap at her side.

"Bitch!" A boot this time, smashing into her cheek. Her teeth caught her lip, filling her mouth with blood. She gagged and coughed on the thick fluid, dragging herself up onto all fours, her head lowered to stop herself from choking.

"*Alex?*" Somewhere in the alley, Jack was shouting frantically.

The beam of his flashlight cut across the room, but it was only a fleeting glimpse of rescue, extinguished completely when a hand clamped over her mouth and she was pulled farther into the building. She bit at the fingers straying carelessly close to her teeth and had the satisfaction of hearing her tormentor shriek in pain, but then his fist connected solidly with her face and her knees buckled. Sparks of light danced in her eyes, her head lolling forward as she tried and failed to hold herself up. Something long and thin lashed into the small of her back, and she realized dully as she hit the concrete that one of the brothers had taken her own nightstick to beat her with.

"Stay down."

Manny wasn't giving her a choice, his bony fingers grinding her face into the filth that coated the floor, while Tomas straddled her hips. She could feel Tomas tugging at her uniform, tearing at the straps on her Kevlar vest, and she heard him laugh wildly as he finally yanked her T-shirt halfway up her back.

"Can I? Can I?" That same tone of jumpy excitement, undoubtedly fuelled by the same liquor she could smell on Manny's breath as he gave his answer.

"Sure, li'l bro."

Cold metal pressed against the skin Tomas had exposed. Alex closed her eyes and curled her hands into fists, determined not to utter a sound as she felt the blade begin to slice smoothly into her flesh.

❖

There was a smell of cordite and clotted blood and a buzz of overlapping voices. As Alex clawed her way back to consciousness, she could still feel hands holding her in place, but it wasn't like before; this time their touch was careful and her own hand was being tightly gripped by another.

"Jack?" The word was little more than a croak, her throat sore and parched. She had been screaming—why had she been screaming? The answer was provided by an ill-advised attempt to push herself upright.

"Oh, Jesus Christ." She panted for air, the pain unanticipated and brutal.

"Whoa, lie still. Oh shit, just—please, don't try to get up." Jack's voice bore an unfamiliar edge of stress and Alex obeyed it at once, forcing herself not to struggle as she tried to cope with the agony ripping across her lower back.

"Wh…happened?"

Tomas had cut her; she knew that. She could feel blood pooling beneath her and the draft of air on raw wounds, but she had no memory of anything else that he might have done.

"You're going to be fine. They're bringing the paramedics in now."

She shook her head in frustration, which only made the throbbing in it more relentless. "Not what I asked, Jack."

He sighed and she heard him shift uncomfortably. He knew her too well to try to placate her with platitudes and half-truths. "We could hear you, but we couldn't find you, not straight away." He spoke in a monotone, and Alex recognized it as a tactic that they both relied on at times, a way of recounting events while trying not to connect with them. "Manny had a semi-auto. He took two bullets, died instantly. Tomas was pulling at you, trying to use you as a shield. He was shot in the shoulder, but he'll live. He, uh…" Jack ran his hand through his close-cropped hair. "He didn't rape you."

She let out a soft sob of relief, her shoulders beginning to shake with the effort it was taking not to fall completely apart in front of her colleagues.

"Did he…?" Her question trailed off as Jack put his hand out and touched her cheek.

"Yeah, he had enough time for that."

The young girl whom the brothers had attacked had been found with the word *BITCH* carved into her back. Tomas had signed his mutilation with his gang tag.

"Shit," Alex whispered. An unrealistic part of her wanted to grab something, *anything*, and cover herself up, cover the wounds so that no one would see them, but she knew it was already too late for that. It seemed as if half the division was crammed into the small room, and the other half would know within the hour. That was how it worked; that was how it had always worked. It had never bothered her before, but in the five years she had been on the force, nothing like this had ever happened to her. Nausea rolled over her in waves. She closed her eyes miserably and tried to shut it all out.

❖

Manchester, England

It took less than a minute for Sarah Kent's life to be smashed apart. Five seconds for the driver to succumb to the alcohol with which he had washed down his business lunch, ten for him to swerve from his own lane and into that of Sarah's family. Ten seconds of tearing metal, screaming, and the impact that hurled her violently against the side window of the car. Twenty seconds of pain, obliterating everything else in a razor-sharp barrage. Three seconds for it all to fade to black.

❖

The touch on Sarah's throat was warm but not skin-to-skin, the sensation artificial and rubbery. It pressed and held, and then jerked away suddenly.

"Bloody hell! This one's breathing. It's okay, love. It's okay. You're okay. Shit." Fainter then, as if the man had turned from her. "John, get the stretcher right up here. Spinal board, small collar. Pass me the oxygen before you go. Tell Control we have two Code One, one critical, one walking wounded. Make vehicles four."

Another man answered, his voice wavering with stress. "Okay. Make vehicles four. Will do."

"Oh-two, John."

"Yeah. Shit. Sorry."

Cold air flooded out from the mask as it was hurriedly fixed over Sarah's nose and mouth. She tried to raise a hand to loosen it, but her effort amounted to little more than a twitch of her fingers. Something pressed heavily on her chest, making it almost impossible for her to pull in a breath, and she heard a panicked cry for assistance an instant before hands reached in and hauled her from the wreckage. There was a brief lucid moment in which she recognized that she was probably going to die, and then darkness claimed her again.

❖

Overly bright strip lighting and an odd rocking motion made Sarah blink and squint in confusion. Incapable of processing complex thoughts, her mind gave precedence to the baser instincts telling her that she was cold and that every part of her hurt. She whimpered, her hands flexing against the restraints pinning them to her sides.

"Shh, try not to move, love." A man's voice that she vaguely remembered from some time earlier. "You're in the ambulance. We'll be at the hospital in just a few minutes. Can you tell me your name?"

He used a piece of gauze, already blood-soaked, to stop more blood from trickling into her eyes. She licked her lips, tasting something salty-sweet and coppery.

"Sar…" Her head ached horribly when she tried to shake it, though a hard collar and two rubber blocks prevented the movement from being anything more than a gesture. "Sarah."

"Sarah what?"

"Molly…"

"Is that your surname, love?" The paramedic's brow wrinkled in confusion, his pen poised above his clipboard. He moved toward the gurney and pulled Sarah's mask up slightly, straining to hear her.

She tried again, each word punctuated by a gasp as her breathing faltered. "In the car, my sister. My mum. They okay?"

He lowered the mask again and leaned back in his seat. He didn't give her an answer, but then he didn't need to. The bleak expression on his face told Sarah everything that she needed to know.

❖

Sarah's gurney came to an abrupt stop at the side of a hospital bed. Faces loomed above her, their expressions intent, some more overtly worried than others. Several hands fumbled in their rush to release the safety belts, and she heard the paramedic tell the medical team that he and his colleague would deal with the straps. In a voice strained by tension, he began his handover as a series of jolts raised the gurney to the level of the bed.

"This is Sarah. Twenty-five years of age. Rear seat passenger in a rollover, two-vehicle collision. Seat belt worn, air bags deployed. Main impact to the driver's side, but severe widespread damage to the car. Unconscious at scene. Rapid extrication when her resps dropped off."

He paused while a disembodied voice counted to three. Without further warning, the board to which Sarah was strapped was lifted across to the hospital bed. Even though it landed with only the slightest impact, she cried out at the pain that ricocheted through her. The paramedic resumed his handover and she tried to listen, but she only half-understood the medical terminology in the rapid-fire list of her injuries.

"Right femur's gone, left tib-fib. Reduced breath sounds on her left side. Complained of left upper abdominal tenderness. BP initially unrecordable, she's had a liter of saline and it's hovering around seventy systolic now. She's got a scalp lac that was bleeding heavily, but I couldn't find any other head injury."

She choked back a sob as someone began to cut her clothes off and a needle was slid into her arm with only the most perfunctory of warnings. The paramedic drew a blanket up to cover her and then deliberately stepped into her line of sight.

"Hey there. You're in the hospital and they're going to take really good care of you, all right?" He squeezed her hand, the one without the IV line, and she caught her breath at the pain his gesture unintentionally caused. He looked horrified and placed her hand carefully back down on the board. "Her left wrist is broken," he said quietly.

He stepped away then, toward a young nurse who didn't seem to have a role in the team and was watching the proceedings with wide eyes.

"What happened to her?" the nurse asked, eager for details. They hadn't moved far enough from the bed; even through the wail of monitors and the babble of voices, Sarah could hear their conversation.

"Drunk driver took out a car of three. Double-fatal on scene." The paramedic nodded toward Sarah. "She's a real mess."

"Damn. The drunk?"

"Busted nose, minor lacerations. Bloody typical. The bastards always seem to walk away from it. The police arrested him."

The nurse nodded and patted him sympathetically on his back. "Go get yourself a cup of tea, mate."

"Yeah. Yeah, I might just do that." After one final glance toward the bed, he pushed through the door of the trauma room. Sarah stared at the doors as they closed behind him, and then she squeezed her eyes tightly shut and did her best not to scream.

❖

"Are you sure you're okay to continue, Officer Pascal?"

Alex set the plastic cup back down on the table, all too aware that the tremor in her hand must have been noted by the detective sitting beside her.

"I'm fine." She really wasn't fine. Her lower back burned constantly, the pain exacerbated by the infection that had taken hold over the past twenty-four hours; apparently, weapon cleanliness was not something that gangbangers considered a priority. The IV antibiotics were strong enough to upset her stomach. She had gone cold turkey on the morphine in preparation for giving her statement, and—to add insult to not inconsiderable injury—the detective investigating the case looked as if she had just walked out of a fashion shoot.

The detective raised one perfectly shaped eyebrow, but finally nodded and un-clicked the pause button on the small tape recorder.

"So, just to confirm, it was Tomas Alvarez who had the knife and Manuel Alvarez, his brother, who was holding you down on the floor."

Alex gave a small nod before realizing that wouldn't be enough for the tape. "That's right. I tried to fight them, but I didn't have any strength left." She cleared her throat and reached for the water again, shame at the admission of her own weakness making her cheeks hot. "I couldn't do anything to stop them…"

❖

The door to Alex's hospital room had opened almost soundlessly, but the low whistle from her visitor was a good deal less subtle.

"Well, you look like hammered shit." Jack was standing in the doorway with his arms full of flowers. He grinned toothily and made his way to the bedside.

"Thanks, partner, I love you too." She smiled as he planted a wet kiss on her cheek.

"Still a little warm, Officer Pascal." His hand rested on her cheek and then her forehead, the pleasant coolness of his palm the only reason that she made no attempt to swat him away.

"Doc said the fever's on its way out. I actually felt like eating something earlier."

Jack set the flowers down and pulled up a chair. "I swear, you losing your appetite was like the first sign of the fucking apocalypse. I told Burke and Toledo, and they were both genuinely freaked out."

Alex laughed. "Idiot," she said without malice, her fingers tracing the edge of a petal. "These are beautiful."

"Guys had passed the hat, and I think"—he lifted the larger bouquet and pulled out a spray of roses—"these are from the paramedics who came out that night. They're glad you're doing okay."

"They didn't need to do that." She closed her eyes before they could tear up and took a breath of the sweet scent. "Tell them thanks, if you run into them."

"Of course."

"So, you coping without me?"

He gave her a look that set her off laughing. "You know they paired me with Rookie Road."

"I know." She was trying to keep a straight face, but she wasn't trying all that hard.

"He's a *rook*, Alex."

"I know."

"He eats ice cream. Constantly."

"I know." Her shoulders were shaking. "Hence the nickname."

"I hate you," he growled, not at all convincingly. "Please come back soon."

❖

Awareness returned to Sarah in a series of fractured images. Lights blinked on monitors, numbers flashing, their values never static but constantly fluctuating in response to the slightest change in her condition. Her right leg was suspended in traction, weights keeping the shattered bone in alignment. A plaster cast prevented her left ankle from moving no matter how hard she tried. Intravenous drips and blood transfusions hung in a line alongside syringes in pumps that bleeped shrilly whenever the tubing became kinked, like infants demanding attention.

Gradually, as she managed to stay awake for longer periods, she began to recognize the faces of the medical staff: nurses with singsong voices and gentle hands, doctors who peeled back her eyelids and spoke in terms too convoluted for her to understand. As soon as someone deemed her strong enough, and with a nurse standing solicitously by the cubicle door, a police officer confirmed what Sarah already remembered even through the haze of drugs, the condolences he offered, professional but utterly sincere. She nodded and thanked him politely for taking the time to visit. The nurse hovered, waiting for Sarah's inevitable breakdown, but it never came. She hurt too much to move. Crying would have been unbearable.

After another week of fading in and out, she turned her aching head to see her stepfather sitting at her bedside. Caught unawares, he dropped his gaze from her face, and then looked up a few seconds later with a relieved smile that didn't reach his eyes. Even doped up on morphine, still half-anesthetized from whatever surgery her doctors had deemed necessary the day before, Sarah had been able to decipher his initial expression. He left soon afterward, the question still unvoiced but lingering in his eyes: why had she survived, when his wife and his little girl had died?

❖

The gentle drift of oxygen from the tubing beneath Alex's nose wasn't enough to hide the scent now wafting through the room. Heady and expensive, it might have been pleasant in lesser quantities, but its wearer was more concerned with announcing her wealth than with the subtle effect that a more judicious application might have achieved. Only hours out of surgery, Alex was still nauseated from the anesthetic, and the smell was enough to tip her over the edge. She reached for the bowl that had been positioned strategically near her by the nurse who had cared for her after her first two surgeries, and had barely managed to tuck it beneath her chin before she began to vomit. Through a fresh onslaught of pain, she dimly heard an exclamation of distaste from the person at her bedside. An urgent buzzer sounded, followed by a series of sharp clacks as her visitor rapidly exited the room in a pair of designer heels. Shortly afterward came the welcome approach of someone wearing shoes that were far more appropriate. Alex nodded gratefully as gloved hands kept the bowl in place for her and then wiped her face and her mouth clean.

"Same old, same old, huh?" Ella, the nurse who always seemed to draw the short straw—the post-surgery shift—offered her a spoonful of ice chips before injecting another drug into her IV port. "Should help with the nausea."

"Thanks." Unthinking, Alex took a deep breath before she realized her mistake and had to fight not to gag again. Desperate to distract herself, she shifted slightly in the bed, wincing at the now-familiar pinch of fresh sutures in her back. "How'd they do?"

On this occasion, the skin graft had been taken from her right thigh, in the third and hopefully last stage of a painstaking process to cover up the legacy Tomas Alvarez had left her with. She would still have scars, her plastic surgeon had already warned her of that, but at least the epithet Alvarez had cut into her would no longer be legible.

With a smile, Ella gently but firmly lifted Alex's hand from where it was straying toward the dressing on her back, and placed it onto the sheets.

"They did good. Dr. Rachman was really pleased. He said he'll come by just as soon as you stop puking." She held her hands palm up in apology. "His words, not mine."

"Yeah, sounds about right." Alex crunched an ice chip between her teeth and then grinned as Ella shuddered at the noise.

"I wish you wouldn't do that."

"I wish you'd let me have a beer," Alex countered without hesitation.

Ella made a show of ignoring her. She took a quick note of the vitals displayed on the monitors and then tucked her pen into her pocket. When she dared to look back up, Alex greeted her with an expression of complete innocence. Ella shook her head in exasperation. "For the last time, Alex, I am not smuggling beer in here for you!"

"You're no fun."

"Yeah, yeah, and you're stalling."

"That obvious, huh?"

"'Fraid so, hon." She ran a hand through the unruly mess of Alex's hair, smoothing it back from her face in an attempt to make her a little more presentable. "You want me to send her in?"

"No," Alex said, "but I guess you should."

The door closed behind Ella, only to reopen seconds later. Celia Pascal stood in the doorway, her hair and makeup immaculate, her clothing unruffled by her time spent sitting in a hard plastic hospital chair. The draft from the corridor brought her familiar scent rushing back toward Alex. Clutching a fresh bowl, she swallowed hard and managed a weak smile.

"Hi, Mom."

"I came as soon as I could, darling. Your father and I were in the Mediterranean when we heard."

Alex nodded but made no reply as she watched her mother dab a handkerchief beneath eyes that were yet to actually shed a tear. She knew that Jack had contacted her parents on the night she had been assaulted, and she had been in and out of the hospital for almost a month now, yet her mother's sun-bleached hair and freshly suntanned arms strongly implied that she had chosen to finish her cruise before putting in an appearance at her daughter's bedside.

"My poor baby, what they did to you..." Loud sniffles were added to the face blotting.

Alex closed her eyes, too tired to deal with her mother's histrionics. She wondered whether another bout of vomiting would be enough to get her a reprieve, and then cursed the anti-nausea meds for having finally worked.

She let her breath out between her teeth. "I'm fine, Mom. They've got me fixed up, mostly." She tried to ease the pressure on a sore spot by tucking her knees up, but all that did was make the pain from the donor site on her thigh more pronounced. Even though she managed to repress a moan, she saw her mother eye her suspiciously. She forced herself to smile. "I think they're letting me go home in a few days."

As if this was the cue her mother had been waiting for, she abandoned the handkerchief and handed Alex a small business card she had taken from her purse. "Your father plays golf with this fellow once a month. He's an absolutely wonderful surgeon. He reshaped Effie Thayer's nose, and honestly, you'd hardly recognize her."

Alex arched an eyebrow, certain that she wouldn't recognize Effie Thayer if the woman were the next to turn up in her hospital room. Her mother had never introduced her circle of friends to her, and Alex had her doubts that the more recent additions were even aware of her existence. She placed the card face down on her bedside table without giving it a glance.

"I have a plastic surgeon, Mom. I don't need another."

Her mother pursed her lips and huffed with exasperation. "Well, we'll see what he has to say about that during your first consultation." With a flourish, she opened a leather-bound diary and used a dampened finger to flick through the pages. "I have it all set up for the eighteenth. That will give us plenty of time to get you settled in at home."

So far, counting the drops of saline steadily falling into the chamber of her IV had been enough to keep a check on Alex's temper, but she felt that control slipping as she stared open-mouthed at her mother. Digging her fingers into her palms, she shook her head. "I'm not going back to Boston with you, Mom." It took a lot of effort to keep her voice level, but she was just about successful, though the soft flesh of her palms stung from the force of her nails.

The diary closed with a snap. "Of course you are. Your father and I had a long discussion, and we have both decided that it really is for the best, Alexandra."

The all-too familiar tone her mother had wrapped around Alex's full name made her flinch as if she had been slapped.

"I haven't spoken to my *father* in over five years." She sounded each word deliberately; it was the only way she could force them out. "He made his feelings perfectly clear before I left, and I am not going back."

Her mother patted her arm lightly. "But you're all over that business now, darling. You aren't even with that girl anymore."

For a long moment, Alex wasn't sure whether to laugh or cry. In the end, she merely lifted her mother's fingers away from her arm. "That doesn't mean I'm sleeping with men. Being gay isn't something I'm going to grow out of."

Her mother's face paled beneath its bronzed façade, but she quickly managed to compose herself and gave a high, short laugh. "Well, your father doesn't need to know that, does he?"

"He does know that, Mom. I'm guessing it's the reason you're here on your own."

The laugh again, wilder this time, a little more desperate. "Oh, you know how busy he is. He had a meeting that he really couldn't reschedule and then he has a series of conferences in England and France next week." Her mother's voice faltered slightly, and when she spoke again, she sounded tired and defeated. "He'll probably be away for the next month—"

"Mom—"

Ignoring Alex's attempt to interrupt, her mother continued to speak, her words falling over each other in feigned enthusiasm, even though she was unable to meet Alex's eyes. "But we have it all arranged for you, and he's happy you're coming home. Really."

"Mom, it's okay." Alex took hold of her mother's hand and gave it a gentle squeeze. "I'm okay."

This time when her mother managed to look up, the tears in her eyes were genuine. "You don't look okay." Her bottom lip trembled and a tear spilled down her cheek. "I wanted to come straight away, but your father…" With a shake of her head, she tucked a loose piece of hair behind Alex's ear. "I like it like this, longer. It suits you."

"Yeah?" Alex smiled and relaxed back into her pillows. "I'm glad you came, Mom."

"But you're staying here, aren't you?" Her mother already sounded resigned to the inevitable.

Alex nodded. "Yeah, I'm staying here."

❖

"You have got the worst case of bedhead, my darling."

The brush caught on a tangled strand of Sarah's hair, but it was the familiar voice of her best friend and not that small discomfort that made her open her eyes.

"Well, look at you." Ash was standing at the side of the bed, her face lit up with a grin.

Sarah managed her own tremulous smile, ignoring the sting of slowly healing wounds.

"Didn't mean to wake you up," Ash said, gingerly extricating the brush from where it had become ensnared. "I'm crap at this. It's been years since I had long hair."

Ash had had short, spiky hair for as long as Sarah had known her, and the thought of her with anything so overtly feminine as a ponytail made Sarah start to giggle.

Narrowing her eyes, Ash folded her arms indignantly. "I don't know what you're finding so funny, young lady. I'll have you know I had a beautiful perm in the eighties."

Sarah's hand flew to her left side, trying to splint fractured ribs and a fresh surgical wound as she laughed harder. "Oh fuck, please don't. Oh, you bugger, that hurts."

Ash steadied the morphine pump Sarah was fumbling for. The dose Sarah administered had been long overdue, and she lay completely still until she felt the drug slowly begin to take effect.

"Better?" Ash asked. She stroked the back of Sarah's hand, encouraging her to relax her grip on the pump.

"Mm, yes." Sarah sighed with relief. "Thank you."

"For what? Busting your stitches open?"

"No." Sarah passed the brush back to Ash, who resumed the task of unknotting her hair. "I can't remember the last time I laughed."

"Hardly surprising, love. You've had a pretty terrible few weeks."

"I know."

Ash set the brush down and pushed the last few strands of sweat-damp hair from Sarah's forehead with her fingers. "Richard phoned me, said he'd arranged for me to be allowed to visit you in here." The intensive care unit had a strict *immediate family only* policy, which meant that Sarah's stepfather had been her only visitor since the accident. Ash, often forthright to a fault, now looked unusually reticent. "He said to tell you that he was going away for a while, that he didn't know when he'd be back."

"But that..." Sarah frowned in confusion. "That means he'll miss the funerals."

Ash was already shaking her head, her expression stricken. Sarah stared at her in disbelief.

"I'm so sorry, Sarah."

"No. *No*. I wanted—"

"Your mum and Molly were buried two days ago."

Sarah slammed her fist against the side rail of her bed, her body trembling with rage. "He must have known..." Anger gave way instantly to grief, and she started to cry, the words choking off in her throat as she sobbed. "He must have known and he did it anyway."

Ash perched on the bed and gathered her close.

"I just wanted to say good-bye to them," Sarah whispered, tears soaking the front of Ash's shirt. "He couldn't even give me that."

❖

Cruel hands held Alex to the floor, pressing her face into the ground and forcing the breath from her. She couldn't shout for help, she could barely breathe, and she couldn't fight them off. The hands moved lower, a man laughed, and a blade dug into her back. With the one breath she managed to take, she started to scream.

"Oh fuck..."

She covered her face with her hands and fought to stop herself from hyperventilating. Thin, early morning light was already creeping in beneath her drapes and the air in her bedroom was stifling. She kicked her legs, freeing them from the mess of twisted sheets, and then pushed herself into a sitting position, her knees drawn up and her arms wrapped around them. She shuddered as she tried to rid herself of the residual terror still clinging to her. The nightmare was always the same; sometimes she managed to wake herself up before the cutting started, but more often, she failed.

The water in the glass on her bedside table was warm and stale, but she drained it regardless, pulling a face at the taste. Her alarm clock ticked over to 3:17 a.m. In the corner of her room, her police uniform was just about visible, neatly laid out over a chair. Feeling more exhausted than she had when she'd gone to bed, she closed her eyes and rested her chin on her knees. For the past week, she had been attending sessions with the departmental therapist, a mandatory step on the road back to active duty. He had been reassuring her that nerves were only to be expected, that a sense of trepidation was normal and healthy, and that he would have been more concerned if the trauma she had suffered hadn't affected her. As cold sweat soaked her tank top and set her off shivering, Alex wasn't so sure that she wanted to be normal. She wasn't sure what she wanted anymore.

CHAPTER TWO

The bar beneath Sarah's fingers was slippery with sweat. She gripped it more tightly, trying to find the purchase that would give her legs the support they needed.

"You're doing great, darlin'." Standing at the far end of the parallel bars, Ash waggled the gift-wrapped bar of chocolate she had brought as motivation.

"Fuck off," Sarah muttered, her teeth gritted as she tried to summon the strength necessary to take another step. Her left leg obeyed her without too much complaint, but her right, its femur held together by a titanium rod, told her in no uncertain terms that it had had enough. "I can't." An uncontrollable trembling started in her arms. She shook her head. "I can't do this."

"Three more steps." The warm hand in the middle of her back belonged to Isaac, her physiotherapist. He had shown infinite patience, surprising in such a young man, first in coaxing her out of her hospital bed and then in getting her to the point where she was confident enough to stand. Not wanting to let him down, she concentrated on slowing her breathing and then straightened her shoulders. She reached out with her right hand, making sure of her grip before bringing her weaker left arm forward.

"Good, that's good." Isaac was close behind her, poised to steady her if necessary but allowing her the space to make her own move.

"This really is a *huge* bar of chocolate," Ash announced, before making a show of zipping her lips shut when Sarah scowled at her.

"Not helping, Ash," Sarah gasped as she lifted her right leg. It dropped down clumsily, but she had succeeded in taking a full step, and she glanced up. "Okay, if it's Cadbury's then you're helping a little bit."

"Dairy Milk," Ash confirmed. "Two more steps and it's all yours."

"Yeah, no problem." Lowering her head, Sarah ignored the pain coursing through her battered body and slid her fingers along the rail again.

❖

Alex's first day back in uniform passed in a haze of comradely smiles, careful claps on the back, nods, and well-wishes. She had been assigned desk duty for the week: a gentle and mandatory reintroduction to the job she had lived and loved for five years. Immersing herself in reading through a stack of case reports, witness testimonies, and official bulletins helped the morning pass uneventfully. With a pleading expression, Jack had dropped a tub of ice cream on her desk as he wandered through, his temporary partner in tow. She had laughed, waved at him as he headed out again, and then eaten the ice cream in lieu of lunch.

As the clock on the wall crept around to five p.m., the regular clerical staff started to straggle toward the exit, their complaints about aching backs, budget cuts, and the inevitable snarl up on the freeway filtering through the desk partitions. Lights dimmed one by one, leaving Alex with only the glow of her computer screen and a bulb that flickered intermittently above the fax machine. Somewhere down the corridor an industrial vacuum cleaner began to hum, the rise and fall of its volume as it was steadily moved reassuring Alex that she wasn't entirely alone.

The case file she had located earlier that day was easy for her to access, no one having had the presence of mind to lock it against her username. For the space of two breaths, she stared at the small icon, her hands slick against the plastic of the keyboard. One tap of her finger gave her an index: ballistics, CSI, crime scene photography, medical reports, witness statements. Calmly deciding on an organized approach, she started with ballistics.

The vacuum cleaner and its operator had gone and the corridors had long since fallen into silence. After three hours, the caution Alex had initially employed had been subdued by her own exhaustion and the repetitive, often impenetrable nature of the forensic analysis. With only two items remaining on the index, and her mind already distracted by thoughts of a long, hot bath, she was largely functioning on autopilot as she opened the penultimate folder.

"Jesus."

The sequence of images filled the screen rapidly and without warning. Instinctively, she pushed her chair back, trying to distance herself from photographs she could not remember being taken, photographs that recorded in unflinching detail the injuries she had suffered. Unable to close down the images fast enough, she resorted to shutting her eyes, cursing herself inwardly for being so stupid and then cursing herself with more vehemence for being such a coward.

In her last counseling session, the therapist, sitting in his cozy office with its lofty view and its expensive coffee maker, had blithely told her to confront her fears. She had just about resisted the urge to throttle him at the time, satisfying herself with a sarcastic comment that had drifted right over his head as he smiled infuriatingly and nodded in unthinking agreement. She was quite certain this scenario wasn't what he'd had in mind, but she decided that for once she would follow his advice. On the count of five, she opened her eyes.

The woman in the photographs seemed like a stranger. Bloodstained and beaten, she stared unseeing at the camera as gloved hands guided her into position. Alex could remember only the terrible sense of disorientation, the clamor of multiple voices, and finally, the irresistible pull of strong narcotics. The medics had obviously waited until she was unconscious before they unwrapped her back.

Cleansed of blood, the lettering was easy to decipher, the H slipping away clumsily where her assailant had started to lose his nerve. In the hospital, she had compulsively traced her fingertips first across the lines of sutures and then across the raised scars, but she had never actually seen the initial damage. It was only now, weeks later, that she appreciated the tact of the doctors and the fierce, protective determination of the nursing staff. She closed the images one by one, to leave only the snow-capped mountains of her desktop wallpaper. The computer shut down with a cheerful tune. She wiped her face dry and reached for her jacket.

❖

The grass was brittle underfoot, an unusually prolonged spell of hot weather having scorched the green from its stems so that they crackled as Sarah negotiated a careful route through the stones. The walking stick that the hospital had given her tapped and jarred against the flattened markers, guiding her path and just about enabling her to keep her balance.

"Only another minute or so," Ash said, keeping close but being careful not to hover by her side.

"I'm okay." Sarah paused to push her hair away from her forehead, tucking behind her ear the strands that routinely escaped her haphazard ponytail. The sun was bleaching the color from everything around them, and she raised a hand to shade her eyes and regain her bearings. She set off again immediately, following Ash's directions and trying to quiet her labored breathing.

"Oh!"

She had suddenly caught sight of her mother's and Molly's names, and she stopped abruptly, any sense of preparation abandoning her in an instant. The intense physical effort and a surge of uncontrollable grief made her vision gray momentarily. She reached out to grip onto the smooth granite of the headstone. It was warm beneath her fingers, and she stroked it back and forth as the dizziness abated.

"Sarah, here." Ash held out the bouquet.

Sarah took it from her, the candy-sweet scent of the roses mingling with the cut grass surrounding the graves. It smelled like blissful hot summers, summers when she would come home from university and make up for lost time by playing in the back garden with Molly. She shook her head, her shoulders heaving as tears splashed onto the funeral wreaths that were already faded and wilted at her feet. She dropped to her knees, ignoring the pain from her legs as she tried to clear a space for her own flowers.

"Let me get rid of these, okay?" Ash waited until Sarah murmured her consent and then gathered the older tributes together. "That's better, bit tidier. I think your mum would want things tidy."

"She would." Sarah wiped her nose and face with her shirtsleeve and shrugged apologetically at Ash's expression of horror.

"Here." Ash rooted in her pockets until she found a packet of Kleenex. "Thought we might be needing these."

"Thanks."

"Any time." She sat beside Sarah, shuffling until she was in a comfortable position. "It's very beautiful here." She held out an arm and Sarah leaned gratefully into her embrace. "We'll just sit for a bit, then, eh?"

Sarah nodded, unable to reply, as the cheerful song of a blackbird perched in a tree above a freshly dug grave drowned out the sound of her weeping.

❖

One by one, the peas dropped off Sarah's fork. She swore beneath her breath, scooping up more potato to stick them into place. Dexterity was proving to be difficult, with one wrist that still creaked and complained when she wanted it to cooperate, but her mum had always told her not to *shovel her peas*, and even though her mum was gone, Sarah was finding that old habits were hard to break.

"You missed one." Across the table from her, Ash snorted in amusement and flicked a stray pea back toward her plate.

Tess, Ash's partner of more years than they could be bothered keeping track of, looked up from the papers she had been engrossed in and noticed Sarah's predicament. "Sorry, love. I'll do carrots next time, something you can stab." She waved her own fork at the printed sheets. "This is quite a lot of money, Sarah."

Her peas successfully glued into place with potato, Sarah swallowed the mouthful before her appetite—what little appetite she had—faded. "I know."

"I can give you advice on investments, try to make it work for you and gain some decent interest. Richard may be a shit, but he's been a generous shit."

Ash made a disgusted noise that caught the top of her beer bottle and projected itself around the room. "Oh, he's proper fucking big on generosity, so long as she leaves him alone."

"Ash..." The warning in Tess's tone was unmistakable.

While Sarah had been lying semi-conscious in the ICU, Richard had put the family home up for sale. Later, he had forwarded via his lawyer correspondence detailing the settlement of his late wife's will and requesting that any enquiries be directed to his legal team. They had told Sarah he was in Italy, but beyond that, they had declined to comment.

Sarah placed her knife and fork neatly onto her plate and pushed it aside. "She's right, Tess. And I'd really appreciate your help."

Before taking a career break, Tess had been a financial advisor to a number of local charities. She nodded at Sarah and gathered the papers together efficiently. "Okay, if the missus would be so kind as to put the kettle on, I'll go through these with you."

Ash's fork made a clang as she dropped it. "Oh, just because you're having our child, I have to be your galley slave?"

Tess grinned as she struggled to her feet, her swollen abdomen straining the limits of her T-shirt. "Want to swap? Be my guest. He was kicking me all night, and for the third day in a row, my ankles are the size of tree trunks."

Ash rolled her eyes. "Tea or coffee?" she asked, and then gave a melodramatic sigh that earned her no sympathy whatsoever.

❖

Sarah sipped her tea, glancing around the familiar layout of the living room. Tess was still reading through the legal papers, and in the kitchen, Sarah could hear Ash washing the dishes, clattering crockery and pans with carefree abandon. The living room of their two-up two-down terraced house was small but cozy, with a sofa running the length of one wall and much of the remaining floor space taken up by a home birthing pool, yet to be unwrapped. Following her discharge from the hospital, Sarah had been sleeping in the only spare room, sharing the space with a baby's crib, a changing table, and stacks of tiny outfits knitted by proud grandparents-to-be.

A burst of rain hit the window, breaking into her thoughts, as the rumble of distant thunder signaled a break in the recent spell of uncomfortably humid weather. Even with the tea burning her throat pleasantly, she found herself unable to relax. Although she had come to terms with her decision over the last few days, she was dreading broaching the subject with her best friends. This was obviously a perfect opportunity, so continuing to tell herself that she was waiting for the right moment sounded like a hollow argument. It was only when her palms began to sting that she realized how tightly she was gripping her mug, and set it on the table.

"Tess?"

"Mm? What, sweetie?" Distracted, Tess didn't look up, which somehow made it easier for Sarah to continue.

"I handed my notice in at the pool."

That got Tess's attention, and her head lifted sharply. "You did? When?"

"Yesterday. I took a walk while you were at the hospital."

"Must've been some walk." Ash stood in the doorway, wiping her hands dry on a towel. "That's a good couple of miles each way."

"Yeah, but I caught the bus home," Sarah admitted with a small smile.

Ash perched on the arm of the sofa and took hold of her hand. "You know I'd have given you a lift. Why didn't you ask?"

"Because you'd have tried to talk me out of it." And probably succeeded, Sarah added silently. "But I can't stay here." She held up her hand as both Tess and Ash drew breath to protest. "I *can't*. I love you both, more than I can probably ever tell you, but you need your space. And with the money, I've been thinking…" She squeezed Ash's hand, a wordless plea for support, for her not to make this any harder than it already was. "I want to use some of it to travel."

"Sarah—"

Sarah shook her head at Tess, breaking into whatever she was about to say. "Please don't."

Ash ran her fingers lightly through Sarah's hair as Tess came to sit on the sofa.

"You've thought all this through?" Tess asked quietly.

"Yes." Sarah sounded more confident than she felt. "I never really knew what I was doing before. I got lucky, somehow drifted into a job I enjoyed, but I'm not sure I want to teach swimming for the rest of my life. I'm not sure what I want."

"So," Ash said lightly, "you're going to run off, have fabulous adventures, have fabulous sex with fabulous exotic women, find the real you, and then come home to tell us all the gruesome details?"

Sarah blinked slowly and then looked up at Ash. Ash ignored Tess's horrified expression and smirked as Sarah started to laugh helplessly.

"You're a bloody idiot," Sarah managed to gasp. "I'm not sure about all that *finding the real me* crap, but the rest of it sounds great."

❖

Blue and red flashed steadily, splashing color across the magazines at the front of the store and giving unnecessary prominence to their lurid headlines: *Angels Murdered by their Mommy*, *Stars With Cellulite: Exclusive Photos!* Blue then red, blue then red.

"I didn't mean to do it. I didn't mean to do it." The kid was sweating, hopped up on who the hell knew what, as he stared glassy-eyed at Alex. Mucus and tears ran together on his face and clogged his throat, giving his voice a perversely childlike quality. In one hand, he still gripped the bag of money he had taken from the cashier, and in the other, his gun was beginning to waver.

"We know you didn't mean to," Jack said, unbelievably calm at Alex's side. "Just put the gun down."

"I'm sorry. I'm sorry."

Her wrists aching from the strain of keeping her weapon trained, Alex tried not to allow the crumpled form behind the counter to distract her. Blood still seeped from its ruined skull, and the thick metallic smell was making it hard for her to breathe.

"If you put the gun down, we can help you. We can help *him*."

Alex nodded when Jack looked to her for confirmation, but she couldn't speak, and for a split second, she saw a flash of fear in his eyes.

"What's your name, kid?" he asked.

"Michael." Barely a murmur, but Jack was undeterred.

"Okay, Michael, I need you to trust me. Here's what we're gonna do: you're gonna hand me your gun and we'll walk out of here together before this gets any bigger than it needs to, okay?"

The strobes from their patrol car lit up Michael's face, catching the blond streaks in his hair and the sheen of his semiautomatic. Perspiration trickled down Alex's neck as she battled the almost overwhelming urge to just run for the door, to let someone else stand in front of a trigger-happy kid with nothing to lose.

"Put the gun down," she whispered, almost a plea, and Michael flinched at the unexpected edge of desperation in her voice. "Just put it down."

The kid's hand shook violently, rattling the coins in the bag, and Jack opened his mouth to reassure, to placate, to try to bargain some more.

"Just..." Alex raised a finger from her gun, stilling Jack as Michael slowly lowered his weapon.

"Please don't shoot me." His gun dropped to the tiles, spinning lazily in place until Alex, reacting quicker, kicked it beneath the magazine rack. The paper bag split, scattering coins as the kid lifted his hands in surrender. Mesmerized, Alex watched nickels and quarters flip and slide while Jack moved in front of her to cuff Michael's hands. The cashier's life had been worth less than twenty dollars.

❖

The technicians from the medical examiner's office were respectful even in their well-practiced efficiency, but Alex still shuddered as the weight of the body bag thudded onto the gurney. The Styrofoam cup of coffee someone had thrust into her hands was too strong, and the few sips she had managed were already churning in her stomach. Her shift had finished more than two hours ago, but they weren't letting her go home; hours of debriefings and statements were still to come, and she was already so tired. Despite the sultry temperature, she turned the heat up in the car. She pulled her jacket tighter and hunched forward with her arms folded across herself.

"You okay?"

She nodded without looking up. It was not the first time that Jack had asked.

"Wanna talk about it?"

"Not really." That was the last thing she wanted to do. It was much safer all tucked up inside her, tormenting her with aches in her gut, cold sweats, and sleepless nights. If she talked, that would be it. Jack would know everything; but then she remembered the look he had given her in the store and she realized he probably had a damn good idea anyway. "I'm fine," she said, the lie well rehearsed but still completely unconvincing.

"Alex…"

"I'm *fine*." The coffee splashed onto her fingers as her hand shook. It suddenly felt as if there was no air in the car, and she clicked the button to lower the window, her finger blanching from the pressure.

"Slow your breathing down."

She shook her head. How could she slow it down when there was something crushing her chest?

"Alex, slow it down."

Lights danced across her vision as she took huge gulps of air, but some distant, rational part of her brain told her that that was only making things worse. With a massive effort, she closed her mouth and forced herself to breathe through her nose.

"Shit." The lights faded, and Jack's worried face gradually came into focus.

"Better?"

She nodded, her legs trembling as adrenaline flooded her body.

"That cramping in your hands should ease off soon." At some point, he had taken the cup of coffee from her clawed-up fingers.

"Thanks." She wiped her face as best she could.

"They happen a lot?"

"No." Her answer was automatic, but she was too strung out to keep up the pretense, and she looked across at him. "All the time," she whispered, pushing aside the instincts that were warning her to say nothing, to give nothing away. "They happen all the time." Her eyes slid shut; she couldn't look at him and still make this admission. In the dark it was so much easier, and she felt the tightness in her chest begin to loosen its grip. "Jack, I don't think I can do this anymore."

CHAPTER THREE

The rhythmic rush and retreat of the waves across the sand had lulled Sarah to sleep, and it was the first thing she heard as she awoke the next morning. Stretching her arms above her head, she kept her eyes closed for a moment, breathing in the tang of salt and seaweed and the lingering smoky scent of the small fire on which she had cooked her supper. The sun had already been low in the sky by the time she had found the right turn-off for the campsite and walked down to the deserted beach. Although it was late October, the weather throughout her journey up the West Coast had remained unseasonably warm, and as she peeked out from her tent, another cloudless morning promised that that would hold true for at least one more day. She blinked against the glare of the sun, shielding her eyes with her hand as she tried to decide whether she was hungry enough to leave the comfort of her sleeping bag.

As it often did around this time in the morning, the buzz of an incoming text message cut short her procrastinations. She smiled and shook her head as she scrambled in her bag for her phone. Across the Atlantic and eight hours ahead of the West Coast of America, Ash or Tess would be attempting to convince their demanding son that sleep really would be in his best interests. Much to the amusement of Sarah and the despair of her two closest friends, he was seldom easily persuaded.

Morning, gorgeous. Where you at today? Oh, Jamie just puked in your honour, how sweet. Tess says hi. Well, she would if she was awake. Let us know what you're up to. It's raining here. Again. A x

Sarah opened the image attached to the message and her smile broadened. Jamie had just turned two months old and seemed to have inherited the hair color of one mother and the grin of the other. The message had taken over an hour to make its way to her, but she sent a reply regardless.

Morning from just south of Seattle. Slept on the beach again, so yes, Ash, I do have sand in all my unmentionables, before you ask! Planning to go hiking in the mountains next. Tell Tess not to look so worried (because she will as soon as she finds out). I've got the hang of this camping lark. I'll be fine. Love you all. Big kiss to the boy. Sarah x

She attached her own photograph of the postcard-perfect little cove and then sent the message. Wide-awake now and sticky with dust and sweat from the previous day's drive, she eyed the water longingly. A quick glance around confirmed that no one had joined her during the night, which made her decision that much simpler.

At the shoreline, she peeled off the tank top and thin sweatpants she had slept in and dumped them next to her towel. The water was cool as it lapped at her toes, and then colder by degrees as she waded farther in. She had swum countless times as she had traveled across Europe, gradually regaining the stamina and musculature that weeks in the hospital had stolen from her. Unwilling to expose herself to the curiosity of tourists and the pitying expressions or questions that would inevitably follow, she had made a habit of hiking out to beaches far off the beaten track or plunging into Alpine lakes in the dimness of the pre-dawn. Here, as on those occasions, there was no one to stare at the twelve-inch scar that bisected her right thigh or the ugly mess left behind by the surgeons as they fought to stem the internal bleeding in her abdomen. Her only audience was a gull that squawked indignantly at her before quickly losing interest. She jumped the first few waves that hurtled toward her. Then she dove into a large breaker and swam strongly into the deeper, calmer water. The pull and burn of her muscles felt good after being cramped in her Jeep for far too long. Loath to leave the water even when she finally ran out of energy, she flipped over onto her back while she caught her breath. The sky was cobalt blue, small wisps of cloud just starting to form. Closing her eyes contentedly, Sarah lifted her face to the sun.

❖

Standing on the cabin's rickety front porch, Alex straightened her back and massaged the base of her spine with both hands in an attempt to work the kinks out of it. She ached all over, but it was a good ache, an ache that came from working outside in the fresh air all day, and, she reflected with a wry grin, air didn't get much fresher than this.

A small figure ambled into view, shadowed as ever by a black and tan dog. Alex hurried down to meet them and at least attempt to relieve the man of the tools he was carrying.

"Hey, Walt. Hey, Kip."

The dog licked her hand in greeting, his demeanor as stoical as that of his owner. Five foot four and sixty-eight years old, Walt was a man of few words, but he possessed an energy that constantly astounded Alex. Nodding his thanks, he handed over the lighter part of his burden without breaking his stride, and they walked back to the cabins together.

"Coffee's about ready," she said.

Walt grinned, two rows of perfect white teeth standing out brightly against his weather-beaten face. "I knew you were a good gal the day I hired ya."

"Yeah? No regrets?" Although she kept her tone light, there was a trace of genuine concern underlying her question; she was aware how big a leap of faith it had been for Walt to take a chance on her in the first place.

The advertisement she had answered had been vague: *Help wanted to run small farm. No experience required, accommodation incl.* The salary had been a pittance, the hours unspecified, and when she tried to find the address on a map, she searched for over an hour before having to admit defeat. Despite Jack's incredulity and against his well-intentioned advice, she had posted an application off that night, never daring to anticipate the letter and hand-scrawled map that would arrive three days later.

Walt's "small farm" was a vast tract of woodland bordering the North Cascades. Stepping from her car that first time, Alex had gazed upward to see towering Ponderosa pine and jagged, snow-capped mountains. The only sound to break the stillness had been birdsong, and the air had seemed to rush into her lungs after so long breathing in the thick smog of the city. It was only when the view had misted over that she had realized she was crying. Walt had made her coffee, sat her on the porch, and offered her the job. She had spent the last three months working herself to the bone in an attempt to justify his faith in her, but still sometimes she worried.

"You got good instincts, Alex." Walt picked up the mugs she had just filled, and she followed him back out and sat beside him on the top step of the porch. Kip settled at their feet, worrying at a well-gnawed bone. "You're doing fine."

"Oh." She took a sip of her drink to try to hide her relief.

"Plus, you make a damn good cup of coffee." He nudged her with his shoulder and succeeded in coaxing a smile out of her.

"You sure know how to charm a girl."

He laughed and she leaned into him briefly. Lapsing into an easy silence, they cradled their mugs as the air turned cooler and the shadows across the clearing began to lengthen.

❖

The steam from the hot water made Alex shiver in anticipation as she lowered herself inch by inch into the battered metal tub. Finally accustomed to the heat, she ducked her head beneath the water to rinse the accumulated sweat, dirt, and wood smoke from her hair. She added shampoo to the mix and ran her fingers low down her neck, searching by habit for the hair that had been cut away in a no-frills salon just outside Snoqualmie that doubled as a taxidermist when business was slow. Her mother would almost certainly disapprove, but Alex had always liked her hair short, and the new style was nothing if not practical.

A bath was her once-a-week luxury, and—like most of what passed as amenities in her new life—she had had to work hard for it. All the water for her tiny cabin had to be hand-pumped from the outside well and heated pot by pot on her wood-burning stove. It was something else that would appall her mother. Alex had spent pretty much every week of every childhood vacation camping or bivouacking with her two elder brothers, however, and it had been surprisingly easy for her to slip back into a lifestyle that was short on modern conveniences.

Before she left Los Angeles, Jack had taken her to dinner, and over steak and one too many beers he had let fly, telling her that she was making a massive mistake, that running away and hiding was only a temporary fix, something she would regret within weeks. He hadn't been able to change her mind, but their heated conversation replayed itself as she lay back in the tub, and in spite of several resolutions she had made and easily kept thus far, she found herself thinking about Los Angeles. Day by day, the contact she had with friends back in the city was fading as letters became less frequent and a patchy signal on her cell phone dissuaded them from sending messages and e-mails. She was surprised by how little that troubled her. She had thought that the camaraderie of the force would be the one thing she would miss, but in the weeks she had been back at work after the assault, something had changed fundamentally. Friends and colleagues had treated her differently, unwilling to engage her in conversation for fear of saying the wrong thing and more inclined to give her a wide berth in order to make their own lives easier. She had found herself pushed to the periphery, set to one side as damaged goods, and had rapidly grown tired of the sympathetic glances, given that she suspected her mental state and reliability under fire were probably the hot topics of locker room gossip.

She closed her eyes as the warm water began to ease the aches from her limbs. Outside, an owl hooted softly, its call gradually becoming more distant and then fading completely to leave nothing but silence and a pitch-blackness unbroken by the sodium glow of streetlights. There was no constant rumble of traffic or wail of sirens, no voices raised in dissent, no television blaring in the background or intermittent buzz of messages on her cell phone. It had only taken a month for the nightmares to stop and for her appetite to return. She had regained the weight she had lost, and working with Walt, she had found muscles she had never even known were there. Drowsing in the steadily cooling water, she carefully weighed both sides of the argument that Jack had raised so vehemently and came to her own conclusion: if this was running away, she really didn't have a problem with it.

❖

Sarah moaned with relief as she lowered her bare feet into the cool water of the stream. With the chill rapidly numbing the pain of blisters long since burst, she leaned back on her hands, wiggling her toes in the water and laughing as tiny curious fish swam away, startled.

"Sorry, little guys."

Her toes now motionless, the fish slowly approached her again. They nibbled gently at her feet before realizing that she wasn't actually a food source and returning to bask in the sun-warmed pools at the edges of the current.

As soon as she had sat down, an energy-sapping weariness had settled in. The sun was already beginning to cast a pink tinge across the glacial peaks that framed Ross Lake, and the prospect of pitching her tent loomed as large as a Herculean task. It had taken her a full day to hike out to the campsite from Milepost 138 where she had left her Jeep, but she could not deny her sense of achievement at having reached even this far.

For over a week, she had followed State Route 20, driving through the heart of the North Cascades National Park. At regular intervals, she had stopped off to hike some of the countless miles of trails. She had encountered no problems, gotten accustomed to the rules and regulations governing the park, and finally felt capable of tackling one of the more challenging routes. Looking at her options on the map, she had wondered aloud at the dire names given to such magnificent surroundings. A coin toss had made the decision for her, turning her away from an exploration of the trails around Mount Fury and toward a hike up to the summit of Desolation Peak.

At the Ranger Station, Marilyn, a long-serving stalwart with a lovely smile and boundless enthusiasm, had cemented Sarah's choice of trails, recommending the Desolation Peak hike as a relatively safe and easily navigated route. She had explained how it had become something of a pilgrimage for fans of Jack Kerouac, who, she said, had worked as a lookout on the peak back in the fifties and subsequently used the experience as inspiration for one of his novels. The good weather of the weekend had seen a steady stream of hikers making the trip, but as Marilyn issued her backcountry permit, a quick perusal of the itineraries submitted had given Sarah a little thrill of excitement: only one other person would be hiking her route, and that person would be an entire day behind her.

"Be mostly on your own up there," Marilyn had said. She had cast an appraising eye over Sarah before nodding and handing over the permit. "You'll be fine."

And Sarah had been fine. Although long, her first trail—the East Bank trail—had been clearly marked and obviously well traveled, making it a pleasant hike even with the burden of her camping gear. She had made good time, stopping on occasion to rest and to exchange pleasantries with hikers heading in the opposite direction. Those who had made it up to the summit of Desolation Peak described it as one of the most spectacular viewpoints in the entire park…

It was only when Sarah's head dropped to her chin that she realized she was on the verge of dozing off. She splashed her face with cold water and clambered reluctantly to her feet. Her tiny two-person tent took barely any time to pitch, but she couldn't muster the strength to start a fire and settled instead for a dinner of beef jerky, granola bars, and chocolate. When she wandered down to the stream to collect water, she noticed a second small tent pitched close to the edge of the lake. A young man carrying a pan gave a cheery wave as he walked toward her.

"Hi there."

"Oops, no you don't. Daft little bugger…" Sarah stooped low to stop an overly adventurous fish from ending up in her water bottle, and then smiled at her companion. "Hello."

"Johnno." His accent was broad Australian.

"Sarah."

They shook dirt-streaked hands and then laughed self-consciously.

"My better half spotted you. Got sharper eyes than me. Wondered if you and yours fancied a beer?"

She gazed longingly over his shoulder at the fire burning brightly by the side of their tent.

"Not sure about the beer, and there's only me," she said, licking her sun-chapped lips. "But I'd kill for a cuppa."

"Zach, get the kettle on, love. We have a guest."

She smiled as Johnno made a show of presenting her to his partner, who shook the hand she held out.

"Sit down and ignore him. He's always been an idiot," Zach said, in an accent nowhere near as pronounced as Johnno's.

Johnno set the kettle on the fire and dropped a teabag into a mug he had taken pains to wipe clean. "If I'd known you were English, I'd have offered tea first. So you're out here on your own?"

"I am."

"Heading up or back down?"

"Up, tomorrow. You?" She kept her question casual. Although it was nice to chat to someone after spending most of the day in solitude, she was hoping not to have to tag along as a third wheel.

"Down. We're taking the lazy option and getting the boat out. Zach got the whole Kerouac thing out of his system today and is now craving a feather bed, a bath filled with bubbles, and room service."

A bottle top hit Johnno's head with a resounding thud, and Sarah tried hard to keep from laughing.

"Ignore him, darling. *I* try to." Zach handed her the mug of tea, and she leaned back against an old log with a grateful sigh.

"Thank you."

"No worries." They drank contentedly for a while before Zach broke the silence. "Hey, you got a radio?"

Puzzled by the random nature of the question, she hesitated before answering. "No. I've got a mobile phone, but the service is really patchy out here."

He stabbed three marshmallows onto sticks and distributed them. "Heard the weather forecast today, that's all. They reckon we've got maybe another day like today before the rain sets in."

She nodded. Marilyn had told her pretty much the same thing, except that Marilyn had given her a window of three days of good weather. "I'm going to set out early tomorrow, get back down before dusk. I don't mind a bit of rain on the low trail out."

"Torrential rain," Johnno corrected her, "of Biblical proportions."

With a frown, she raised her head to the cloudless sky, thousands of stars dizzying her for an instant. Night after night, the weather had been settled like this, but she supposed it had to end at some point. When she lowered her head again, her marshmallow was ablaze.

"Bollocks," she muttered, and ate it anyway.

Johnno seemed to have caught the change in her mood and threw the packet of marshmallows toward her as a means of apology. "Oh, you ever tried a s'more?"

"A what?"

"S'more. Not as disgusting as it sounds, I promise you."

Graham crackers and Hershey's chocolate were quickly produced from their bear-proofed larder and Sarah watched wide-eyed as the alleged delicacy was constructed.

"Oh God, really?" Marshmallow and melted chocolate oozed from the center of the crackers and across her fingers.

"Delicious. Try it."

She took a dubious bite and then a larger one. "Oh, yum."

"One of this country's finest culinary contributions," Zach declared seriously and refilled her mug of tea. "To great adventures."

All thoughts of bad weather banished, she happily tapped her mug against their beer bottles. “To great adventures,” she said, and stabbed another marshmallow.

❖

“Oh, just one second…” Alex tightened the last rope across the flatbed of Walt’s truck and stood back to evaluate their handiwork. “Good to go, I think.”

Walt slapped the tailgate firmly into place and nodded his agreement. “Yup.”

“How many you expecting?”

“Marilyn reckoned on ten or so. Less if the weather breaks.”

“Set to, on Thursday.”

“Yup.”

Alex cast a glance over her camping gear, somehow squeezed in between several large blocks of wood and all the tools of Walt’s trade. “I should get two good nights out there at least.”

He followed her gaze, one gloved hand scratching through his unkempt beard. “You watch, mind. It’s gonna be earlier than Thursday, and it’s gonna break hard.”

Even after so little time in his company, she knew better than to argue with him. For days, the weather had been hot and humid, clouds threatening to mass in the late afternoons but then dispersing as if only a preview of a main event yet to come. Despite the twinge of unease that his warning instilled, she was loath to cancel a hiking trip that she had been looking forward to all month. From what Walt had told her about the winters up here, there would be precious few opportunities for her to access the higher trails in the coming months.

They were both heading into the North Cascades National Park, where Walt regularly gave wood carving demonstrations to tourists and where Alex had barely begun to explore the myriad tracks and trails that weaved their way through thousands of acres of protected wilderness. Walt, who knew certain areas of the park like the back of his hand, had spent hours poring over maps with her, pointing out the less well-known routes, useful water sources, and natural places to find shelter. He had never asked and she had never told him, but somehow he knew how important it was that she find the confidence to strike out on her own, and the only caution he had ever voiced was in regard to the weather conditions. It was Walt who had suggested leaving well before dawn, and she knew that was for her sake not his. The head start she would gain on the first trail would give her the option of continuing to the summit that same day, cutting her trip slightly short but ensuring that she didn't miss out on any part of the route she had chosen.

He opened the driver's door and gave a thin whistle between his teeth, prompting Kip to scramble into the cab. "East Bank Trail, then?" he said as Alex pulled her door shut.

She smiled, relieved that he wasn't going to try to talk her out of her plans. "Just kick me out somewhere near One Thirty-eight."

"Got your radio?"

She patted the conspicuous bulge at her hip. The two-way had been a gift from Walt, and it was open to one of the public channels used by the park rangers. "Present and correct."

"Not been up Desolation for a while. Let me know if you carry on up there today and I'll square it with Marilyn." He shifted the truck into gear. "Wish I was coming with ya."

"Yeah, yeah." She waggled her eyebrows at him. "And let that poor woman down? You know she'll have been up all night baking brownies." The crush that Marilyn Eagle had on Walt was the stuff of legend.

The truck bounced through a pothole that Walt made no attempt to avoid or slow down for, and the impact jarred Alex's teeth.

"Sorry 'bout that," he said amiably.

"No, you're not."

He grinned. "I was apologizing to Kip."

❖

"About here okay?"

"Wh—?" Startled, Alex turned toward Walt when she realized he was slowing the truck. She had been staring out the window at the scenery as it passed by. Silver light flooded down from a full moon, giving a ghostly hue to the blackness of lakes that she could just about detect through the rolling forest. Waterfalls tumbled from unseen sources, and unidentifiable nocturnal creatures dashed away from the truck's approach to take shelter among the trees. Although she had driven this route on numerous occasions, it had always been in the daylight, and now she felt like a privileged guest in some strange, secret version of what should have been familiar surroundings.

It seemed as if they had only been traveling for a few minutes, and yet Walt was already unfastening the ropes from around her kit.

"Sorry." She jumped out to help him. "Not been much company, have I?"

"When I first came here," he said, his voice his usual leisurely drawl, "all's I did was stare. Felt like there was just too much to take in, like I didn't deserve to be here. Been here fifty-seven years now. Still feel like that some days."

She nodded, her throat tight. "Thanks, Walt."

He made a gesture as if to dismiss himself as nothing but a sentimental old man shooting the breeze. "Trailhead's that way. Let me know where you're at."

"I will. Say hi to Marilyn."

This time his gesture was far less polite, and Alex laughed, waving through the cloud of dust as he accelerated away. She adjusted her pack, altering the strap lengths to find a comfortable balance, and then checked her watch. The official distance to her first campsite by Ross Lake was sixteen miles, and she wondered whether it really was an option for her to continue to the Desolation summit that same day. With a shrug, she decided that over thinking the matter would only result in her rushing or getting stressed. She would hike at a decent pace, try to judge the weather, and see how she felt.

Standing alone by the side of the road, she took a deep, slow breath. The sharpness of pine resin intermingled with the earthier scents of vegetation decaying underfoot. Water trickled over rocks somewhere off to her right, a constant melody that sounded at once amused and ethereal. She set off walking past a beat-up old Jeep, feeling light-headed with a mixture of nervous anticipation and simple happiness.

A skittering through the fallen leaves made her pause just as she reached the trailhead. She tiptoed in the direction of the sound and then crouched low to pan her small flashlight across the ground, but it picked out little from the shadows. She shook her head at herself.

"Not gonna get past halfway if I go chasing after every little critter," she muttered, feeling faintly ridiculous. She was turning back toward the trailhead when the glint of metal caught in the beam of her light.

"What the…?"

No one would have seen the truck from the road, and it was unlikely that she would have noticed it either, had she not wandered slightly out of her way. Midnight black and obviously a victim of some rough handling, the SUV had been concealed in a large patch of undergrowth. She cast her flashlight over it, picking out the numerous dents in the bodywork, tires that were only borderline legal, and a side window that was splintered like a spider's web. It certainly wasn't the vehicle's value that had motivated such an effort to hide it away. She knelt by the rear bumper, flicked a finger beneath a loose corner of the truck's license plate, and pried the plate upward. The original plate beneath the false one had been hacked at with something sharp before the owner had given up and tied the upper one into place.

Alex pulled out a pen and scribbled what little she could decipher of the lettering onto the back of her hand. She was reaching for her radio when she realized that Marilyn would still be in bed for a good few hours yet. Reluctant to make a nuisance of herself with one of the rangers whom she didn't know, for something that could have a perfectly innocent explanation, she moved away from the truck.

"Probably nothing," she said. "Kids with no backcountry permit."

Her theory sounded reasonably plausible, and she picked up her pace as she passed the East Bank trailhead. The dawn chorus was starting early, countless birds waking to defend their hard-won territories with fierce song. She listened to the variations, trying to identify the species from what Walt had taught her. It was an effective distraction, allowing her to bury a little deeper the nagging suspicion that her *reasonably plausible* theory was utter crap. Permitless kids might hide their truck, but they wouldn't go to the trouble of hanging false plates. Staring straight ahead into the darkness, Alex found herself listening for noises other than birdsong, noises that might alert her to the presence of other people, that might tell her exactly who else was with her on this trail.

CHAPTER FOUR

The sun had only been up for a few hours and the day was already too hot. For Sarah, taking a break was an ungainly exercise in finding a decent rock to sit on and then wrestling her pack from her shoulders, but her mouth was desert-dry, and sweat was soaking through the thin cotton of her shirt, so she persevered. It was a minute or two before she was able to drop her bag onto the ground and dig into it for her water bottle. Despite her thirst, she took care to limit how much she drank; the trail up to the summit was a notoriously dry one. With the last of the snow long melted from the lower peaks, there were no reliable water sources, and the route was taking her longer than she had anticipated.

Pressing the cool of her bottle against her forehead, she stretched her legs out in front of her and took a moment to catch her breath and enjoy the view. Some distance below the tree line, Ross Lake cut an azure swath through the valley, its vast shape defined by the mountains that rose sharply from its shores. At the campsite, she had only been vaguely aware of the true scale of the peaks, but from this higher position, the range seemed endless, soaring skyward with its summits carved out in glistening white against the sky. She felt incredibly lucky to have such a beautiful place all to herself, and the heat and the momentary discomfort faded into insignificance. She rummaged in the side of her bag, found a packet of dried fruit, and decided that this would be an excellent spot for a snack.

She had slept reasonably well, waking in good time to have breakfast and say good-bye to Zach and Johnno. Zach had given her his old transistor radio, insisting that they had no further use for it now they were "returning to civilization." She had accepted it with good grace, not really expecting it to work on the trail but appreciating the gesture regardless. When she stowed her water back in its place, it knocked against the radio's plastic casing, and she pulled the radio out, curious to see what stations she might be able to intercept in the middle of nowhere. Once she had fathomed how to switch it on, a slow turn of its dial brought her an earful of static. She winced, lowering the volume just in time to avoid a blast of some terrible heartfelt anthem that she recalled Ash once dismissing as *emo shite*. More static followed.

"—armed and dangerous. Public are warned not to approach but to contact the—"

The report faded into a buzz of white noise. Curious, she lifted the radio, angling its aerial to try to sharpen the signal.

"Once again, the violent hijack of—led to the escape—"

She snarled with exasperation. "Oh, you bloody thing, you start a good story—"

"In the direction of the—license plate—Hotel November Foxtrot. And now to other news. A seventy-seven-year-old man has defended his decision to marry a go—"

Finally admitting defeat, Sarah clicked the radio off. "I hope to hell that was a gold digger," she muttered, fastening the top of her bag and then threading her arms through the straps to hoist it into place.

She stood slowly and turned to look back at the distance she had covered. The trail had been climbing for the last three miles, and the relative cool of the lower forest had given way to more exposed terrain. Somewhere off to her left, a marmot spotted her and barked a warning, its shrill yelps carrying easily across the meadows. She spun around to try to find it, and snapped a quick photograph of it standing up on its back legs to act as group lookout. With her attention still focused on her camera's viewfinder, a sudden change in the light momentarily confused her, until she realized that the sun had gone behind a cloud. She lowered her camera to squint upward. Small white clouds were scudding harmlessly across the vast expanse of blue sky. The cloud that had dulled the sun moved quickly on, leaving untempered heat beating down on her once again.

"Onward and upward," she declared brightly.

The marmot, almost as if it had understood her intention to leave its territory, frantically yipped its encouragement.

❖

Alex was singing softly beneath her breath when the crash and thump of something unhurried, something undoubtedly larger than the deer and squirrels she had encountered so far, stopped her in her tracks. Her own progress, apart from the song she had been cheerfully but almost inaudibly massacring, had been largely silent. The forest had hemmed her in, its needle-covered trail muffling the sound of her footsteps while the hemlocks and cedars towering above her head allowed her to walk comfortably in dappled shade. For hours, she had been hiking without a care. Marilyn had promised to get back to her with any word on the mysterious SUV, but as time had passed, Alex had drawn the conclusion that no news was good news. Now she crept off the trail, carefully dropped her pack, and crouched low among a cluster of ferns that were thriving beside a small stream. Beads of water left over from early morning mists dropped steadily from their fronds, the intermittent splatter as they hit the ground not nearly loud enough to muffle the pounding of her heart.

Another thump and a snap of brittle wood, closer this time, made her head jerk up, her hand automatically reaching for the holster she no longer wore and the gun she no longer carried. She hissed a curse, pressing herself back against the rough bark of a stunted larch as if that would somehow let her merge into the very fabric of the forest. The ferns less than three yards away shuddered violently and she held her breath, only letting it out again when a large black bear emerged from the cover of the vegetation. It rose onto its hind legs, sniffing the scents being carried toward it on the breeze, before dropping again and moving quickly across the open territory, back into the safety of the trees.

Once it was well out of sight, Alex swayed forward onto her knees as she tried not to laugh too hysterically. She had seen bears before on numerous occasions; she gave herself a mental slap for having allowed her imagination to run roughshod over her common sense. She fastened her pack back into place and stepped gingerly out of the ferns onto the trail.

She had only been walking for a few minutes when she heard the dull rumble of thunder in the distance.

❖

Sarah gave a cheer as she pressed her hand against the sun-warmed wood of the lookout station on the summit of Desolation Peak. The slatted planks of the shelter formed shutters, sealing the small building from intruders, and she traced the planks with her fingers, following them around until she came to three low steps that led to a secured door. The air was cooler with the altitude she had gained. The keen wind chilling the sweat that had stuck her hair to her forehead felt glorious after so long in the baking sun. She hurriedly shrugged off her pack so she could perch on the steps and catch her breath. Elation at having made it so far pushed aside the unease caused by the crack of thunder she had heard as she reached the summit. She drank sparingly from her last bottle of water, then propped it beside her bag and took up her camera instead. She felt the muscles in her legs protest at standing again so soon after she had promised them rest, but to the west a menacing blanket of gray cloud was swirling over the mountaintops, and she didn't dare stay on the summit for too long, however much she would have liked to linger.

Through the viewfinder, she lined up a panoramic shot of the mountains whose names she had committed to memory: Mox, Redoubt, Spickard, Heart of Darkness. Layers of pristine snow softened the sharp edges of their summits, but their collective mien was one of hostility, the sweeping backdrop they formed undeniably majestic but unforgiving all the same. She gradually made her way around the shelter, any inclination to rush tempered by the sheer grandeur of her vantage point. Far below, with reflections of storm clouds boiling on its surface, Ross Lake seemed to stretch for an eternity, effortlessly filling the void where glaciers had retreated. Squinting hard, she tried to work out by which shore she had camped, before laughing at her own ineptitude and taking enough photographs to ensure that she had all of the possible options covered. An eagle circled overhead, its cry piercing the grumbling unrest of the threatened storm, while she crouched low and used a pencil and a scrap of paper to take a rubbing of the embossed US Geo Survey benchmark that was fixed onto a rock near the shelter.

Scrubbing her pencil across the paper, she wondered uncertainly why she hadn't just taken a photograph. Her answer came as she stared down at the paper in her hand: an echo of Molly's voice chattering with excitement as she ran her crayons across textured bark or stone walls to transfer their patterns onto her sketch pad. Molly would spend hours searching the garden for rough surfaces, only giving up when she finally ran out of pages in her pad. It had been Sarah who had first shown her little sister the trick…

The pencil dropped to the ground and Sarah blinked. Her fingers ached where they were clenched around the paper and her legs felt leaden and cramped; she had no idea how much time had passed. As she rubbed her eyes dry with her knuckles, the white of the paper in her hand suddenly darkened. She looked up at the sky, nervous tension twisting in her gut.

"Shit."

If her exposed position had afforded her better protection, the rapid progress of the storm through the valley would have been truly spectacular to behold. She watched wide-eyed as a surging mass of charcoal-black cloud began inexorably to swallow up what remained of the blue sky. The sun submitted without a fight, plunging the summit into an unearthly twilight. That was enough to shake Sarah from her stupor, and she ran across to the lookout station, slipping and skidding on rocks already slickened by the first drops of rain. By the time she reached her pack, the mountains and lake she had photographed not half an hour earlier had vanished entirely. Mist drifted toward her, blurring the edges of the landscape, making everything instantly alien and unfamiliar. She quickly pulled on her waterproof jacket, drew the hood up, and fastened it tightly against the hail and rain that was now pouring down. The walls of the shelter were protecting her from the worst of the wind, so she huddled next to them, trying not to panic, trying to weigh up her admittedly limited options: to stay where she was or to attempt to make her way down.

A bolt of lightning split the sky, static electricity charging the atmosphere and making the hairs on her arms prickle. Thunder immediately followed in its wake, a furious percussion that smashed off the mountains. As the freezing rain lashed her, she tried and failed to prize open any of the shutters fastened across the windows of the shelter. The door would not budge an inch, even when she shoulder-charged it. Soaked to the skin and shivering uncontrollably, she winced at the electrified hiss and roar of the storm. She tried to console herself with her experience of the European Alps, reminding herself that even the most ferocious of storms there could sometimes burn out and pass over within minutes, sweeping out as abruptly as they swept in. In the absence of any real plan, that made her decision for her. She returned to the side of the steps, where she unfolded the survival bag she had packed almost as an afterthought, and she somehow managed to wriggle into it in spite of the wind ripping and tugging at the thick plastic. She tucked her hands between her thighs for warmth, raised her knees to her chest, and settled down to wait.

❖

Through vertical sheets of rain, Alex could just about make out the shape of the small boat nearing the jetty on Ross Lake. A gust of wind barreled into it, throwing it wildly off course, until its skipper managed to correct its bearings and its tentative progress resumed.

“Hey there!”

Her hail carried on the wind, and one of the two young men waiting on the shore waved cheerfully as she walked over. The smile left his face as she drew closer, and he turned to confer urgently with his companion.

"Don't worry. I'm sure the skipper's done this hundreds of times," Alex said, as soon as she could be heard without raising her voice.

"Sorry, we thought you were someone else," the taller of the men said in a strong Australian accent, continuing to scan the trail behind her as he spoke. "Friend of ours—well, a friend as of last night. She went up Desolation on her own this morning, and…" He gestured in the direction of the mountain and then shrugged helplessly. Its lower slopes were barely visible, the summit completely shrouded by the storm.

His companion squeezed his bicep in reassurance. "We were going to go up after her," he said, "but it got so bad we figured we'd only be causing more problems, and then there'd be three of us wandering aimlessly out there." He opened his hands in frustration. "We're fucking useless at this survival lark. We tried to phone the ranger station, but there isn't a hope in hell of getting a signal in this."

Alex nodded, her brow furrowed with concern. "I've got a radio. Should be able to get through to them. I can give them a heads-up that there might be a rescue pending. Oh, whoa, catch hold of that."

The sodden rope hit the jetty with a thud, and the Australian stamped his foot on it to stop it from slipping into the water. Together, the three of them managed to haul the boat into place while the boat's skipper jumped out to moor it securely. Without pausing to exchange pleasantries, he began to throw their bags aboard.

"You getting on too, ma'am?" he asked, his voice strained with the effort it had taken him to negotiate the crossing safely.

Forcing her gaze away from the storm that was battering what should have been her destination, Alex shook her head. "No, you get on out of here."

The skipper nodded brusquely, disinclined to waste time by arguing with her, but the other two men hesitated.

"What are you going to do?" The Australian had obviously tracked her line of thought.

"I'm not sure," she admitted. "Carry on up a little way, hope that I meet her on the way down." She gestured for them to get on board. "Go on. I'm sure she's fine."

The men climbed onto the boat, where they hung on to the sides as the wind buffeted them and the lake roiled. The Australian seemed the steadier of the two, raising his hand in reluctant farewell.

"Her name's Sarah. Tell her that Johnno and Zach said hi. Get her to ring us, will you?" he called.

"No problem." Alex slipped the knot free from its mooring post and threw the rope for Johnno to catch.

"Oh, hey," she shouted as the boat's engine coughed and then fired up. "Why'd you hide your truck?"

"Our what?"

"Your truck, back at the highway."

Both men looked completely mystified. "We don't own a truck," Johnno yelled back, the wind tearing at his words. "Neither of us can drive…"

❖

A full hour had passed, but the storm showed no signs of abating. Her eyes fixed on the sky, Sarah listened to the wind clatter and howl around the shelter, and gradually realized that this wasn't one of those flash in the pan weather fronts that washed humidity from the air and left everything fresh and sweet smelling. Thick cloud had descended on the mountain, rain continued to fall heavily, and visibility had narrowed to less than half a yard. Her phone sat silent and useless in her hand, her fingers numb with cold as she gripped it like a lifeline that she wasn't yet ready to give up on. She knew she had to try to descend, try to find the right trail and lose enough height to drop beneath the cloud cover. She also knew that finding the right trail might well prove to be impossible; it had tapered out just below the summit, and there were no landmarks left for her to fix upon. Unwilling to wander blindly, she fumbled for her compass and used the only thing she could see—the shelter—as a reference point. Her calculations and her memory were leaden with cold and panic, but they both urged her in a vaguely westerly direction. She kicked her way out of the survival bag and then wrestled with the slick plastic until she had managed to fold it and stuff it back into her pack.

"You can do this and you'll be fine," she whispered as she stood to her full height and the wind immediately knocked her sideways. "And you'll laugh about it in the morning."

Her bottom lip was trembling, so she bit it. Bowing her head against the rain, she took a deep breath and set off walking.

❖

"This is stupid," Alex muttered, "really, seriously stupid." She splashed through yet another in an endless series of puddles, mud and cold water sinking through the long-defeated waterproofing on her boots and soaking into her socks. On the bright side, she could no longer feel her feet, which was definitely a blessing. Ahead of her, smoke billowed from the blackened stump of an ancient pine. A bolt of lightning had cleaved the trunk in two, shattering hundreds of years of painstaking growth and neatly blocking Alex's path. Back at the camp, she had decided to leave the heaviest items of her gear and switch to carrying a day pack, and she was glad of that now as she hefted the smaller bag over the tree before climbing over it herself. The forest surrounding her creaked ominously as she dropped back down onto the trail. She already knew the storm had been severe enough to cause real damage. Before setting off, she had spoken to Walt on the radio, the reception fading in and out as he told her that several of the access roads into the park were blocked by debris or flash flooding. He had advised her to sit tight at the campsite and wait for a rescue party to reach her, although when pressed, he had admitted that the storm was forecast to last for several days and that any evacuation attempts would be delayed until the conditions improved. At that point, she had changed her mind about telling him of her slightly less than sensible plan to find the missing hiker. She didn't intend to go very far, he couldn't do anything to help, and she really didn't want him to worry.

For a second, she allowed herself to rest. She leaned forward to grip her knees with her hands and pulled in a ragged breath. She didn't sit down; her legs were already shaking simply with the effort of holding her upright, and if she sat down she was certain she wouldn't have the energy to stand again.

"Sarah? *SARAH*?" After the first two miles, she had started shouting intermittently, and she continued to do so, more out of habit now than with any real hope of success.

Her only answer was the moaning of the wind through the trees.

❖

The premature dusk that had fallen at the onset of the storm was gradually darkening to true night, and with a sickening certainty, Sarah knew that she was lost. With no way of second-guessing herself, she had picked up a trail that had initially seemed to be heading in the right direction, but a series of switchbacks, steep descents, and equally steep ascents since then had completely confused her. Still enveloped by thick cloud, she had continued to follow the trail in the hope that it would lose height, but several hours later, the nature of the terrain suggested that she remained at a considerable altitude, and she was utterly exhausted.

The trail was sodden, but she sat down regardless, too wet and too weary to care. She forced herself to eat a handful of dried fruit, washing it down with gulps of water that chilled her even further. As she was steeling herself to push to her feet once more, she heard a voice crying out.

CHAPTER FIVE

The mist muted everything. It drifted at the mercy of the wind, twisting around Alex's feet to conceal her path and hide the trees until she almost walked into them. It dulled sound to the point where she was painfully aware of her own heartbeat, the effort her body was making thumping too fast and too hard in her ears. The forest had tapered off some miles ago, the remaining scattered trees and shrubs providing her with little shelter from the wind, driving rain, and seemingly endless swirling of gray. Every few minutes she promised herself that she would turn back, take Walt's advice, and return to the lake to wait for rescue. Then another five minutes would pass and she would decide to go on just a little farther. She was walking largely on autopilot now, and the sudden shock of the radio vibrating at her hip made her stumble into a small bush. Carefully extricating herself from its thorns, she slumped down at the side of it and pulled the radio free.

"Go ahead, Walt."

A buzz of static assailed her, forcing her to scramble onto a high rock to try to clear the signal.

"—Don't know if—stay the hell away from them—killed one man already."

Her hands slick with sweat, she hesitantly raised the radio to her lips. "Walt, say again. Over."

The stress in his voice was apparent even through the breaks in the reception. "Cops got a hit on the partial plate you gave Marilyn.

The truck was used to hijack an ambulance transferring a prisoner to the hospital. Alex, are you getting this okay?"

"Yep." She was already scanning her surroundings, waiting for something to leap out of the mist at her. She lowered the volume of the radio as far as it would go yet still be audible. "I hear you."

"Convict's been named as Nathan Merrick. Cops think his girlfriend Bethany played a part and they might be traveling together. No idea what they'd be doing in the park, but Merrick spent two summers up here working trail maintenance about fifteen years back."

Alex nodded, even though there was no one there to see her. She felt surprisingly calm, her years working on the force coming into play as she compartmentalized the information. "What was he in for?"

A pause, before Walt answered with obvious reluctance. "This time around, aggravated assault and armed robbery…" He hesitated and Alex said nothing, the inference hanging in the static. She could sense his indecision and dreaded what else was to follow. It only took him a second or two to steel his nerve. "He was on a federal watch list for his links to a number of white supremacist groups. Apparently, he was their go-to guy for weapons, explosives, clean cash. Two trucks were used in the breakout. One was found burned out and traced back to a lieutenant in one of the bigger groups. I guess Merrick was too valuable to lose for twenty-five to life."

She gave a short, humorless laugh. "I'll bet."

"There's something else, Alex." If it were possible, Walt sounded even more troubled. "They killed one of the prison guards, and a second is missing."

She stared with loathing at the radio in her hand as if it alone was responsible for the bad news that just kept on coming. When she finally answered, anger made her voice hard. "They could be anywhere by now."

"I know. They're not likely to be by the lake, so just hang tight. The cops and the feds'll be all over this as soon as they can get up there."

"Yeah, uh…" She wiped a hand across her face, raindrops immediately re-gathering on her eyelashes and obscuring her vision. "I'm not by the lake, Walt."

"Where you at?"

"Not exactly sure. Most of the way up Desolation, I guess. Two guys told me about a friend of theirs. She went up there earlier today and didn't make it back. Figured I'd try and find her." She kept her tone light, as if to imply that this wasn't anything to make a big deal about. After all, she'd had nothing better to do, had she?

The radio emitted a series of high-pitched beeps followed by an ear-splitting wail. There were only two bars left on its battery, and she hadn't thought it necessary to bring a spare. In fits and starts, the signal cleared again, and despite the circumstances, she couldn't help but smile. Walt obviously hadn't been fooled by her attempt at nonchalance.

"—'king stupid-ass things to do—middle of nowhere—'king storm with the gods only know—running about out there—"

She gave him a few more seconds to calm down. "Sorry, Walt," she said, genuinely contrite, when he ran out of steam. "Just…she's on her own up here, and besides, she won't know anything about this guy Merrick."

His sigh was perfectly transmitted. "I know. Doesn't make you less of an idiot, mind."

"I'm hoping she's on the trail somewhere or holed up at the summit."

To her surprise, he didn't try to talk her out of continuing, didn't try to persuade her to return to the relative safety of the lake. It had only been three months, but apparently, he knew her better than that.

"Keep your head down, Alex."

"I will. Promise."

"Keep in touch."

"I will."

Her hand was shaking as she clipped the radio back onto her belt.

"Shit," she whispered. She lowered herself from the rock and winced at the noise of her boots landing heavily in a puddle.

With dusk now rapidly giving way to night, the trail ahead of her was almost completely invisible. She pulled a flashlight from her pack, tempering its beam with a spare sock so that the dull light was just about enough to guide her, and set off again, painfully aware of every sound she made and every sound that filtered through to her out of the mist.

"You sure as hell pick your moments to try and be a hero." She shook her head at the sheer scale of the odds stacked against her. She knew that if she didn't laugh about it, then her only other option was giving up and turning back.

❖

The relief surging through Sarah gave her the energy she needed to push toward the sound of the voices. Her narrow trail was winding precariously along the edge of a steep drop-off, the depth of which she couldn't gauge with the thin beam of her flashlight. The tenuous nature of her path had hampered her progress, but she was close enough now that she could distinguish the cadence, if not the actual words, of a man and a woman. She was about to draw breath to shout across to them when the quiet buzz of her phone made her hesitate.

"Typical, you bloody work now that I've found someone," she muttered, pulling it out to find a text that Ash had sent over twelve hours ago. The signal on her phone was wavering between one bar and two, and her mood lightened immeasurably as she grinned at the photograph of Jamie, a picture of innocence with chocolate cake smeared all over his face.

Deciding to delay replying until she was somewhere warm and dry, she returned the phone to her pocket. Then she tilted her head to one side, listening and trying to reestablish the direction she needed to take. The ledge she was negotiating gave her no protection from the wind that whipped rain into her face, wind that tormented her by intermittently lifting the mist to give her a few precious seconds of clear visibility before casting it down to conceal everything once again. Her gloves were soaked through, her fingers numb from trying to find purchase on the slippery rocks, but as she strained to concentrate, the chill that suddenly made her shudder had nothing to do with how cold she was.

At first it was just sounds: a thud and a short cry of distress, but then a voice carried toward her with perfect clarity. It was a man's voice, different from the first one, wavering with fear but fighting to stay calm.

"Just let me go, please. Look, I don't know where we are. I don't know where you're going. Who could I tell?"

No one answered him, but there was another thud, followed by a weak groan. He coughed, and Sarah winced at the thick, wet gurgle of his breathing. She turned off her flashlight and huddled low as she attempted to make sense of what she was hearing. Torn between a desire to stay hidden and an urge to try to intervene, she held her breath, slipped her pack from her shoulders, and tucked it out of sight behind a boulder. Then she crept forward, navigating a path through a maze of oddly shaped rocks to reach one that was far larger. She climbed atop it and lay flat on her front. For what seemed an interminable length of time, she stared across the small clearing, struggling at first to comprehend exactly what she was seeing and then simply not wanting to believe it.

A man and woman clad in wet weather gear stood a short distance away with their backs toward her. In front of them, starkly lit by the flashlights they were training on him, knelt a second man. The thin white shirt he was wearing was torn and bloodstained, with epaulettes on his shoulders suggesting he had been at work before he had somehow ended up here, struggling to hold his position on the rain-slickened scree with his hands bound behind him. He was shaking his head, blood running from his nose and splattering onto the ground as he repeated the same words over and over again like a delirious mantra.

"Please don't kill me. I have a family. Please don't kill me."

Locked in a heated debate, his captors were ignoring him. The woman walked around him to peer tentatively over the edge of the cliff face, and then turned back to her companion. With mounting horror, Sarah watched the woman laugh and shrug, before the man standing beside her kissed her savagely. When they broke apart, he took one step, placed a gun against the forehead of the kneeling man, and pulled the trigger.

Too stunned to look away, Sarah gasped involuntarily as a gout of blood exploded from the back of the man's skull, the wind hurling it forward to cast a fine spray across the face of his murderer. As if in slow motion, the body slumped to one side, its eyes staring blankly in the twin beams of light as blood continued to leak out onto the scree. With a look of disgust, the woman pushed her toe beneath the torso and tried to roll it, cursing in exasperation when she was unable to shift its weight. His expression impassive, the man took a firm hold of the body and flipped it into the void. He tracked its progress down the mountainside and then, seemingly satisfied, wiped his hands on his pants to clean them.

Sobbing silently, Sarah edged backward, her fingers still clamped around a loose piece of rock that she had taken hold of but never had the chance to throw. She felt sick, her legs weak and clumsy as she tried frantically to move; she needed to get back to where she had left her bag. Ignoring the sting of her abraded palms, she half-fell, half-jumped down from the rock she had been lying on. The impact forced a moan from her, and the crunch of the footsteps heading in her direction halted immediately.

"What the fuck?" The woman's voice, low and wary, followed quickly by the snap and click of a round being chambered.

The man gave a derisive laugh. "You really think someone's gonna be wandering out here in this? Don't be fuckin' stupid, Beth. Gunshot got some critter spooked, is all."

Sarah didn't wait to hear whether the woman had been persuaded by the man's argument. Throwing caution to the wind, she turned the flashlight on, instinct and adrenaline taking over to plot the simplest route back. The light bounced as she ran, a sudden glimpse of color catching in its beam as she reached the outskirts of the rocks. She stooped to grab the bag, swinging it onto her shoulder without pause and only realizing as she did so that something was wrong, that it was a duffel bag, not her rucksack. The additional weight unbalanced her, and she staggered slightly, her shoulder colliding with a rock. Momentarily stunned, she tried to catch her breath, casting the light around to look for her own bag. She couldn't see it; all she could do was hope that this one would contain enough supplies to replace hers.

As she readjusted her burden, a choppy burst of wind lifted the veil of gray for an instant. A glare of light caught her full in the face and a startled shriek was drowned out by the man's guttural yell of "You little bitch!" before the mist dropped again, and the two figures, so close they had almost blundered into her, disappeared.

Sarah was already running. There was no path for her to follow, just the certain knowledge that she needed to get as far away as she possibly could. As she was about to hurdle a boulder, a sudden bang made her ears ring. To her right, shards of stone flew into the air. She ducked left, losing her footing and skidding a short way down an incline before she grabbed hold of something stunted and prickly and came to a jolting stop. Below her, rocks and debris continued to slide, clattering loudly as they gained speed before finally coming to rest at the start of the sparse tree line. Gravel and scree shifted beneath her feet, edging her irresistibly downward as she tried to stand. Terrified, she took a huge gulp of air, but another gunshot effectively made her decision for her. She forced herself upright and began to run down toward the trees, the fragile formation of the slope collapsing and disintegrating as she sank her boots into it. Her momentum was too swift for her to control her descent effectively and she tumbled, crashing onto her side but continuing downward regardless.

The tree line loomed ahead. With a desperate effort, she dug her boots into the slope and pushed herself to her feet once more. She dared a glance over her shoulder, able only to distinguish two faint beams of light. They were moving slowly toward her, the progress of her pursuers more cautious than hers as they attempted to follow her without falling. In front of her, a vague path threaded through the gnarled firs and then led into a massive tract of thicker forest. As she set off again, the duffel bag shifted suddenly and she had to pause to move it back. Almost immediately, she heard the crack of gunfire. Three shots rang out in a rapid salvo, followed by a shock of pain that ripped through her right side.

"Oh God." Wavering unsteadily, she clamped a hand to her side, able to process little other than the fact that she was still standing and just about able to walk. Not daring to use her flashlight any more, she staggered down into the trees, the trail forgotten, her priorities narrowed to staying on her feet and finding out how badly she was injured.

Minutes passed with no additional shots fired. Blood oozed unbearably hot against her freezing fingers. She balled her hand into a fist, pushed down hard where it hurt the most, and ran deeper into the forest.

❖

Even in the middle of the wilderness and in the middle of a storm, there had been no mistaking what the noise was. Alex had automatically dropped into a crouch at the sound of the gunshot, and she had still been crouching there minutes later when the second shot was fired. Several others had followed at uneven intervals, and—having already realized she was in no immediate danger—she had attempted to work out where they had come from. The scream of the wind and the distortion from the valley made that next to impossible, though they had been somewhere off to her left and possibly at a level slightly lower than her own. She found herself fervently hoping that the gunshots had been necessary to ward off an animal, but knew that was unlikely to be the case.

She switched her flashlight back on and cautiously retraced her steps, her beam concentrated on the right-hand edge of the trail. It took her thirty minutes to find what she was looking for: an overgrown trailhead that had obviously been long abandoned in favor of the route she was on. Her map still had it marked, a dotted line creeping around to cut into a huge expanse of forest, down toward where she now thought she needed to be. With a whispered but heartfelt apology to Walt, she stepped over the rocks that had been placed to keep hikers on the official trail to the summit, and did her best to pick up her pace.

❖

At first, Sarah mistook the noise for thunder, a tumultuous barrage of sound that seemed to be coming from everywhere at once. She swayed on the spot as she listened, her breath coming in painful gasps, her fist cramping and sticky at her side. She felt sick, dizzy, and so exhausted that it took her several minutes to realize there was no thunder, and the flickers of rushing movement filtering through the trees in the first weak light of dawn were actually a river. Her feet sloshed in gathering pools of overflow as she neared its banks. It had been swollen to bursting by the storm, and the force of the water was sweeping massive pieces of debris along as if they weighed nothing at all.

There was no way that she could cross it. There would be no bridge so far from any of the trails and there was no possibility of her wading or even swimming safely to the other side. Her legs began to buckle as she stood staring at the water, and before she even recognized what was happening, she was down on her hands and knees with her vision slowly fading out on her.

"No, no." In desperation, she deliberately ground her knuckles into the wound on her side, the pain bringing everything sharply into focus again. Blood streamed through her fingers and she swallowed convulsively against a sudden surge of nausea. Her head hanging low, she forced herself to stand. For hours now, there had been no sign of anyone behind her, but the riverbank at this point was too open, too exposed, and she knew she wouldn't be able to carry on for much farther. For what seemed like the hundredth time, she pulled her phone from her pocket and squinted through the mud and blood smeared across its display. The signal jumped to one bar and vanished again in a heartbeat. She kept it clutched in her hand as she made her way back to the cover of the tree line. With one eye on her phone, she slowly followed the course of the river downstream and began to search for somewhere to hide.

The rain had settled into a relentless drizzle, cloud blanketing the forest and ghosting eerily through the trees. The dawn chorus had been muted by the storm, and the occasional quiet crunch of

Sarah's boots sinking into the carpet of pine needles was the only regular disturbance of the stillness. Her attention was divided between breaking a trail and scouting the territory, and she didn't see the raised mess of roots from a lightning-blackened fir until she fell over them. This time, she didn't have the strength to get up again.

"Shit."

Snared like an animal in a trap, she twisted and kicked weakly until her boot came free. She immediately drew her legs up and rested her head on her knees. She was wondering vaguely whether she would pass out before she threw up, when the phone that she was still gripping buzzed once. Barely daring even to hope, she turned it over to find a new text message from Ash.

Hey, you. Guessing you're out of range (yes, Tess is worrying). Hope you're getting up to all sorts of mischief. Details as soon as you can. Love A x

"Jesus." The unintentional irony of the message was lost on her as she watched the signal strength hold steady at two bars. With shaking hands, she searched her contacts until she found the park's emergency number that Marilyn had insisted she take with her. The call was answered in three rings.

"You have reached the emergency helpline for the North Cascades National Park. Due to the extreme weather, we are experiencing a high demand for emergency assistance. Please leave your name, number, and a brief message after the tone."

As the high-pitched beep faded, Sarah wondered despairingly what she should say. She didn't want to risk hanging up without speaking, since she didn't know whether she would still have a signal the next time she tried.

"My name is Sarah Kent. I got lost near the Desolation summit." She shook her head, tears streaming down her cheeks as her voice broke. How could she possibly fit everything that had happened into one phone message? "I saw a man kill someone and he shot me. I'm bleeding and I don't think I can run anymore. Please, if anyone is there, please—"

"Hello?" The person on the other end of the phone sounded breathless. "Sarah?"

"I'm here." She closed her eyes and wiped her face with the sleeve of her jacket. "I'm here."

"It's okay, sweetie, it's Marilyn. You're on the loudspeaker and we're all gonna try and help you, okay?"

"Okay."

"Sarah, we have someone out there looking for you. Are you able to describe where you are or what direction you went in?"

With her eyes still closed, Sarah tried to talk through her route, starting with her failed attempt to find the path down from the summit. She gave them the direction she thought she had traveled in, before describing the ledge she had followed. When she told them what had happened there, some logical part of herself registered the fact that they seemed to know more about the perpetrators than she did.

"Did you see any landmarks? Anything unusual up there?" Marilyn had been coaxing the information out of her bit by bit, seeming to sense that Sarah was teetering on the verge of collapse.

"Rocks," Sarah murmured. "Right near where it happened, one big one was flat like a tabletop. I ran down from there into the woods and I came out into a clearing." She laughed suddenly, shaking her head at her own ineptitude. "Oh fucking hell, I'm right near a fucking river."

She heard Marilyn begin to confer urgently with a man whose voice had been in the background throughout the call.

"There's a tree about twenty minutes down," Sarah said, fighting to remember anything else that might help. "A fir, struck by lightning. I fell over it."

"That's really good, Sarah. Try not to go too far from there." The line crackled and faded, and Sarah shook her head as if her will alone could strengthen the signal.

"They're going to find me," she whispered. "They're going to find me before you do."

When she looked down at her phone, it was already dead.

❖

Still chewing the granola bar she had dispatched in two bites, Alex refolded her map and set off again with a renewed sense of urgency. From the information Sarah had managed to provide, Marilyn and Walt had been able to plot her likely route and give Alex a good idea of her current whereabouts. It was by no means an exact science, but it was certainly better than nothing, and the old trail Alex was following headed in the right direction. In a guarded tone, Marilyn had warned her that Sarah was injured, but Alex was loath to start worrying about the implications of that just yet. *Don't go borrowing trouble* was one of Walt's favorite sayings, and she had decided that was sage advice, given her situation.

Her trail was descending at a steep gradient, and she had to step carefully to stop herself from slipping. Loose stones rolled beneath her boots, making the path treacherous, so she moved to its edge to try to walk on the grass and moss that had taken root there. She followed the zigzagging route for an hour, her knees and lower back aching with the stress of tempering her speed. Small streams sluiced across her path at regular intervals, impromptu waterfalls cascading down the mountainside to further increase the volume of the river she could hear pounding its way through the valley.

Her caution now had little to do with losing her footing. Instead of remaining on the trail all the way down, she began to break a route of her own, keeping the path in sight but weaving through the trees above it until she was low enough to catch glimpses of the gray foaming rapids that split the forest in two. Descending farther still, she could see that the river was completely inaccessible, huge rocks tumbled by avalanches creating an unbreachable barrier, and yet she knew that at some point Sarah had found a clearing. This made her plan an incredibly simple one: find the same clearing, walk for another twenty minutes, and then look for a tree felled by lightning. It sounded so easy in theory, but in practice it would probably be akin to finding the proverbial needle in the haystack.

Despite her misgivings, however, the clearing proved surprisingly easy to spot. An obvious natural opening had been formed by the path of an old avalanche, and grasses and ferns had taken full advantage over the years to create a small lea. She had seen nothing like it so far, and peering downstream into the mist rising from the water, she could see no other similar clearings, masses of rocks quickly dominating the landscape again. Confident of being in the right place, she was setting off to start her search for the stricken tree when a flash of movement ahead of her made her drop quickly into a crouch. Any hopes she had had that it was Sarah were immediately dashed when a second figure joined the first. Keeping low, Alex crept toward a thicket of new-growth firs and watched as the man and the woman conferred and then slowly turned full circle to scan the area.

Alex froze as the man looked across to her hiding place. His face was pinched and pale, but anger and frustration blazed in his eyes, and his attention did not linger for long.

"She's not here, Nate." The high whine of the woman's voice carried her words easily to Alex.

"I fucking know that."

The man—who Alex now knew was Nathan Merrick—was already walking onward, not bothering to wait for the woman to catch up with him. He was going in the exact direction Alex had been heading. At a loss as to what else she could do, she timed a minute on her watch and then set off behind them.

❖

Beads of water dripped from the moss with the regularity of a ticking clock. With her hands cupped beneath it, Sarah waited patiently for her palms to fill and then gulped the water down. No matter how many times she did this, her thirst still raged, but she didn't dare move to the stream she could hear trickling close by like a particularly cruel form of torment. She leaned her head back down on the duffel bag and pulled her knees close to her chest. Something low on her abdomen gave her a sharp stab of pain, and warm wetness began to soak into the sweater she had wrapped around her wound. With a moan, she twisted to sit up again, pressing the sweater against herself and trying not to cry out. Her feet scuffed in the gravel as she struggled to find a comfortable position, and she was about to try lying on her other side when she heard the crunch and snap of a twig and then the unmistakable sound of footsteps approaching. She shrank back into the shadows as far as she possibly could, clenched her fist, and waited.

It happened almost before she knew anything about it. There was a rustle of cloth above her, a slithering of mud and small stones, and a hand that clamped across her mouth. An arm wrapped around her waist and pulled her close while a second hand gripped her wrist. She struggled briefly, straining to wrench free.

"Shh." Little more than a rush of breath against her cheek. "I'm not going to hurt you. It's okay. You're okay."

A woman's voice, young, and sounding as scared as Sarah felt. She shuddered once, fatigue and relief draining all the fight from her. The hand covering her mouth was cautiously lowered, and she relaxed her own hold on the shard of rock she had readied as a weapon.

"Hey, Sarah."

The whisper was only just audible. Sarah turned her head slightly but could still only sense rather than see the woman's smile.

"My name's Alex. It's good to finally meet you."

CHAPTER SIX

It had all been due to dumb luck in the end. Both Alex and Merrick had heard the rattle of stones as Sarah moved, but from her position twenty yards behind him, only Alex had seen the flash of black and yellow on the sole of Sarah's boot. Unable to pinpoint the source of the noise, Merrick had eventually walked on to continue his search. Alex had waited for him to move out of sight and then waited a few minutes more before she dared to approach Sarah's hiding place. Now, pressed next to her in a water-worn hollow at the base of a rock, Alex listened to Sarah's labored breathing and tried to figure out what to do next.

"Are they still out there?"

They were the first words Alex had heard Sarah speak, and she found herself smiling in surprise at the British accent.

"No, I think they've gone. How you doing?"

Sarah laughed quietly, as if unsure exactly how to answer, but her hand flew to her side and the laugh turned into a moan of discomfort. "Oh shit, I've had better days."

Her hand was freezing cold when Alex squeezed it. Trying not to show her concern, she edged around until they were sitting side by side.

"Sarah, how badly are you hurt?"

When Sarah tipped her head to look at Alex, the hazel-green of her eyes was the only color that remained in her face. "I don't know," she admitted a little sheepishly. "I thought if I could still run then it couldn't be so bad, but I can't get it to stop bleeding for long."

"So we need to find somewhere we can patch you up, then." Alex realized that she did have a plan after all; she just wasn't sure exactly what Sarah would think of it.

❖

"You want to go back up?" Sarah sounded exhausted by the very idea, and Alex shook her head quickly.

"Not all the way up. We just try to keep following the river and then go up to here. See…" She traced her finger along a blue line on her map and stopped at a small black square. "I'm not sure what this is. It may be an old lookout post or logger's hut." She could sense Sarah watching her as she refolded the map, and she swallowed hard, hating what she had to say. "We can't keep going down, not yet. Not while Merrick is looking for you. Most of the access roads are blocked, no one can get in to help us, and you look like you're gonna fall over as soon as you stand. We need somewhere we can hole up for a while. I don't…" She opened her hands, unaccustomed to feeling at such a loss. "I don't know what else to do."

Sarah took a measured look at the cramped space they had been sharing for the past hour and then held her hand out to Alex. With a grin, Alex carefully helped her to her feet, wrapping an arm around her when she wavered.

"Do me a favor?" Sarah said, once she seemed confident of staying upright.

"Sure. What?"

"Carry that for me?" She toed a bag that Alex hadn't even noticed. "I can manage your pack, but that's really bloody awkward."

The bag was a small duffel bag, difficult to carry for any length of time and not the type of pack an experienced hiker would be using. Slightly confused, Alex passed her pack over, wincing in sympathy as Sarah shouldered it. She swung the other bag onto her own shoulder.

"This yours?"

Sarah shook her head. "No. I sort of nicked it."

"Nicked?" Alex couldn't place Sarah's regional accent, but it certainly wasn't one typically found in British costume dramas.

"Sorry, I *stole* it. When I, after they—" She shivered and wouldn't meet Alex's eyes.

"It's okay, you don't need to…I know what he did."

For a second, Sarah looked utterly lost, but then she straightened her back and nodded at Alex. "We should go."

For almost four hours, they walked in silence. The wind whipped away anything they did try to say, and the effort that the trek was demanding and the fear of being discovered stopped them from attempting to shout over it. There was no path, just the line of the river and landmarks they had both memorized before setting off. They had been walking for little over an hour when Alex realized that Sarah had stopped taking notice of their route, as if only sheer force of will was making her put one foot in front of the other. Alex stayed close by her side, not close enough that Sarah would notice but close enough to catch her if she fell.

❖

"Okay, easy, easy. Sit here for a second. I just need to commit a misdemeanor." Alex steered Sarah to sit on an old log, then dropped her bag and hunted around for something she could use to smash the padlock on the door of the decrepit-looking hut. "Why the fuck would anyone lock this?" she muttered, selecting a decent-sized rock and eyeing the best angle of attack. With a hard swing, she smashed the rock against the metal and then stared open-mouthed when the lock disintegrated immediately and the door swung open.

"Oh." Hearing something that sounded suspiciously like a stifled giggle, she turned to find Sarah bending double with laughter. Alex smiled. "Think I overdid that?"

"Possibly, just a little."

"C'mon." She tucked her hand beneath Sarah's arm. "Let's get you inside."

Despite the dull light enveloping the valley, it took a minute for their eyes to adjust to the near-total darkness in the hut. Constructed entirely from wood, its single room was windowless and smelled strongly of mildew and animal musk.

"It's bijou," Sarah said lightly.

"It has a certain charm," Alex agreed. She panned her flashlight around the tiny building. A large crate and a wooden chair were the sole furnishings, but against one wall stood a small log-burning stove with a pile of kindling stacked up beside it. "Oh, now, that's more like it."

As Sarah sat wearily in the chair, Alex wedged an old ax beneath the wooden crossbeams of the hut door to hold it closed and then turned back to the stove. Newspapers mixed in with the kindling bore dates from the 1980s. Her initial optimism fading, she struck one of her waterproofed matches. Despite the dampness evident in the hut, the small piece of paper she lit burned brightly and smoke curled up toward the chimney. She held her breath, hoping against hope that after thirty years it was still functional. The smoke disappeared within seconds and she rocked back on her heels with a quiet whoop of joy. She selected the driest pieces from the woodpile and soon had a fire crackling in the belly of the stove. Amber light flickered across the filthy floor, revealing a covering of straw and moldy carpet. On one of the walls, hung on a single nail, was a photograph of a stern-looking young woman, its edges smudged by greasy fingerprints as if it had been taken down and put back up many times over.

"She looks like she was loved." Sarah had followed Alex's gaze to the photograph.

"Yes, she does," Alex said softly, but the pang of remorse she felt at trespassing in a stranger's home was swiftly tempered by the practicalities of their own circumstances.

The hinged lid of the crate was stiff with lack of use, and it creaked noisily as she opened it. Inside, she found three dusty blankets, a pair of overalls, a length of rope, and a set of tin cooking utensils.

"What if they see the smoke?"

Her hand poised to unzip the duffel bag, Alex hesitated and turned to look at Sarah. She was watching the fire as if mesmerized, but didn't seem to want to take advantage of its heat until she was certain that it wouldn't be snatched away from her.

"The mist should be enough to hide it. Here, stand up for a second." Alex pulled Sarah's chair right up to the stove and then nodded at her to sit back down. "They don't know which direction we headed in, and with the weather this bad it'll be dark in a few hours. I think it's worth taking the chance."

"Oh, okay. That's good," Sarah mumbled, her head nodding as she fought a losing battle to stay awake. Alex carefully leaned her forward and took her sodden jacket off. The sweater underneath was equally soaked and Alex could see dark stains on the one wrapped around her abdomen, but she seemed to be comfortable enough for the moment.

Leaving her to doze, Alex turned her attention back to the duffel bag. It had been packed with military precision: packets of dried food stacked above two complete changes of clothing, a flashlight with spare batteries, a generous supply of cigarettes, and a wash kit that included a bottle of hair dye. A Ziploc bag contained a passport, driver's license, and Social Security card. The photograph on the papers belonged to Nathan Merrick, but all three bore a new name. At the bottom of the bag were a rudimentary first aid kit, a leather pouch, and a filthy oilskin. She unsnapped the fastener on the pouch and let out a whistle as a thick wad of hundred dollar bills fell out first. She set the cash aside and drew out what remained. It was not a handgun as she had hoped, but a handheld GPS device.

"Nice," she muttered, not needing to be an expert to recognize it as an expensive piece of gear. It turned on with a welcoming beep but then stubbornly requested a passcode. Her optimistic guess of a factory-set 1, 2, 3, 4 was quickly rejected, leaving her with only three opportunities prior to being locked out of the system. She slid the GPS back into its pouch and picked up the oilskin instead. Flakes of dried mud fell off as she untied the leather straps that had been bound tightly around it. The outermost layer of the skin showed some sign of degradation, but when she spread the cloth out, its inner layer was dry and completely intact. The skin had been used to protect a small plastic box, the lid of which had been sealed with duct tape. Slightly wary now, she shook the box. A quiet metallic rattle sounded from within. She peeled the tape off and flicked open the lid before she could second-guess herself.

"What the hell?"

She tipped three small keys into the palm of her hand and then held them up one by one to study them in the firelight. They appeared to be intricately designed security keys, all similar but not quite identical in cut and thickness. Despite her mounting suspicion that Merrick had only recently unearthed them, their condition was pristine. She dropped them back into the bag as if they had burned her, possibilities and theories racing through her mind until only the most obvious one remained. "Shit." She glanced over at Sarah, startled to find not only that she was awake but that she had been watching Alex empty the bag of its contents.

"It's not really me they're after, is it?" Sarah said.

It suddenly all made sense to Alex; that Merrick would be so persistent in hunting Sarah down, when in all likelihood she would have died from exposure or her injuries long before she could tell anyone where he was or what he had done.

"No, I don't think it is." Alex looked uneasily at the keys. "Before I found you, Walt—the guy I work with—spoke to me on the radio. He told me Merrick was pretty heavily involved with white supremacist organizations. They were probably the ones who busted him out of jail." Even this little information seemed too much for Sarah to take in, so Alex simplified things for her sake. "I think he's out here looking for something," she said, as Sarah nodded reluctantly in agreement. "And I think you might have stolen his map."

❖

The rope had been long enough to stretch from one side of the hut to the other, and Alex had hung their coats to dry. Their boots and socks sat steaming in front of the stove, and a pot of water was heating slowly but surely. Curled up on the floor beside the boots, Sarah was fast asleep. Although Alex had tried her hardest to delay what needed to be done next, she had just about run out of ways to procrastinate, and she was concerned enough about Sarah's condition to put a hand on her shoulder and gently wake her.

"No. Don't." Sarah lashed her hand out to slap Alex's away.

"Hey. Sorry, I didn't mean…It's just me."

"Alex." Sarah pushed herself up to sit with her back against the wall. "Shit, was I sleeping? I don't remember falling asleep. I was going to help you." She looked around and nodded with admiration. "Love what you've done with the place."

"Why, thank you, ma'am, but I'm not sure you're going to love me for this." Alex held out a first aid kit. "You're still bleeding, Sarah."

There was a small, fresh pool of blood where Sarah had been lying. She hurt too; that much was obvious in the tight lines drawn across her face and the stiffness that pervaded her movements. She didn't say a word as Alex helped her to take her sweater and her tank top off, but just shivered once as goose bumps rose to cover her torso, and then she dropped her arms to her sides to allow Alex to untie the sweater around her midriff. Her hands curled into fists as the material came loose.

Murmuring a stream of apologies, Alex cast the sweater aside and brought the flashlight closer. "It's a through-and-through," she said, mostly to herself. "God, what a mess." She leaned back slightly and studied Sarah's face. "You managed to run down half a mountain with this?"

"Yeah." Pulling the sweater away had caused the wound to open up, and Sarah was absently watching blood streaming freely again from the ragged hole the bullet had torn in her right side. "I've had worse."

There was no appeal for pity in her tone; it was just a matter-of-fact comment she had made without really seeming to think about it. The piece of gauze Alex was using to clean the streaks of blood from her abdomen gradually revealed a raised spider's web of silvery scar tissue, but Sarah didn't offer any explanation, and, conscious of how exposed she already was, Alex didn't ask the obvious question. She of all people understood Sarah's desire for privacy.

"Oh hell." Now that she had a clearer view of what she was dealing with, Alex realized it wasn't just the bleeding that was going to be a problem. "Sarah, there's a piece of your sweater in here." She could see the small piece of navy blue fabric folded deep within the injury. The cavity originally caused by the bullet's track had collapsed around the cloth, wedging it firmly in place. Alex felt her palms begin to sweat as she considered it. She wasn't a medic, and she didn't really have a clue what to do. Applying pressure to the bleed wasn't stopping it, but for the moment at least, it was giving her time to think. She was still watching stark crimson leak into the white of the gauze when a quiet metallic clink made her look up.

"Wash your hands as best you can and sterilize these." Sarah was holding out a pair of tweezers from the first aid kit. "The cloth has to come out or it'll cause an infection, and then I think I'll need a few stitches." She kept her voice light, but her hand trembled almost imperceptibly as Alex took hold of the tweezers.

"Are you a doctor or something?"

Sarah shook her head with a desperate gasp of laughter. "No, I saw it in a movie once."

Alex stared at her dumbfounded for a moment before she too began to laugh. "You saw it in a *movie*?"

"Yeah." Sarah shrugged. "Hey, it worked. The guy lived. I think he went on to save the world."

❖

"You comfortable?"

"Mmhm, I'm fine." Lying on her left side with her head pillowed on a blanket, Sarah nodded at Alex. "Ready when you are."

"Okay." Alex tried to ignore the butterflies fluttering in her stomach. "Let me know if you want me to stop."

"Don't stop," Sarah said immediately. "Please, whatever you do, don't stop."

"Right. I won't stop. Ready?"

"Yep."

For what seemed like the longest time, there was nothing but the sound of Sarah's teeth grinding together and Alex cursing as she worked to get a firm grip on the tiny circle of cloth. The tweezers were awkward things to maneuver, sliding and jarring when she tried to open them in the right place, while rivulets of fresh blood worked to conceal the old scar tissue as quickly as she wiped it clean. Eventually, with a sharp tug that owed more to luck and frustration than judgment, the cloth came free, and she clamped a thick wad of gauze in place to stanch the bleeding. She looked down to see Sarah's face pressed into the blanket, her upper arm hiding what little of her face would have been visible, her body shaking as she tried not to cry.

"I got it, Sarah. We're halfway there."

Back when her hands were steadier, Alex had threaded the needle she always kept in her kit for emergency repairs, although she had never envisioned using it for this sort of emergency.

Sarah lifted her head and, seeing what Alex was about to do, hurriedly wiped her face dry. "Are you okay?"

With the needle poised, Alex hesitated. "Shouldn't that be my line?"

When Sarah nodded, Alex selected her starting point, pushed the needle through, and made her first stitch before she could lose her nerve completely. It became no easier after that, and although she tried to tell herself that it was just like mending a hole torn into a tent canvas, the analogy was less than convincing. Canvas was never warm and slippery with blood beneath her fingers, nor did it tense or flinch when she pulled a stitch taut. When at last the wound had stopped seeping blood around the bright green cotton, she felt sicker than Sarah looked. She cast the needle and thread aside and wiped her face dry with the bottom of her sweater.

"Sarah, it's done."

"Thank you." The softest of whispers.

Alex pressed two Advil to Sarah's lips to go with the Tylenol she had taken earlier, and held a bottle of water for her to sip from. By the time Alex was smoothing clean dressings over the seven neat stitches, Sarah was barely conscious. Alex covered her up with both of the remaining blankets, tucking them in closely, before adding more wood to the stove. The supplies in the duffel bag had included coffee, dried milk, and sugar, and after she had cleaned the blood from her hands, she made herself a strong, sweet drink. With the mug wrapped in both of her hands, she huddled close to the fire. A small leak marked time by dripping persistently in one corner of the hut. She sipped her coffee and listened instead to the deep, regular breaths Sarah was taking as she slept.

Gray, washed-out light was seeping through gaps in the ramshackle walls when Alex jerked awake. At some point in the night, she had moved to sit beside Sarah, and Sarah's arm was flung casually across her lap, its hand twitching intermittently as she dreamed. Curling her fingers around Sarah's for a second, Alex was relieved to find that dry warmth had replaced the cool clamminess of the previous day. Unconsciously, Sarah returned the slight pressure, and then her eyes opened blearily.

"Shh, go back to sleep. Everything's fine."

Sarah nodded sagely in agreement and settled without ever having woken properly.

Alex disentangled herself from the blankets, collected the pot from the stove, and tiptoed over to the door. When she stepped outside, she was greeted by a wall of fog that reduced visibility to a matter of yards, but she could see that the hut sat in the smallest of clearings. Huge fir trees crowded in on it, effectively sheltering it from sight, while a lively stream provided a useful water source. Walking around its perimeter, she saw no trails through the trees, nothing to make it easy for anyone to find. Any traces of whoever had once lived or worked here had long since been reclaimed by the forest. Feeling confident that they could safely spend at least one more night, she used a rock to dig herself a small toilet, and washed in the stream's frigid water. She was refilling the pot when she heard a thud, and she tensed, turning immediately toward the hut. Sarah was leaning against the doorjamb, wrapped in a blanket. She smiled woozily as Alex dropped the pot and jogged over to her.

"What are you doing up?"

"I, um." She waved a vague hand toward the trees. "I really need the loo."

The phrase was temporarily lost in translation before Alex nodded in sudden understanding. "Right. You, uh, you need me to…?"

"No. I'll manage."

"Right." She took hold of the blanket Sarah held out to her. "Give me a shout if…"

"If I split my stitches pulling my trousers up?" Sarah offered with a grin.

"Exactly."

"I'll shout. I promise."

"Great."

They both laughed, the absurdity of the exchange briefly alleviating the dire nature of their predicament. Alex waited until she was sure that Sarah was safe to walk unaided, and then stepped inside and began to look in Merrick's bag for something suitable for breakfast.

❖

"I can offer you mac 'n' cheese or oatmeal." Alex held the packets up as Sarah came back into the hut.

"I'm not really hungry."

Sarah gripped the water pot tightly. Hoping to save Alex a job, she had managed to fill the pot and carry it back, but she could feel cold sweat dampening the hair at the nape of her neck, and her fingers began to slip from the metal. There was a scramble of movement and a hissed curse, and then she felt Alex grab her arm. Without ceremony, she was half-dragged, half-carried toward her improvised bed of blankets.

"Put your head between your knees."

The last thing she wanted to do was move any part of herself, but instead of thinking up a suitably pithy response, she sagged onto the floor. "I'm going to be sick."

She made no effort to resist when Alex guided her to lie down on her uninjured side, and she closed her eyes as the room swam in front of her. She opened her eyes again at the touch of a warm cloth on her forehead, to find Alex carefully wiping her face.

"Still feel sick?" Alex placed an old bucket within easy reach and waited as Sarah took a tentative breath.

"No, I think it's passed, thanks." She wanted to tell Alex to stop, that Alex had already done so much more than she could ever hope to repay, but the touch felt so reassuring that she kept her counsel and lay still beneath it.

"Let me take a look here." With one hand resting on Sarah's hip, Alex used her other to lift Sarah's sweater and check the dressings she had applied the previous night. Both were speckled with only the slightest amount of fresh blood, and the fear eased from her expression. "Those look good. I think it's shock that's making you feel so bad." She sounded as if she was trying to work it out for herself as she went along. "You lost a lot of blood, and you probably dropped your blood pressure by standing up for so long. I think that's how it works." Her hand and the cloth resumed their soothing motion across Sarah's face, her fingers easing the tangles from soaked strands of hair. "I had a friend who was an EMT, used to get real pissed at people telling her someone was in shock when all they'd had was a fright. 'There are five types of clinical shock,' she would say, 'and that's not one of them.'"

"Are you a police officer?" Sarah asked softly.

The question seemed to catch Alex off guard. She dropped her hand away, her eyes not quite able to meet Sarah's.

"I was," she said at length. "What made you think that?"

"Last night, when you said 'misdemeanor,' it seemed like a police-type thing to say, but I don't know." Sarah hesitated, struggling to follow her logic through. "You also seem pretty good at all this," she gestured around herself, "which confuses the issue slightly."

"I work near the park now. I quit the force." Alex left the statement hanging and stood to balance the pot on the stove. "Oatmeal okay?"

Sarah might have been shocky, but she recognized the end to a conversation when she heard it, and she nodded. "Oatmeal's fine."

"Be about five minutes."

She nodded again, settling down and studying Alex obliquely as she readied bowls and sugar and poured packets of powdered fruit drink into mugs. She was a good couple of inches taller than Sarah, with short hair whose style would probably have flattered the shape of her face had sleep not left her hair stuck out at all angles. Her movements were cagey, as if she knew that she was being watched and was afraid that the simple act of preparing a meal would somehow reveal all her secrets. Remembering Alex helping her to undress the previous night, Sarah averted her gaze and wondered how long she could keep her own secrets.

CHAPTER SEVEN

Battery died on this yesterday." Alex dropped the radio back into her bag, where it landed with a dull thud.

"No signal on this." Sarah set her phone where they could keep an eye on it in case some kind of network miracle occurred and it resurrected itself.

"So, we're here…"

Sitting close together in front of the stove, they were trying to take stock of what they had, where they were, and exactly what they were going to do next. Sarah looked at where Alex was pointing to on the map.

"We're in the middle of nowhere," she said.

"Yup, closest thing to civilization is probably here." Alex tracked downward and miles across wilderness, back to the campsite on Ross Lake. "Oh, that reminds me, Johnno and…Shit, I forgot the other guy's name. They said to say hi." She shook her head in apology.

"Johnno and Zach? You met them?" Sarah found herself smiling. "I hope they got away okay."

"They were the ones who told me you were out here. Last I saw them, they were safely on the boat." Alex topped up Sarah's mug. "Drink more. You need the fluids."

Sarah obediently took a sip and then made a face. "Ugh, my bloody eyeballs are floating."

It took Alex several seconds to decipher her meaning, but when she did, she snorted with laughter. "That's disgusting." The fact that she was still laughing somewhat belied her declaration. "Okay, I've tried to work it out and I have no clue. Where the hell in Britain are you from?"

"The north. Well, northern England, which is way below Scotland." Sarah sketched a vague outline over their map and pointed in the right general direction. "I was living with friends. Oh, it's easier to show you. Here we go. This is Ash and Tess, and their son, Jamie. I've not met him yet." She handed Alex her phone. "They'll be worried sick. Tess has been fretting since I set off traveling, and with good reason this time." Alex passed the phone back, and Sarah closed the image down with some reluctance.

"They look real happy," Alex said, a wistful note in her voice.

"They are. They've been together for years. Ash has been trying to play cupid for me in the Village for as long as I've known her, but she reckons her arrows shoot about as straight as her."

Alex looked slightly bemused. "The village? What, like an English country village, with a bowling green and a duck pond?"

Sarah all but choked on her drink. "God no, not quite. This village is a patch of gay pubs and clubs in Manchester. She'd drag me down there, try and fail to set me up with someone, and we'd head home together with fish and chips to tell her wife all about it." She shifted a little, curling her knees up in an attempt to alleviate the throbbing in her side. "They're as good as family to me." The tears that suddenly blurred her vision had nothing to do with the pain. She wiped them away quickly and forced brightness into her tone. "So what about you?"

In response, Alex held up a finger to call a temporary halt to the conversation. She thrust her hand deeply into her pack and felt around until she found what she needed. She made short work of the wrapper, then snapped the bar of chocolate in two and offered Sarah half.

"If you're getting my life story, we're definitely going to need chocolate," she said, scooting down a little and crossing her legs at the ankles.

"Shit. Did I open a can of worms?" Sarah sounded genuinely worried, but Alex waved away her concern.

"I was brought up in Boston, lived there for…" Alex paused to work out the math. "Twenty-three years. I have two older brothers, and parents who liked to leave us with our nanny while they entertained friends, played golf at the country club, or took cruises to far-flung parts of the world for months at a time." She swallowed the last of her chocolate and licked her fingers. "Needless to say, Father did not approve when I joined the Boston P.D., and he pretty much cut me off completely when I started seeing Meg."

"Ah," Sarah said pointedly. She didn't seem to be shocked by the direction the conversation was taking.

"Yeah, *ah*," Alex repeated, mimicking her intonation. The empty wrapper crinkled in Alex's hand as she twisted it nervously. Her parents had made coming out such an ordeal that she was more than a little gun-shy on the issue, even when she was obviously in good company. Fingers gently wrapped around hers, loosening their grip on the paper, and she looked up.

"Go on," Sarah said. "But only if you want to."

Alex took a couple of seconds to study Sarah. Although she'd only met her a few hours ago, there was something about her that seemed familiar: a look in her eyes that Alex had seen in the mirror countless times since that night in the alley. Suddenly conscious that she was staring, and not wanting to make Sarah feel uncomfortable, she lowered her gaze, but Sarah hadn't let go of her hand, and that alone was enough for her to resume telling her story.

"Meg was an artist from LA, and back then when I was young and stupid, I thought she was the most beautiful girl I had ever seen." She rolled her eyes at the cliché. "When my dad threw me out of the house, I transferred to the LAPD, and twelve months later, Meg ditched me for a performance artist whose sole work of genius comprised five minutes of her standing naked in front of a black screen, screaming and crying." She tried to smile, but she was unable to disguise the bitterness in her voice, bitterness that was partly aimed at the way she had been treated, but mainly at her own blind naivety.

"Is that when you moved out here?"

"No, that came later. I stayed in LA for five years. There wasn't a whole lot for me to go home to."

As much as Sarah looked like she wanted to ask what had happened next, she didn't push the conversation in that direction.

"Maybe later," Alex murmured, in response to the unvoiced question. "Maybe later we can both swap our war stories."

Sarah nodded, one hand pressed protectively across her abdomen as if that would somehow erase the marks that Alex had already seen. "Need something stronger than chocolate for that," she said, and Alex gave a short laugh of agreement that managed to sound at once terrible and completely without humor.

❖

The cigarette flared and crackled as Nathan Merrick took a deep, agitated drag on it. Smoke billowed from his nostrils when he exhaled. The fire he had managed to keep alight for the past hour hissed as rain began to fall again. Large scattered drops battered ground that was already saturated, picking up momentum and finally driving him back to the small tent where Bethany was sleeping. He sat just within its confines and aimed his smoke out the open flap. Behind him, Bethany muttered and turned over, the thin blanket she had covered herself with tangling awkwardly around her. Merrick watched her struggle for a long moment before he turned back to the night and to the storm that he hoped would continue to rage until he had the chance to sort out the mess he had gotten himself into.

Three days' grace. That was all Nicholas Deakin had given him. Three days to get to the safe-box, collect the order, and rendezvous for the pickup. Initially, everything had run smoothly; his escape had been far easier than he had anticipated, the weather forecast had conveniently emptied the park, and even the storm hadn't really hampered their schedule. Heat rising to his face, he flicked what little remained of his cigarette onto the ground and lit a fresh one. That left the pack in his hand empty, and he screwed it up furiously in his fist. That bitch had stolen everything, and he knew that running out of cigarettes was going to be the least of his problems. Deakin had sounded wary at their last radio check-in but had grudgingly agreed to extend his deadline by two days, a concession that probably owed much to the fact that Beth—his niece—had corroborated everything Merrick had told him and begged her uncle for more time. As if it had been necessary, Nicholas had reminded Merrick exactly how much the group had risked for him so far and how great a payoff they were expecting.

"Nate, it's cold with that open." Bethany's voice drifted out of the darkness.

He ignored her, laying out his map instead and casting his flashlight over it. "She can't have gotten this far," he muttered, mainly to himself, but he felt the warmth of Bethany's arms as she wrapped them around him.

"We missed her, then." Bethany stroked the hair back from his face.

He brusquely shrugged her off. "Go to sleep." He pushed her again, more forcefully this time, and she fell back against her crumpled blanket. "First light, we head back up. We're not gonna miss her again."

❖

The hut door was slightly ajar, and the faint breeze filtering in through it was enough to wake Sarah. Comfortable and drowsy, she breathed in the fresh scent of moist pine and rain, glad that the draft had alleviated the stifling heat that had built up in the small room through the night. She shifted experimentally, trying to gauge whether the pain in her side was any easier and finding that it was nowhere near as severe as it had been. When she pushed herself up to tell Alex, she saw that the space beside her was empty, Alex's blankets already neatly folded and piled together. In their place, the map was spread out, with all of Merrick's falsified identity papers scattered on top of it alongside the GPS device that Alex had found in his bag.

Dizziness reminded Sarah why it wasn't such a good idea to change her position abruptly, and she had just settled down again when Alex came back into the hut. Barefoot and wearing only a sports bra and combat pants, she had obviously been bathing in the stream, and her short hair was damp and spiky where she had ruffled her hands through it to dry it. Her eyes unaccustomed to the hut's dull light, she hadn't noticed that Sarah was awake, and Sarah was on the verge of speaking when Alex turned her back and stooped to pick up the rest of her clothing.

The firelight cast a butter-yellow glow across her back, dancing over lean muscles honed by months of manual labor, and picking out in perfect delineation the jagged edges of the scarring that marred the lower third of her torso. Horrified by her unwitting intrusion, Sarah quickly turned her face away, but she had already seen the telltale mismatched tones of neatly positioned skin grafts. Remembering Alex's earlier reference to their respective "war stories," she shivered despite the warmth of the room. She heard a whisper of cloth as Alex pulled a sweater on and the murmur of happiness she made when she realized that it was dry. Although Sarah was desperate to apologize for what she had seen, instinct and her own miserable experiences told her that that would only make matters worse. With her eyes still tightly closed, she exhaled slowly into the scratchy wool beneath her cheek and forced herself to keep quiet.

❖

Sarah ducked her head beneath the small waterfall and allowed it to pour over her. The water was cold, the sort of cold that made her catch her breath, and made her skin tingle painfully before suddenly bringing a rush of heat to its surface. She had always loved that rush. At school, when her friends dipped their toes into the pool and pulled them out shrieking, she had jumped straight in, having learned at an early age that the best way to deal with that first shock of icy water was simply to get it over with and swim through it. During her convalescence, she had returned to and adapted that philosophy of taking the plunge and pushing through the pain countless times.

She splashed water on her face and used a torn scrap of cloth to give herself as thorough a wash as was practicable. Alex hadn't been too keen on the idea of Sarah heading out on her own, but she had insisted that she felt strong enough to manage without help. It was true that she was feeling better, although when she had finished she sat beside the small stream for a while to catch her breath in preparation for the walk back to the hut. She watched a tan-colored bird take an early morning bath and tried very hard to convince herself that she wasn't going crazy. That instead, she really was stranded in the middle of the wilderness with an armed man chasing after her, an armed man who might or might not have hidden some mythical treasure out here. That she had been shot and somehow managed to survive. But mainly that she had been rescued and cared for by a young woman who was starting to give her funny fluttery feelings in her stomach, and who absolutely should not have been dragged into this mess in the first place.

Her soaked hair whipped against her face as she shook her head. She pulled it back to wring it between her hands. She and Alex couldn't stay here. The hut's very remoteness was what made it such a dangerous place to linger; it was the only shelter marked in the area. Once Merrick realized that she had not continued her descent, it would not take too much of a leap to work out where she was hiding. Although she appreciated Alex giving her time to rest, she was not willing to endanger her more than she already had. Anticipating a struggle to persuade her of that, she set her jaw and strode across the stream.

When she entered the hut, she found Alex sitting in the middle of the floor, surrounded by Merrick's falsified papers and scowling at the GPS in her hand. Her face brightened when she saw Sarah.

"You look positively shiny," she said with a grin.

"Mountain water is amazing for the complexion," Sarah told her in a voice that owed a lot to ridiculous cosmetics commercials. "It's all the rage, darling." She sat on the floor at the edge of the papers and felt the smile fade from her lips. "Alex, we need to leave," she said without preamble.

Alex set the GPS down carefully and looked at her. "We'll be good here for another day or so. Just until you're stronger." But she sounded uncertain even as she spoke, as if she was aware that her argument was built on shaky foundations.

Sarah shook her head. "It won't take Merrick long to figure things out. When he does, he'll double back and this is the first place he'll look." She could see Alex drawing a breath to argue but didn't give her the opportunity to interrupt. "I'm not going to risk your life by staying here," she said fiercely, but a tremor crept into her voice as her composure began to slip and the rest of her words came out in a harsh whisper. "God, you shouldn't even be here in the first place."

Alex grabbed hold of her wrist before she could hide her face away. "Don't go blaming yourself, now." She lowered Sarah's hand into her lap and covered it with both of hers. "I don't remember you inviting me to this party; I just sort of gate-crashed it. Best fun I've had in years."

"Liar." The word choked and stuttered in Sarah's throat. She didn't know whether to laugh or cry.

"Well, yeah." Alex nodded in easy concession. "I'm scared shitless really."

"You are?" Sarah met and held her gaze. "Me too." She felt Alex stroke the back of her hand gently and laid hers on top.

"You're right about moving on, Sarah."

"I know." She took a breath, not bothering to hide her relief. She patted Alex's uppermost hand once. "How about I make breakfast, you carry on trying to crack the Enigma code there, and then we get packed?" She made as if to move and then paused, confused when she realized that Alex was staring at her. "What?"

Alex grinned. "Anyone ever tell you that you're real cute when you're bossy?"

❖

The smell of ersatz cheese warming on the small stove was making Alex's stomach rumble. Despite her earnest attempts to ignore it, she couldn't help but go and linger by the pot, watching the bubbles rise and burst as the macaroni simmered.

"Packet says ten minutes, Alex." Sarah made a show of checking her watch. "You've had two."

"Two?" Alex stirred the pot as if that alone would make the food cook faster. Beneath her spoon, the pasta still felt rock-hard. She moaned dramatically. "But I'm so hungry. Think it'd be okay like this?"

Sarah took the spoon from her, looking aghast. "No, I think it'd be absolutely revolting, but feel free to prove me wrong. Just leave my half in the pan for another…" she glanced at her watch again, "seven and a half minutes." Trying not to laugh, she shook her head as Alex slumped back down by the map and sulkily took up the GPS device.

"Got that figured out yet?" Sarah asked in a transparent attempt at distraction. She liberally sprinkled into the pasta the contents of a small bag that she then slipped back into her jacket pocket. After adjusting the pot slightly, she came to sit beside Alex.

"Yep, think so." Alex held out the device, tilting it away from the firelight to take the glare off the screen. Whoever had programmed the security code for the device had not been very imaginative, using the year and month of Merrick's newly assigned date of birth, and Alex had cracked it shortly after Sarah had poured the macaroni into the pan. "He was heading…there." She pointed to the location. Although she had never used a GPS, preferring the old-fashioned method of map and compass, once she had worked out the referencing system, it had been relatively simple for her to find Merrick's intended destination on their map.

"There's nothing there," Sarah said, looking at where Alex indicated. "It's in the middle of the forest."

On the map, Alex's finger was resting on a spot approximately six miles from the hut, slightly higher than their current location and farther into a dense tract of forest. While they had no intention of going there themselves, she knew that being able to pinpoint the spot for the police would make their job easier.

"Good place to hide something you don't want anyone to stumble across accidentally," she said.

Sarah nodded, following Alex's logic through. "And an absolute bugger to find if someone's stolen your fancy electronic map-type gadget."

"I'm guessing you're not his favorite person about now."

"I'm not too fond of him either," Sarah countered. "He bloody shot me."

Alex couldn't help but smile at her indignation, and Sarah slowly smiled as well.

"It bloody hurt," she muttered, before returning to the stove and tasting the pasta. "Not bad if I do say so myself," she said, and laughed when Alex held her plate out expectantly.

Alex peered into her dish and did a slight double-take at the strange color of the concoction.

Sarah had obviously been expecting this reaction. "Just try it," she said.

Alex dutifully dipped the tip of her tongue into the sauce. It tasted exactly like mac 'n' cheese was supposed to taste. Encouraged, she swallowed the spoonful. After a couple seconds, she noticed the pleasant heat that lingered in her mouth and a subtle smoky flavor that hadn't been evident immediately. She looked at Sarah, who was trying not to laugh at her.

"This is the best mac 'n' cheese I ever had." She licked the back of her spoon. "Why does mine never taste this good? I buy exactly the same brand."

Sarah retrieved the sealed baggie from her jacket, and threw it to Alex. "I keep them in my pocket so the bag doesn't get ripped. Never travel without them," she said.

Alex held the baggie up to the light and gave her the dubious look she traditionally reserved for street corner dealers.

"They're *herbs*, Alex. All perfectly legal herbs. Rosemary, sage, thyme, and paprika, which, along with a good sprinkle of black pepper, is what I've added to your breakfast. Livens the sauce up a bit and makes it taste slightly less like it was put together on a production line."

"Yes, it does," Alex said before sneezing as the pepper she had just sniffed irritated her nose. "I can't cook for shit. Living out here is a great excuse to eat crap out of a can every night." She shrugged at Sarah's dismay. "My family had a cook. My mom just assumed I would marry well enough to be able to do the same. I boiled an egg dry once. Set off all the fire alarms. After that, I was banned from the kitchen."

Sarah accepted the herbs back and tucked them safely away again. "You make a very fine oatmeal," she said, managing not to sound at all condescending. "If you can follow instructions on a packet, you can follow a recipe."

"Mm, maybe." Alex suspected Sarah's confidence in her was misguided. "As a kid, I always wanted my mom to show me how to bake a cake for my brothers—their birthdays were only a couple of days apart—but she never did, and I guess I just stopped asking."

"I'll show you how to bake a cake. Soon as we get out of here," Sarah said, her eyes blazing with anger on Alex's behalf.

Alex smiled shyly, unaccustomed to having anyone willing to fight in her corner. "You will?"

"Yep, chocolate cake, fruit cake, whatever you like."

"I like chocolate."

"Chocolate it is then," Sarah said easily and knocked her fork against Alex's spoon to seal the deal.

The GPS beeped once and then again in quick succession, making them both jump. Alex gave a low cheer, turning it toward Sarah. The display read: *coordinates stored, calculating distance.*

Sarah stuck her fork in her mouth while she applauded. "I had every faith in you," she mumbled around the metal. "Never doubted for a second."

Alex gave a little bow, but then her eyes widened as she read the display.

"Christ, we really have wandered off course. This shows it's thirteen miles back to Ross Lake from here, but that's as the crow flies. There's the small matter of a mountain in between." Although she'd had a good idea where they were in relation to the lake, she hadn't had the chance to think about how they were going to get back there.

"Ouch." Sarah gave a heartfelt grimace.

"If we stay on the level, follow the contours, it's probably twice as far." Alex gestured to the map, her initial optimism fading as she thought about the trek they were going to have to attempt. She switched off the GPS to conserve its battery and looked at Sarah. "It's not going to be easy. We're going to have to hike off-road to start with. Using the map and the GPS, we should be able to find a trail, but we're nowhere near any of the official tracks here. Whatever trail we do find, we'll just have to hope it's passable."

Sarah inclined her head, trying to gauge distance and walking speeds against the weather and their own physical condition. "So maybe two to three days if we're lucky and the storm settles."

They both jumped, startled, as a sudden gust of wind slammed the door shut and rain began to beat against the roof.

"Oh, me and my big mouth." Sarah laughed hopelessly. She leaned into Alex, who wrapped an arm around her.

"We'll be fine," Alex murmured into her hair. "Marilyn'll have teams out looking for us as soon as she can. All we need to do is meet them halfway."

"Okay, we can do that."

"We can do that," Alex said. "We'll finish breakfast and get packed up."

She felt Sarah nod but make no attempt to move away. Holding her close, Alex could smell the faintly herbal scent of stream water in her hair. Her heartbeat thudded strong and reassuringly steady against Alex's chest, the rhythm gradually slowing as her breathing became softer and more relaxed. Alex closed her eyes. The pounding of the rain faded into the background, taking with it the wind and the persistent clatter of something loose on the doorframe. She didn't want to leave the hut. They were safe here. At least until the man with the guns showed up. She shuddered once and felt Sarah edge more tightly against her in response.

"It'll be okay. We'll be fine," she whispered, but then wondered how the hell she could expect to convince Sarah of that when she was so very uncertain herself.

❖

Alex had found the old khaki backpack buried at the bottom of the trunk. Dirt and cobwebs flew into the air when she shook it, but the straps were all sound and it would be far easier to carry than Merrick's duffel bag.

Blankets, a sizable piece of plastic sheeting, rope, and two each of the pots, plates, and mugs were already set to one side, ready to pack, and she was now sorting through Merrick's supplies. She added all of his food, his clothing, his flashlight, and his identity papers to the pile. The papers would be useful evidence for the police and the FBI, who might be able to trace them back to their source, but more importantly, the last thing she wanted to do was leave them behind for Merrick to find and use to flee the country.

Sitting cross-legged on the floor, Sarah began to pack the items Alex passed her. She laughed when she looked up to find Alex deliberately tearing all of Merrick's cigarettes in half.

"What?" Alex asked innocently. "They're very bad for him. I'm doing him a favor."

Still laughing, Sarah picked up a pack and began to help her out. "Oh well, if he wasn't pissed off with us before..."

"Yeah, what have we got to lose, right?" Alex tore into another handful, but Sarah's hands had stilled and she was staring blankly at the wall. "Hey." Alex reached out and unfolded Sarah's fingers from the pack she had all but crushed. "You okay?"

Sarah didn't answer right away, and when she did, her words were little more than a whisper. "He just shot him," she said, her gaze still fixed and distant. "That night, the prison guard. Merrick was so casual, like it was nothing. He didn't even blink." She licked her lips and slowed her breathing with a visible effort. "I heard the guard begging for his life, Alex. Telling them he had a family. I wanted to help him, but I was so scared and I couldn't think fast enough."

"What could you have done?"

The directness of Alex's question made Sarah pause.

"I don't...There must have been something."

"One tired, terrified young woman weighing about a hundred twenty pounds soaking wet, against two armed criminals." Alex used her thumb to wipe a tear from Sarah's cheek. "There wasn't a thing you could've done, Sarah. Not a fucking thing. You can't keep beating yourself up about it."

In lieu of an answer, Sarah took the cigarettes back and tore into them viciously.

"I know where the body is," she said at length. "That'll help, won't it?"

Alex stopped brushing tobacco and paper from her pants. "Yeah, that'll help."

For a few minutes, Sarah continued to destroy the last pack of cigarettes, dropping the pieces into a tin bucket that seemed to have more holes than actual tin. When there was nothing left but the empty pack, she pushed herself to her feet, screwed the cardboard up, and tossed it into their makeshift trash can. Alex looked up at her and Sarah nodded toward the corner of the room where the chair sat with the first aid kit at its side.

"Shall we just get it over with?" she said.

Alex set the bucket down. She looked about as enthusiastic about the prospect as Sarah felt. "Let me wash my hands."

When Alex came back from the stream, Sarah had already stripped off her sweater and was busy studying the dressing on her side. For the first time, it was completely free of fresh bloodstains. The wound was tender when she laid her hand across it but the discomfort was bearable.

"Okay, stay still," Alex said.

"I can't, that tickles." Sarah squirmed as Alex began to peel off the dressing and then she caught her breath when the tape suddenly came away in a rush. "Shit, now it hurts. I liked it better when it tickled."

"Sorry." In a familiar routine, Alex carefully felt around the edges of the wound, trying to detect any swelling, heat, or discharge that might signify an infection. "Looks good," she said, before asking in a lower tone, "You ready?"

"Mmhm." Sarah's answer was always the same, as was the sensation of the rough wood beneath her fingernails as she dug them into the arm of the chair.

Without further hesitation, Alex quickly wiped an antiseptic-soaked cloth across and around the wound, waited for the air to dry it, and then pressed a clean dressing into place.

"Nothing to it," Sarah said shakily. She allowed herself to be helped up. Gripping onto the back of the chair, she waited for the pain to fade. The hut was dark and cool, the stove already extinguished. As she pulled the rest of her clothes on, she could hear rain falling steadily, and she would have given almost anything not to have to leave the tiny sanctuary they had found. When she fed her arms through the straps of Alex's pack, it settled too low on her back and rubbed unbearably against the raw wound.

Noticing the problem, Alex adjusted the straps and the pain gradually eased.

"Any better?"

"It's fine, thanks."

A quiet beep sounded from the GPS when Alex switched it on. Without another word, they walked out into the rain.

CHAPTER EIGHT

Nathan Merrick was pacing, five steps back and forth. It was still early, but he and Bethany had set off just before dawn, the beam of their flashlights cutting through the trees as they tried to regain the ground they had lost. Late the previous night, poring over the map, he had cursed himself for not seeing it sooner. Previously, he had been assuming that the girl would continue downward in an attempt to find help, because that had seemed to be the only sensible course of action for her to take, since there was no map in the bag she had stolen and the GPS was passcode protected. And yet…

He paused, turning around in dirt already scuffed and trampled beneath his restless passage.

And yet there, on his map, obvious once you knew where to look, was the small black square symbolizing the only possible source of shelter for miles around. It was only supposition, but he knew in his gut that the girl had gone there. Maybe she'd had a map tucked into her jacket. Maybe she just knew the park well. He wasn't really interested as long as he found the little bitch. He stopped again and spat into the mud, trying to remember in which direction Beth had chosen to go when she had announced that she needed the toilet. He had started to walk across to a clump of bushes when she came hurrying out, tucking her shirt back into her pants and then clipping her radio onto her belt.

"Sorry," she said quickly, her cheeks reddening despite the cool air.

"Took you fuckin' long enough." He spat again, mostly for the satisfaction of seeing her disapproval.

"I said I was sorry." Her hands were moving nervously, patting her clothing down as if she were afraid she had misplaced something. She had been twitchy since setting off, and he was growing weary of adjusting his pace to accommodate her.

"That way." Pointing straight ahead, he set off immediately, no longer caring whether she could keep up. He had far greater problems to worry about.

❖

Blinking like a prisoner emerging from solitary confinement, Sarah shielded her eyes with her hand and raised her face to the sky.

"Bloody hell."

Standing beside her, Alex followed her gaze upward. "Well, would you look at that."

The rain had petered out an hour or so ago, but as they walked beneath the thick canopy of the forest neither of them had been able to see the patches of blue gradually forming in the sky. The small clearing they had just reached was bathed in sunshine. Tall grasses and ferns seemed to sparkle as light glinted off the beads of water evaporating from their surfaces, and thin wisps of steam rose from the ground as it warmed up. Sarah closed her eyes blissfully as she felt fingers of heat start to chase the chill from her skin and dry her sodden hair.

"Good a place as any for lunch, I reckon," Alex said, pointing toward a group of stones large enough for them to sit on.

Sarah followed her across the clearing, enthusiastically shrugging out of her coat as she walked. She spread it to dry on one of the rocks. Her boots came off next, swiftly followed by her socks. She wrung them out and pulled a face as gray water oozed from them.

"I would give quite a lot right now for a clean pair of socks," she declared, arranging them a strategic distance away from where she and Alex were about to eat.

"Yeah?" Alex raised an eyebrow. "What kind of offer might you have in mind?" She set her equally grim pair alongside Sarah's.

Sarah blew her breath out between pursed lips as she contemplated the question. "Oh, I don't know. Dinner somewhere fancy, all expenses paid. Nice hotel with Egyptian cotton sheets, spotless white fluffy robes, and tiny bottles of posh toiletries. Full English breakfast in bed, with mugs of tea big enough to drown in." Her eyes had inadvertently closed as she spoke, and she opened them with a start when something soft brushed against her knuckles.

"You had me at 'dinner somewhere fancy,'" Alex said with a smile. She pressed the clean pair of navy blue socks into Sarah's hands. "But the rest sounded great too."

Sarah laughed, a flush of heat spreading across her cheeks. "Hey, a deal's a deal. I said Egyptian cotton and I meant Egyptian cotton. Where the hell did—" Holding the socks up, she saw how large they were and realized they were Merrick's. "I hope he gets trench foot," she muttered vehemently. She was just about to pull them on when she hesitated. "Oh, have you got a pair?" She offered one of the socks to Alex, who waved it away.

"I'm good. He had two sets. They were brand new as well. I snipped the labels off them back at the hut." She solemnly held out another offering to Sarah. "In case we get really desperate."

Sarah removed the plastic wrapper from the small bundle of cotton, her eyes widening as she opened out and then gaped at a pair of bright red and green striped boxer shorts.

"Nice," she managed, before laughter made her double over. Tears brimming in her eyes, her side aching from the motion, she shook her head as Alex displayed a blue and yellow polka-dotted pair. "Bloody Nora, I think those are worse. I'm keeping these. Who knew master criminals had a sense of humor?" She carefully refolded the shorts and tucked them into her backpack. "I don't know why I'm laughing," she said, when she had finally managed to compose herself. "Everything I had was in that bag I lost. I already am pretty fucking desperate."

❖

They had only been walking for two hours after their lunch break, and Alex had slowed the pace considerably, but she could tell that Sarah was tiring. Sarah hadn't said anything—Alex doubted that she ever would—but her breathing was rasping noisily as she walked, and she was clearly having difficulty keeping up. Alex stopped near a fallen log that would make a convenient seat, pulled the map out, and crouched low on the ground. She didn't really need to try to work out their position on the map and she wasn't sure that it was even possible, but it would give Sarah a chance to rest without making her self-conscious. After less than a minute, two boots appeared at the edge of the map. Alex squinted upward as Sarah's shadow fell across it.

"I'm okay, Alex." Sarah spoke with as much conviction as she could muster. In truth, she was struggling and had been for a while. Although the wound in her side seemed to be healing cleanly, the niggling pain had been a constant companion throughout the day and was eating away at what little energy she had left.

Alex made no comment, merely handing Sarah a bottle of water and two Advil and watched until she swallowed the pills.

"How far have we come?" Sarah passed the bottle back to Alex, who drank deeply before screwing the lid back on.

"At a guess, about seven miles."

The route had been tortuous, forcing them to make countless detours around obstacles that the GPS either didn't feature or didn't seem to consider a problem. It had been grueling and frustrating in equal measure.

"Not far enough, then," Sarah said, and held out a hand to help pull Alex to her feet.

❖

"A bath. Sinfully deep and boiling hot, with bubbles up to my chin."

Sarah gave a low moan of agreement. "Oh God, yes. All of that and a bar of Cadbury's chocolate to eat while I'm soaking in it."

They had been playing the "What will you do first upon reaching civilization?" game for the past half-hour and it had proved to be an entertaining distraction.

"I have no clue what Cadbury's chocolate is," Alex said, laughing quietly at Sarah's exaggerated look of horror. Seconds later, her smile faded as she came to an abrupt halt. "Oh crap."

In front of them, their narrow track was dominated by a flat slab of rock that stretched for three or four yards. Until now, the path they had been following had been narrow but reasonably uncomplicated, since the terrain gave them little option but to continue forward. To their right was a high, unscalable bank of crumbling rocks and dirt, while on the opposite side, the forest floor fell away down a steep embankment. The rock slab was angled slightly in the direction of the drop-off, water coursing across it to make its surface doubly treacherous.

"Sometimes," Alex said, staring at the slab with undisguised loathing, "I don't think life is very fair."

"We can't go back." Sarah tried to sound decisive, but Alex caught the edge of fear in her words.

"No, we can't."

Back was several miles of the same thin track, with no option to deviate until they were almost at the clearing where they had eaten lunch. The light had been failing for the past hour, their breath fogging in front of them as the clearer sky made the temperature plummet. At least if they continued onward there was a chance of finding somewhere to make camp; they knew for certain there was nowhere suitable behind them.

Taking a firm grip of Sarah's hand, Alex edged her boot onto the rock. The stone was greasy with wet lichen, and for the most part perfectly smooth, and she immediately felt her sole begin to slip. She stepped back and looked again, searching for flaws in the rock's surface, for an irregularity that might provide her with a foothold.

The first fissure in the rock was only just perceptible, and it was a good stride's length from where they stood. Using her flashlight, she pointed it out to Sarah, who nodded and then carefully adjusted the pack on Alex's back.

"Just making sure you're balanced," she said in response to Alex's puzzled look.

"Right. Thanks. Here goes nothing," Alex murmured and stretched out with one leg to plant her boot along the rough edge of the small crack. She knew as soon as she took the step that the choice had been a good one and that it would be enough to anchor her safely.

"You see another one?" Sarah called out, unable to go anywhere until Alex had moved.

"Yeah, just about. It's to my left. Bit closer to the edge than I'd like, but it looks bigger than this one."

"Okay. I'll be right behind you."

From Alex's position, she couldn't see Sarah, but she heard her take a shaky breath. She wiped the sweat from her palms onto her pants, angled herself to face the next foothold, and then wriggled her boot toward it. She set her left boot in place, and then pushed off with her right.

"Shit!"

Sarah had just made the first step, which gave her a perfect view of Alex's arms pinwheeling as she scrambled to regain her footing. Without thinking, Sarah launched herself toward a faint bulge in the rock, slightly above Alex but close enough to reach out to her. Feeling her feet slide, she instinctively dropped to her knees, catching hold of Alex's hand as she did so. Her own motion dragged Alex down, and she winced at the thud of Alex's knees landing on the rock, but Alex was no longer falling, and three hard tugs brought her back up to Sarah's level. Still on their knees, they huddled together, panting to catch their breath, arms wrapped around each other. Sarah could feel Alex shaking uncontrollably as the adrenaline worked its way out of her system.

"You okay?" Sarah finally whispered.

"Yeah." The word came out hushed as if she wasn't quite convinced. "That was a bit fucking close." She seemed to realize that she still had hold of Sarah's hand in a death grip. She disentangled herself and rubbed Sarah's hand gently in both of hers. "Sorry, I think I crushed you a little."

"Sooner have crushed fingers than you end up at the bottom of that." Gazing toward the edge, Sarah shuddered. Then she indicated their kneeling position. "This seems to help though. Maybe it'd be easier to crawl across."

"Seems so obvious now." Alex sounded faintly embarrassed that she hadn't thought of that in the first place.

With the traction provided by their clothing and the additional security of being able to find handholds, they were soon clambering to their feet on the opposite side.

"Didn't much like that," Sarah said in a tone wry enough to acknowledge the extent of her understatement. "Are you all right?"

Alex was rubbing her sore knees, bending and flexing them to check for damage. "I'm good. I think my pride is slightly more battered than my knees."

Sarah surprised herself by leaning into Alex and kissing her quickly on the cheek. "If it helps any," she said with a hint of mischief in her voice, "you and your wounded pride can lead the way."

❖

Merrick tucked his Glock back into his belt and stepped into the hut. The door creaked shut behind him. Ignoring the smell of smoke and decades old mildew, he slowly panned his flashlight around the place. His eyes narrowed as he tried to pick objects out of the gloom, but the dark stain in front of the stove stood out even against the filthy carpet. He crouched beside it and touched his fingers to it. They came away dry, but it was unmistakably a bloodstain. His duffel bag had been left neatly on a wooden chest, and in the far corner sat a tin bucket full of torn up cigarettes.

Grinding his teeth together, he ignored the flush of anger that made a pulse throb in his temples and consoled himself instead with the certainty that he was on the right track, that the girl had definitely been there. He placed his hand against the stove, felt the residual heat of its metal, and smiled grimly. He and Beth were probably less than a day behind her, and considering the bloodied dressings lying half-charred in the ashes at the base of the stove, they were in far better shape than she was.

He searched the rest of the hut thoroughly but found no sign of his GPS, his keys, or his ID papers. The only thing she had left behind was a bottle of hair dye. She had taken everything else, even his fucking toothbrush.

"Goddammit."

He stormed out of the hut, kicked the door closed, and looked around. Beth was several yards away, kneeling in the grass, retrieving something she had dropped. She held the radio up sheepishly as he walked over to her.

"I thought I heard you calling me on it," she said, "but I think it was probably the wind. I just got a bit creeped out." She looked at the hut and shuddered. "We're not staying here tonight, are we?"

"No." He wasn't planning on staying anywhere near there that night. He was planning to search the clearing until he picked up the girl's trail and to follow it until the light died completely. He gestured at the radio. "Keep that fucking thing off. Those batteries won't last forever."

Beth nodded quickly. "Sorry, Nate."

He was already walking away from her toward a small, flattened area of undergrowth. It seemed as good a place as any to start looking.

❖

The ancient stones seemed to teeter perpetually on the verge of tumbling down the mountainside. It was only the well-established growth of moss and lichen on their surface that gave any suggestion of how long they had rested in their places and for how many thousands of years they would continue to do so.

Sarah followed Alex as she waded into the bracken growing rampantly at the base of the rocks. Once she seemed certain they would be adequately hidden, she lowered her pack from her shoulders.

"I think we'll be good here for the night." She lifted Sarah's pack down, and with both hands on Sarah's shoulders she guided her to sit on a low rock. "I'm gonna scout around, see if I can find some wood, grab some water from that stream we passed."

Sarah muttered her agreement and made as if to stand, but Alex easily held her still. "If you need me, yell. I'll be close by and I won't be gone long, okay?"

"Okay." Sarah's nod was reluctant, but she knew that she had pushed herself as far as she could go. She waited until Alex was out of sight and then lifted her sweater up. "Crap."

Bright moonlight made the fresh blood glisten on the dressing, and when she touched her fingers to it they came away warm and coated. It was nothing that she hadn't expected; she had felt something tear as soon as she lurched for Alex's hand back on the slab of rock. She pulled Alex's backpack toward her and opened it. She set aside the plastic sheeting and the blankets—things she knew they would need that night—and found their small first aid kit.

The dressing came away easily, the blood already weighing it down and pulling it loose. Holding her flashlight with one hand, she clumsily used a swab to mop up the blood that was leaking from one corner of the wound. Although she couldn't really see what she was doing, she tore at a packet of butterfly bandages with her teeth and then swore as the strips fell all over the ground.

"I got them." Alex's hand covered hers, bringing it back to rest against her abdomen. "Keep some pressure on it, Sarah."

Sarah blinked, bewildered. She hadn't heard Alex return, but now she could see the bottles of water and an armful of wood scattered where they had been hurriedly abandoned. Alex knelt in front of Sarah and angled the light to see what the damage was.

"You've popped a stitch here." As the bleeding tapered off, she tilted her head to look up at her. "Did that when you grabbed me, didn't you?"

"Yeah, I think so."

"Weren't planning on telling me, were you?"

Sarah shook her head. "Wasn't planning on it, no."

"Figured you'd just fix it up yourself?"

"Yep."

"And how's that working out for you?"

She narrowed her eyes. "Not all that well, actually."

Alex's teeth flashed white in the moonlight as she grinned, but her voice was soft when she spoke. "Gonna let me help you?"

"Please."

"Okay, just untuck this a bit more."

Sarah tugged at the tank top that was half in, half out of her pants and lifted it and her sweater clear.

"That's better," Alex said, busy trying to unpeel the butterfly bandages from their backing. "I think two or three of these will be enough to hold it closed."

"No more embroidery?" Sarah asked, waiting nervously for the answer. She had coped with the suturing back when she was half-stupefied with shock, but she wasn't sure she could go through it again.

Alex easily caught her meaning. "No, no more embroidery," she said firmly.

She sealed two of the artificial sutures into place and then added a third for good measure. Sarah's hand jerked a little as the final suture made something in her abdomen twinge, and the flashlight she had been holding for Alex to work by shifted its beam by the slightest fraction. She heard Alex's sharp intake of breath and knew without looking what had caused it. For the past two days, Alex had been ignoring the scars twisting the skin of Sarah's abdomen. She had dressed the gunshot wound and taken pains not to touch or allow her gaze to linger anywhere else. Now, kneeling so close that Sarah could feel the warmth of her breath flutter across the damaged flesh, there was no way for her to pretend that she hadn't seen them.

Acutely aware of Alex's proximity, Sarah battened down the almost overwhelming urge to cover herself and waited for the inevitable question. It came only after Alex had carefully rearranged Sarah's sweater to cover her, and it wasn't the one Sarah had been expecting.

"Did someone hurt you, Sarah?" Sorrow and anger fought for dominance in Alex's voice. Sarah shook her head fervently, wanting to say something reassuring but unable to speak through the tears that were choking her.

"Oh no, c'mere." Alex sounded mortified.

Sarah felt Alex reach for her, and for a fleeting second, she stiffened, before her resistance crumbled and she sagged bonelessly into Alex's arms. The suddenness of her capitulation took them both onto the ground, the flashlight slipping from her fingers to plunge them into a silver-limned darkness. Smothering her cries against Alex's jacket, she squeezed her eyes tightly shut and finally broke beneath the misery that months of loss and loneliness had forced her to bear.

❖

"Molly was my half sister. I don't really remember my dad. He died of cancer when I was five, and Mum married Richard ten years later." Sarah cradled her mug in both hands and took a tentative sip of her cocoa. There was a series of snaps as Alex broke up kindling to feed into their small fire, and Sarah watched the smoke curl up from the fresh wood. When she began to speak again, her voice was still hoarse from weeping.

"I don't think they planned to have a child, but Molly was born while I was at university. Mum used to call her their 'happy little accident.'" She tried to smile but shook her head instead as fresh tears made the fire shimmer in her gaze. "She had just turned seven, and she was such good fun: full of mischief and utterly fearless. Last summer, I was teaching her to swim, and that afternoon my mum had come to the pool to watch her attempt her first length. Mum was driving us home. She'd let Molly sit up front because she'd done so well." She closed her eyes, felt tears break and run down her cheeks, and tasted salt when she licked her lips. "A drunk driver hit us, flipped our car over. The police said that Molly and my mum died more or less instantly."

Alex's warm hand took hold of hers, and Sarah turned toward her, unable to keep the pain of that day from her expression.

"I don't remember much of the next month." She made a vague gesture toward her abdomen, and that was enough for Alex to nod her understanding. "But I remember the look on my stepfather's face on one of the few occasions he came to visit me. He held the funerals while I was still in the ICU, sold our house, left me the money from it, and went to Italy. I haven't seen or heard from him since." She set her mug down, no longer able to stomach the sweet smell of the chocolate. "He blamed me," she said, something inside her loosening with the simple release of saying the words aloud. "If I'd been sitting in the front seat of the car like I usually did, Molly might still be alive."

She lowered her head, but Alex cupped her chin and raised it again.

"You know it's not your fault, don't you?"

"I know that," Sarah whispered. "Most of the time, I know that."

Physically and emotionally worn out, she lay back on their makeshift bed of plastic sheeting and musty blankets. The plastic crinkled and dipped as Alex lay down beside her.

"I still dream of that day, over and over," Sarah said into the darkness.

"I know."

Something awful in Alex's tone told Sarah that the response hadn't been merely a platitude. She shivered, thinking of the scars she had seen on Alex's back. Alex shifted closer to her, the warmth from their bodies gradually chasing away the cold that was seeping through the plastic. Sarah's eyes drifted shut, and when she spoke again she wasn't sure whether she was awake or sleeping.

"Every time I have the dream, I'm in the front seat…"

CHAPTER NINE

Alex held her numb fingers out to the fire and tried not to pay attention to the throbbing in her right temple and the nagging ache that a cold, damp night and extensive bruising had left in her knees. Beside her, stirring a pot of simmering oatmeal, Sarah looked about as rough as Alex felt. Her face was pale and dirt-streaked in the early morning light, with dark shadows beneath eyes that were puffy from crying and too little sleep. She had been subdued since waking, though Alex suspected that had more to do with her dread of the day to come than anything that had been said the night before. The continuous stress of being hunted and the physical stress of the hiking were slowly but surely wearing them both down.

A quick appraisal of their supplies had made them halve their breakfast rations, but even so, at their current pace, they were likely to run out of food before reaching Ross Lake. Despite the headache, Alex forced herself to eat the small portion of oatmeal that Sarah handed to her. A bottle of water was passed over next followed by two Tylenol pressed into her hand without comment.

"No, I don't need them. I'm fine," Alex said, holding the pills out to Sarah.

"If you were 'fine' you wouldn't be hobbling around and you wouldn't look like you were about to throw your breakfast back up." Sarah sighed. "Just take the damn pills. Please."

Alex withdrew her hand and stared at the pills resting on her palm. "How many do we have left?"

"Enough," Sarah answered, concern making her voice sharp. She shook her head apologetically. "Enough for you to take those."

Without another word, Alex unscrewed the water bottle and washed the pills down.

"We'll get more water on the way past the stream," Sarah said, already starting to break the camp and pack their gear. "The sky's clearing. Rescue parties will be out looking for us. They might even be able to get a helicopter up." She stopped midway through folding a blanket and dropped to a crouch at Alex's side as if to emphasize the importance of what she was saying. "We just have to keep going."

Sunlight was beginning to filter through the highest reaches of the forest canopy. Alex shaded her eyes to look up at her. She looked back, unblinking, and Alex couldn't help but smile at the sheer determination on her face.

"Got a real fucking headache," Alex admitted quietly.

"I know," Sarah said. "I'm guessing your knees are playing up as well."

"If that means aching like sons of bitches, then yes, they're playing up."

"The Tylenol should help, now that you've actually bloody taken it."

Alex chuckled. "I was trying to be brave."

"You *are* brave," Sarah said, her tone sincere. Then she grinned. "How about you let me play the butch today, huh?"

Alex nudged her with a shoulder. "Gonna carry the heavy bag?"

Sarah's own laughter abruptly faded. "Oh hell, I don't think I'm ready to go quite that far."

❖

The trail leading away from the small clearing had been all the easier to spot for being the only possible option. Merrick had found the route the previous night, and then slept soundly in the certainty that not only was he on the right track, but he was also managing to gain ground. The early morning mist was already thinning and rising as he cooked breakfast, but he wasn't worried that they had slept late. When Beth returned from the stream, he smiled and she blushed prettily. She pulled her hair into a loose braid before sitting by his side and giving him a kiss on his cheek.

"Smells good." She nodded toward the pot of oatmeal.

"Maple syrup makes all the difference," he said with a wink. It was easier to humor her than tell her it was nothing but cheap, processed crap.

They didn't have a future together. He was under no illusions in that regard. It had been four years since she handed him a discreetly designed flyer at a gun show. Always eager to make contacts, he had gone to one of the rallies listed on the leaflet, stood in a crowd of sweating, seething white supremacists, and listened to the ferocious rhetoric of the unassuming-looking man on the stage. It had not taken long to decide that that man would be a very useful contact indeed. As the crowd roared their approval and bayed for the blood of anyone who didn't abide by their particularly limited world view, Merrick had spotted Beth standing close to the stage. He had wandered over, flirting aimlessly with her at first. Then she had proudly named the man on the stage as her uncle, and Merrick had realized that she was his way in.

It had taken several months of dinner dates, church services, and standing reverently at Nicholas Deakin's hate rallies before Beth finally introduced Merrick to the rest of her family. He and Deakin had been kindred spirits, not necessarily in their politics but in their desire to get a job done as efficiently and cost effectively as possible. Deakin and the other trusted groups he put Merrick in touch with had offered contracts worth thousands of dollars, and Merrick had closed on every one of the deals he had made…

"You not hungry, Nate?"

Except for this one.

Merrick tasted the over-sweetened, over-salted, lukewarm cereal. He forced himself to swallow it and then to smile.

"Just thinking, babe," he said.

This deal had been valuable enough to force Nicholas into taking an unprecedented risk, that of organizing the jailbreak that would enable Merrick to see it through to its completion. Nicholas's motives were his own. For Merrick, the outcome would be far simpler: the opportunity to leave the country and retire in luxury on an absolute fortune.

He finished the last of his breakfast and washed the taste away with a mouthful of water. He was tired of living like an animal, tired of the shitty food and wearing the same stinking clothes. As he kicked the smoldering ashes to extinguish the fire, he thought of the girl who had caused him so much trouble and wondered whether today would be the day they caught up with her.

"She better fucking run," he said to no one in particular, but he saw Beth cringe away from the tone of his voice. "She better fucking run."

❖

"I love my love with an F, because she is fabulous…" Sarah took hold of the hand Alex offered to her and stepped onto the wobbly rock in the center of the fast-flowing stream. "Thank you."

"My pleasure, ma'am." Alex gave a little bow and kept her steady as they made the next step together. "One more," she murmured, tilting her head to one side to weigh their options. "That one doesn't look too bad."

"Yep. You going first?"

Alex smiled. "You mean, are you going *in* first?"

"Well, yes, of course that's what I mean." Sarah's tired eyes flashed with amusement.

With the sigh of one long accustomed to being tormented, Alex hopped onto the rock and then quickly onto the bank. "It's fine, not slippery at all." She held her arms out regardless for Sarah to grab on to, but Sarah landed without incident.

"Okay then." Alex made an onward gesture. "So why do you hate fabulous Freda?"

For the last hour, they had been distracting themselves from their myriad aches and pains by playing silly word games. They had already been through the alphabet naming candies and desserts, and this latest was one that Sarah's sister had taught her.

"Hey!" Sarah protested. "I'd not even given her a name yet." She shrugged. "But I suppose Freda's as good as any. Okay, I hate my love with an F because she is..."

Alex glanced over her shoulder in time to catch Sarah furrow her brow in contemplation and then start to giggle.

"Because she is flatulent," she concluded. Her shoulders shook as she laughed.

"Oh my God." Alex stopped in her tracks and turned to face her properly. "Please tell me you've never had a Flatulent Freda as a girlfriend."

"Hell no." Sarah sounded appalled. "Although Ash did once set me up with someone whose main selling point was her ability to burp 'God Save the Queen.'"

"You're shitting me."

She shook her head with exaggerated sorrow. "I only wish that I was."

"And I thought I'd had it tough with Meg," Alex said, surprising herself with her ability to mention that disaster of a relationship with such equanimity. But then she found Sarah incredibly easy to talk to. In spite of the exertion, the discomfort, and the constant fear, there had been many occasions during the past two days where she had forgotten all of it and just enjoyed Sarah's company. It had been a long time since she felt comfortable enough with anyone to lower those barriers that she had firmly established since Meg, but she had quickly become that comfortable with Sarah. She chanced a surreptitious look behind her, but Sarah caught her peeking and waved at her.

"I'm still here," Sarah said, sounding only slightly out of breath. "We're up to G and it's your turn."

Alex turned back hurriedly in an attempt to hide her guilty smile. Sarah's face had been flushed with effort and sweat was sticking her hair to her forehead. She was streaked with dirt, and at some point during the day, something had scratched her cheek and scored an angry red mark across it. And yet, right at that moment, Alex wanted nothing more than to kiss her long and hard, and then see what happened next.

"I'm going to hell," she muttered beneath her breath. She clenched her fingers and attempted to slow her rapid pulse. "Okay," she said, once she was sure she could speak without giving the game away entirely. "I love my love with a G because she is gorgeous…"

Twenty minutes later, as Sarah struggled to find a suitably positive adjective beginning with Z, Alex stopped walking.

"Jesus." She made a grab for Sarah's jacket and wrapped the material in her fist to hold on to it tightly. The force of her effort made Sarah stagger, and she let out a small squeak of protest before she looked up.

"Oh shit," she whispered.

Without needing to be prompted, she stepped back cautiously at the same time Alex did.

A yard in front of them, the mountainside had simply fallen away. Torrents of storm water had eroded the fragile infrastructure of snow-worn rock and crumbling dirt. The force of the landslide had uprooted trees and vegetation and smashed them into pieces. Alex could see where the trail resumed on the other side of the devastated slope, but there was a vast impassable tract between it and the point at which they stood. To either side of them, the forest clung to the mountain. The ground was steep and comprised the same unstable matter that had just collapsed beneath the force of the storm. She was afraid that their own weight on those weather-ravaged slopes would be disturbance enough to cause further slides, and she had no desire to be caught in the middle of one.

She stared down at the GPS in her hand. The red arrow they had been following pointed ahead with unswerving insistence. For hours now, she had assumed the lead, being in better physical shape than Sarah and more familiar with the terrain. Without the issue ever having been discussed, it was Alex who had navigated, who had suggested rest breaks and set their pace. For the first time, she felt the weight of that responsibility bearing down upon her.

"I don't..." She looked up again, a sense of hopelessness gradually engulfing her. "I don't know what we should do," she admitted quietly. She felt Sarah's chilled fingers entwine with her own, and she squeezed them gently, grateful for the unspoken absolution.

"Neither do I," Sarah said, "but I don't think we can get over that gap."

"No."

Even now, there was the intermittent clatter of stones as they were loosened by the water still running down the mountainside. With no protective gear, any attempt to navigate the slope would put them at risk of serious injury.

Sarah pulled Alex farther away from the edge. "Here, sit down for a minute."

"We should keep going," Alex muttered, even as she sat and laid her head on her folded arms.

"Yes, we should and we will," Sarah said, "but not until we've figured out where."

Alex heard a rustling noise as Sarah searched through her pockets. A series of muttered curses was punctuated by a quiet whoop of triumph, and Sarah passed her a slab of something pale brown that smelled sweetly of mint.

"I knew I hadn't eaten it. Here, can't walk straight if you can't think straight."

Alex managed a weary grin. "You want me to make the obvious gag or shall I leave it to you?" She nibbled at the edge of the candy. "What exactly am I eating here?" Whatever it was was tooth-achingly sweet and melted agreeably on her tongue.

"Kendal Mint Cake," Sarah said. "Staple diet of English hill walkers. It's basically sugar, glucose, and peppermint. It'll rot your teeth, but it's a great energy boost." She handed Alex another piece, tucked the remainder away, and unfolded their map. It took both of them a good few minutes to cross-reference their coordinates on the GPS and work out where they were.

"That stream's not marked," Sarah commented absently, her finger tracing over a small grid on the map.

"What stream?"

"It was about half a mile back, cutting down through the trees. I wonder if we could go back to it and scramble downstream about three hundred yards. The stones don't fall that far. Then we could use the GPS to work our way back toward the landslide but cross it at a safe level."

Alex followed her logic through. "And then hope we get lucky and find another stream on the other side to climb back up and regain the trail." It certainly sounded easier than wandering down a mountainside that was liable to collapse at the slightest encouragement.

"Yeah," Sarah said. Her eyes were fixed on the path behind them as if she were waiting for a monster to suddenly appear. "We hope we get lucky."

❖

"It doesn't look too bad." Sarah peered down the course of the stream. Although swollen by the storm, it would give them a clear and relatively straight track down through the forest. The rocks that crowded in on it were slick in places, but she hoped they would be able to scramble down them if the water became too deep or too rapid to wade through.

"No, it doesn't." Alex nodded in agreement.

Sarah felt a small shiver of relief pass through her. She had wanted to take some of the pressure away from Alex, to lead instead of hiding behind the easy option of following, but she had been assailed by doubt as they retraced their steps. The detour she had suggested would eat into what little advantage they had over Merrick, and she knew they didn't have time to make another one.

"Don't know about you, but I'm putting my wet socks back on," Alex said lightly. She was kneeling by her pack and, having pulled her socks from its depths, was now searching through it for something else. When she stood, there was a length of rope in her hands. "C'mere."

Sarah stepped closer to her and raised her arms so Alex could loop the rope around her waist. "Wasn't planning on running off," she said as Alex secured a second loop around herself.

"No?" Alex grinned, testing the knots. "Just don't want to lose you, is all."

"So if I go arse over tits, we both go arse over tits?" Sarah asked, forgetting for a moment that the phrase might not mean a thing to Alex.

Alex laughed as they changed their socks; she didn't seem to have had any difficulties translating that one. "You have such a charming way with words, darling." The upper-class English accent she adopted was actually quite impressive.

"It's part of my Northern charm," Sarah told her with mock seriousness, but then she looked over at the stream and sighed. "So, we should probably do this before we lose the light."

"Yeah, we should."

Alex touched her hand to Sarah's face. Sarah closed her eyes briefly, wishing they were anywhere but here and then wishing that Alex hadn't already dropped her hand away. Straightening her shoulders, she walked to the edge of the stream, where she weighed up her first move. At a reassuring nod from Alex, she stepped into the water.

Even though she'd endured days of cold and miserable damp, growing somewhat accustomed to it, the water that rushed over her feet was chilled enough to take her breath away.

"Oh God, whose bloody stupid idea was this?" she muttered and heard Alex laugh shortly. The current tugged at her ankles, making her wobble. She put her arms out for balance and felt Alex's hand on her shoulder steadying her. Pebbles turned and shifted beneath the soles of her boots, and every drenched rock was covered in a layer of filmy green lichen. She knew then, even as her heart beat faster and urged her to hurry, that this was not something they would be able to rush.

"Just take your time," Alex said, as if she had read her mind. "We get below that point there," she gestured toward a curve in the stream, "and we won't be visible from the trail anymore."

"Okay." Sarah set off again, her feet already numb and uncooperative. A rock that had appeared to be a safe foothold capsized the instant she put weight on it and only a sharp tug from Alex on the rope around her waist prevented her from falling. "Avoid that one," she said, altering her route to step around it.

They made painfully slow progress. Reluctant to speak because of their proximity to the trail, they waded down in near-silence, whispering warnings or advice to each other, with one ear constantly alert to any movement above them. When they finally reached the curve that Alex had indicated, Sarah began to breathe a little easier, but her relief was muted by fading daylight and the nagging sense that they simply weren't going fast enough.

A faint, repetitive, mechanical sound made her instinctively drop low. Behind her, she heard Alex scramble to do likewise, before they simultaneously identified the source of the noise.

"Chopper," Alex whispered. She tilted her head on one side to listen and try to gauge its whereabouts.

Sarah craned her neck back, straining to catch a glimpse of it, but she knew even before Alex spoke again that the helicopter was nowhere near them.

"I think it's over the other side of the peak," Alex said. "Probably heading back in before dusk."

Sarah resumed the task of picking her way downstream. "At least they're looking." She tried to sound optimistic, but the obvious caveat hung unspoken between them: rescue teams wouldn't be any help if they were searching in the wrong place.

❖

Merrick heard the dry snap seconds before he heard Beth's gasp of pain. He turned to find her sitting on the ground, her left foot twisted awkwardly behind her, her face ashen.

"Nate, I think it's broken," she whimpered as he walked over to her.

He could see her ankle now, offset at a strange angle and already beginning to swell. Her foot was still caught up in the tree root she had tripped over. Ignoring her cries of pain, he freed her boot and straightened her ankle.

"Can you walk?" He knew the answer even before he asked the question and was not surprised when she shook her head.

"Please don't leave me here," she said. Her hands grasped out for his and he knocked them away impatiently, trying to think what his options were and finding them extremely limited. Beth attempted to stand but fell back the instant she tried to put any weight on the injury.

"Fucking hell." He stalked away from her and kicked at a diseased piece of tree trunk that crumbled beneath his anger. "You stupid fucking—"

"Call my uncle."

He didn't respond to that, continuing to pound his boot against the rotten wood.

"Call my uncle," she said again, and something, some uncommon note of command in her voice, made him turn around. "Use the radio." She threw it toward him.

"Why the fuck would I want to do that?" He made no move to pick up the radio. "Your uncle is sitting pretty in Seattle waiting for us to bring him something we haven't got a chance in hell of finding right now. You think he'll be happy to hear we have even more fucking problems?"

Beth held his gaze unflinchingly. The set of her face had changed, making her unrecognizable as the timid girl who had obeyed him without question for months.

"He's not in Seattle," she told him calmly. "He's already in the park." She laughed then, and a cruel smile twisted her lips. "You actually believed that he trusted you? You actually believed that I would ever have noticed you at that rally?"

Despite the horrible expression on her face, Merrick found himself unable to look away. He had been utterly confident that he was in control, that he had manipulated every stage of this perfectly, and instead it had been Deakin who had reeled him in from the outset.

"How many times have you spoken to him?" he asked, his voice strangled. He nodded toward the radio, the occasions he had come close to catching her in the act now so obvious in his mind.

"Twice a day. The search parties are slowing him down some, but he could still be here within a couple of days. Leave me some supplies and go on without me."

His answer wiped the smile from her face. "No."

For the first time, she looked uncertain. "What do you mean, no?"

"No," he repeated, and as she lunged for the radio, he kicked it beyond her reach. He picked it up, clipped it onto his belt, and took hold of his gun. "Reckon by the time Uncle Nick catches up with me, I'll have thought of a decent explanation, some tragic accident that befell his favorite niece." He pointed the gun at her head and she stared up at him, hatred burning in her eyes. "Cat got your tongue?" he asked, and moved his finger to the trigger.

❖

The crack of a gunshot was so sudden and so close that it startled Sarah into losing her footing. Her arms flew out as she slipped, her hands grappling for purchase on the rocks. She landed heavily on her side and began to slide, water soaking into her pants and the sleeve of her jacket just before the rope around her waist was pulled taut and she was jerked to a stop.

"Sarah?" Alex hissed. She sounded frightened and short of breath.

"I'm still here." Sarah realized her own voice was just as tremulous as Alex's. She took a quick physical inventory and found nothing more serious than a bump to her thigh. "Thanks."

"Welcome," Alex said. She splashed down beside her and pulled her into a hug. "Sure you're all right?"

"I'm fine." Sarah nodded against Alex for extra emphasis. "If that was him, he's right behind us."

The shot had sounded from the level of the trail, toward the direction of the landslide. She felt nervousness twisting her stomach into knots as she looked over Alex's shoulder. They were only just below the point where the stream dipped out of sight of the trail; as Merrick reached the landslide, they would have no way of knowing which route he chose, no way of knowing if he was in front of them or behind them.

"He can't have been shooting at us," Alex murmured, as if she were musing aloud rather than inviting debate. "So I guess that leaves animal or girlfriend."

"We've not seen anything big enough to be a threat," Sarah said, knowing that the man she had watched calmly shoot a kneeling victim would be more than capable of killing his girlfriend. She didn't want to think what he might do to her and Alex if he caught up with them. That spurred her to move, and she staggered to her feet, wincing at every splash she made and every pebble that shifted and clacked on the streambed. Above them, the sky was aflame with pink and orange, the sun dropping low behind wisps of cloud that weren't going to be substantial enough to prevent a frost. Even now, their breath was visible as they began to walk, and she flexed her fingers repeatedly in a vain effort to regain sensation in them. The only part of her body that she could really feel was the hot area of bruising forming on the outer side of her thigh. She took a perverse sort of comfort from it; it reminded her what it was like to be warm.

The scramble downstream became an annoying stop-start of leaving and then reentering the water. Unlike walking on the trail, which had been, for the most part, reasonably clear, it was impossible to find any sort of rhythm in the water, and she had to force herself not to slam her hands against the rocks in frustration. She felt a gentle tug on the rope around her waist and tugged back to acknowledge Alex's unspoken reassurance. It wasn't the first time Alex had done it, and she always seemed to sense exactly when it was most needed.

"About another fifty yards, then we're good," Alex said.

Sarah nodded, fumbling for the next step even as she warned herself to go slow. *Less haste, more speed,* her mum had been fond of telling Molly. It was a proverb that had never really made sense to Sarah and one that had been gleefully ignored by her younger sister. She repeated it to herself now, soundlessly forming the words. They still didn't make much sense to her, but they stopped her from thinking about Merrick and how long it would be before he found them.

After judging the distance to be about right, Alex gave a quick pull on the rope.

"Here," she said.

Sarah didn't stop, didn't even seem to have heard her.

"Here," Alex said again, giving a little pull on the rope for emphasis.

"Wha—Oh, sorry." Sarah stood still as if in a daze and automatically tucked her hands beneath her armpits to try to warm them. She was shivering violently, the chattering of her teeth audible as Alex took up the slack from the rope and then began to untie the knot at Sarah's waist.

The sun had all but disappeared, taking with it its meager warmth. Alex fumbled with the knot, her fingers stiff and clumsy. Stepping out from the water really didn't help much; her boots and pants were saturated, and the material began to feel even colder against her legs as the cool air circulated around her.

"Dammit." She took Sarah's hands in her own and rubbed the ghost-white skin, hoping the friction would restore some warmth to it. Sarah's face was pallid in the moonlight, and when Alex looked at the sky, she was almost dazzled by the vast array of stars. It was too dark now to continue much farther; she knew they had to find somewhere to shelter for the night. Nocturnal animals were beginning to stir among the trees that crowded in on the stream. Their movement made fallen leaves crackle and rustle intermittently, jangling Alex's already frayed nerves. The forest was no longer clinging to the mountainside at such an acute angle, but even so there was no light within its depths, and using a flashlight would be an open invitation for Merrick to come down and find them.

"Shit." The flashlight wasn't the only thing they would have to forsake that night. She rocked back on her heels. Her socks squelched, and icy water seeped between her toes. "Shit, shit, shit."

"A-Alex?" Her name came out in a staccato from between Sarah's still-chattering teeth.

She swore again, berating herself for having spoken out loud. "Nothing, it's okay," she said, but she could see that Sarah was far from mollified. She pulled Sarah's hood up, tucked her hair into its confines, and then drew the hood tight around her face. Sarah smiled fondly at her, which made what she had to say all the more difficult. "We won't be able to light a fire tonight. Not with Merrick so nearby."

"I know that," Sarah said. She seemed completely calm, as if resigned to whatever fate had in store for her.

Alex squeezed her hand. "Walt showed me a few tricks." She managed to sound more confident than she felt. "We'll be all right, I promise."

Sarah nodded and gave a low murmur of agreement, but the look in her eyes implied that Alex should be careful of making promises that she might not be able to keep.

CHAPTER TEN

Bugger, didn't see it. Sorry."

Sarah took the hand that Alex held out to her, lifted her boot from the small hole it had vanished into, and then scrambled back to her feet. She made a half-hearted attempt to brush dirt and dried leaves from her filthy pants but quickly gave up, seeming to realize that a large quantity of the forest floor was already clinging to her clothes.

For close to an hour, they had been walking in the dark with only occasional light filtering down from the moon to guide their path. Alex had tried to give Sarah an idea of what they needed to look out for, but she knew they had probably already walked blindly past several areas that would have been ideal.

They had continued for an additional half hour beyond the point where Sarah had tripped over, when Alex grabbed her arm to get her attention and then gestured ahead of them.

"There, see? That'll be perfect."

Sarah nodded a little uncertainly. Alex wasn't sure that she really did appreciate the potential of the dead tree in the clearing, but the relief on her face was easy to distinguish.

"Just tell me what you need me to do," she said as, weariness pushed aside, they jogged across to the tree Alex had spotted.

Alex ran her hands over the rough bark of the fallen spruce. The tree's skeletal silhouette had been clearly delineated by the moonlight reaching down into the tiny clearing. The tangled deadfall of the tree's upper branches would give structure to the shelter she planned to build, and for the first time since they started to walk through the forest, there was enough natural light making it through the tree canopy for them to work by.

"Ditch the bags here," she said. "We need insulation for the base of the shelter; spruce branches, bracken, whatever you can gather."

Sarah's lips moved as she repeated the instructions over to herself.

"Sarah?" Alex waited until Sarah looked up at her properly. "Stay within the clearing where I can see you," she said gently, and smiled when Sarah gave her a crisp salute.

Several branches had snapped cleanly off the tree as it had fallen. Alex began to collect the more manageable ones together. She leaned them up against the deadfall and used those that were still full and green to plug the gaps in the walls she was gradually constructing. She had only seen Walt demonstrate this skill once, when he had invited her to accompany him as he and Marilyn ran a weekend course on wilderness survival. It had been the height of summer. The sun had beaten down relentlessly on a group of city thrill seekers who had subsequently gotten back into their air-conditioned SUVs secure in the knowledge that, if they ever deigned to set foot in the wilderness again, they would know what to do should someone steal their Winnebago. Alex had built her own shelter a short distance from Walt's, and Marilyn had stayed late into the evening to share hotdogs and the remnants of the brownies she had baked. Kip, excited to have someone new to play with, had slept with Alex that night, and it had been almost too warm in the shelter for her to bear.

She forced her fingertips beneath another piece of bark that was still stubbornly clinging to the tree trunk and pried it loose to use as a shingle for the roof. With frost already making the grass and ferns glow in the moonlight, she realized that she would give an awful lot right now for a shelter that was half as snug as the one she had shared with Kip.

A swishing noise made her turn around sharply and she saw Sarah staggering toward the tree. Her arms were laden with greenery, and she was simultaneously dragging several larger pieces of spruce that she had hung from her belt.

"I tried to get dry pieces," she said as Alex took some of the load from her. "Oh hey, that looks good." She gave the shelter an appreciative once-over.

"I went for windproof over waterproof," Alex told her, patting the sides where the insulation was thicker. "I don't think it'll rain tonight." The sky was crystal clear, but a nasty little breeze was making the frigid air feel even colder. "Come on. Soon as the floor's done we can get in and get warm."

Together they padded out the tiny floor space, filling the shelter with the scent of fresh pine.

"Smells like Christmas," Alex said, arranging one of their blankets on top of the vegetation.

"Oh, you had to bloody well say it, didn't you?" Sarah muttered without malice. "Now I'm craving turkey with all the trimmings and Christmas pudding with custard." Her stomach rumbled loudly. "God, I'm hungry."

"Me too." Alex's mouth was watering at memories of Thanksgiving and Christmas feasts, and she wondered vaguely at how easy it had been to take such luxury for granted. Never again, she resolved, as she dragged their bags inside the shelter and then pulled into place the two large, leafy branches she had set aside to use as a door. For a few seconds, the only sound was the quiet movement of air as they breathed. Then Sarah giggled.

"Can't see a bloody thing now." She reached her hands out and patted Alex on the face, feeling Alex's lips curl upward as she smiled. Alex dropped away from her and there was a rustling noise before a yellow glow dimly illuminated the shelter.

"Probably be okay to use this if we keep it covered," Alex said, and Sarah realized she had wrapped the polka dot boxer shorts over the beam of the flashlight.

Sarah folded her arms tightly as the warmth generated by their recent exertion was leeched away by her wet clothing. She looked at Alex, who seemed to be considering exactly the same thing, and she shrugged as if to answer Alex's unspoken question. They moved without speaking, kicking off wet boots and socks and then beginning to strip off their pants. Alex sat down first and pulled the blanket aside for Sarah to huddle beneath once she had finally managed to unpeel her soggy combat pants. Their spare socks were still dry despite the trek through the river. Sarah squinted at them in an attempt to distinguish one pair from the other, before distributing them at random. She pressed her bare legs against Alex's, not caring about propriety, and felt Alex try to shuffle even closer to her.

"Summer berries or chocolate chip?" Alex asked, holding two granola bars close to the light to read their packaging.

"Surprise me," Sarah said, and was pleasantly surprised to be handed half of each. She ate each piece slowly, savoring every mouthful and hoping that drinking plenty of water would persuade her aching stomach that it was satisfied.

"We're a bit low on water." Alex tilted the bottle as she took it back from her. "Should have filled up at that last stream we passed."

The stream was fifteen minutes or so from the clearing. Sarah remembered it vividly, having stumbled into that as well.

"There's enough to last us the night," she said. The last thing she wanted to do was leave the shelter, now that she was finally starting to feel warmer. Alex was apparently thinking along the same lines, because she nodded in agreement. "Do we need to keep a lookout?" Sarah whispered.

"I don't think so, not while it's this dark anyway. Maybe from dawn onward."

Sarah felt Alex tug at her arm, encouraging her to lie down. She was bone-weary and made absolutely no attempt to resist. She turned her back toward Alex, suddenly feeling uncertain and terribly shy, but Alex wrapped an arm around her waist and pulled her closer until they were spooning cozily.

"This okay?" Alex murmured, her breath heated against Sarah's cheek.

Sarah nodded, but her throat clamped down tightly on any sound she tried to make, and a warm flush crept across her skin.

"Fine," she eventually managed. "Warm." She squeezed her eyes shut and willed herself to say something of more than one syllable. "Nice." Behind her closed eyelids, she rolled her eyes in despair.

"We're already sharing a damn toothbrush," Alex drawled lazily in her ear. "Hell, Sarah, we're as good as married."

The natural mattress beneath them creaked and rustled as they began to laugh. Any feelings of awkwardness completely banished, Sarah pressed herself back into Alex's embrace and drifted to sleep, trying to imagine what Alex would look like on Christmas morning.

❖

At first it was only a twitch, something easily mistaken for the natural movement of someone who was dreaming. It brought Sarah to that halfway point of being not quite awake but not entirely asleep. She was aware that her toes were cold and that something hard and gnarled was pressing uncomfortably against her ribs, but above all, she was aware of Alex sleeping alongside her, which was why she did not try to alter her position. Another more violent jolt from Alex prompted her to open her eyes. Pitch-black surrounded her. Through cracks in the shelter's walls she could see lines of silver, but Alex had done a good job, and there weren't enough gaps for the light to make a real difference. She could hear Alex's rapid breathing, the rate becoming even more elevated as she attempted to twist free of the blanket. Wide-awake now, Sarah put her hand on Alex's shoulder and felt the muscles tense as if readying for a fight.

"Alex?"

In response, Alex kicked out with a shrill yelp. Her feet caught one of the loose branches of the door and knocked it askew.

"Shit." Sarah scrambled to repair the gap, not wanting to lose precious heat from the shelter and terrified that Merrick would be close enough to hear the commotion. She flicked the flashlight on. "Alex," she whispered with more urgency.

Alex's face was wet with tears. The wall closest to her shook when her fist crashed into it. Acting instinctively, Sarah used both hands to restrain her, and when that failed, she leaned over her bodily in an attempt to stop her thrashing about.

Even in the midst of a nightmare, the sensation of being pinned down had a terrible effect on Alex. Sarah watched horrified as she immediately froze for an instant, and then whimpered and curled herself into a fetal position.

"Jesus." Sarah quickly let go and moved away, but she couldn't bear to sit aside and do nothing as Alex began to cry hopelessly. Unsure how else to help, Sarah shifted herself carefully until she could rest Alex's head in her lap. She rearranged the blanket to cover them both and began to run her fingers through Alex's hair.

Sitting so still, barely daring to breathe, Sarah didn't know how much time passed. It seemed like hours and then no time at all before Alex stopped crying and gradually responded to Sarah's touch, allowing her body to relax. Her fists unclenched, and although her eyes remained closed, she wiped her face with her hand.

"Wh—" Alex heard the croak of her own voice and licked her dry lips. For a disorientating moment, she had no idea where she was, why everything smelled so strongly of pine, or why she seemed to be lying on a cushion that felt distinctly like bare skin. "Fuck." She stopped trying to dry her face and instead buried it in her hands. Bile hit the back of her throat, but she clamped her mouth shut, determined not to compound her humiliation by throwing up. Her entire body ached as if she had spent hours bracing herself for a punch. When she groaned, cool fingers touched her cheek, as if trying to soothe away whatever it was that hurt. That touch felt so good that she kept her eyes closed, waiting for the nausea to pass and the terror that clung to her like a spider's web to melt slowly away.

"Sorry," she whispered, once she was sure that she could speak. "I didn't mean to wake you."

"I know. It's okay," Sarah said, her fingers stroking through Alex's hair again. Without comment, she took her cue from Alex, moving when she moved, until they were sitting side-by-side, close but no longer touching.

Alex unconsciously adopted the position she always did after a nightmare, drawing her knees up to wrap her arms around them.

Setting her feet flat on the floor stopped the shaking in her legs, but she could feel the fine tremors that continued to course through her body. "What time is it?" she asked, for want of anything else to say.

There was a flash of luminous green as Sarah briefly lit the dial on her watch. "Three forty-two."

Alex made a non-committal noise. "Three's about my witching hour."

"Yeah?" Sarah said, the strain in her voice obvious as she tried to keep her tone light. "Mine's a little earlier. Two or so, usually."

"Been doing okay since I came out here." Alex reached out to run her fingers along the rough wall. "I guess all this is stirring stuff up."

"Probably."

Alex heard her inhale shakily, but she didn't say anything else. Alex picked at the wood beneath her hand, hating herself for not having been strong enough or brave enough just to tell Sarah what was going on. Despite the flashlight, it was dark in the shelter, sufficiently dark to hide Alex's face, and as if from a great distance, she finally heard herself say, "I got hurt. That's why I left the force, because I got hurt."

"The scars on your back," Sarah said. It sounded like more of a realization than a question, and the words seemed to come out tinged with sadness.

Alex turned slowly toward her, torn between relief at having part of her story already told and sorrow that Sarah hadn't felt able to ask her about it.

"In the hut, I saw…I didn't know what to say," Sarah whispered. "So I didn't say anything." Her sleeve smeared wet dirt across her face when she wiped tears away. "I'm so sorry, Alex."

Alex used her own sleeve to clean Sarah's cheeks properly. "I don't really tell anyone." She touched her knuckles to Sarah's chin, letting her know she was finished, and then took a grateful sip of the water that Sarah held out to her. "But I don't know." She shrugged. "It was different with you. I wanted so much to tell you everything." She looked around at where they were and gave a small smile. "It was kinda hard to find the right moment, though."

"Is this the right moment?" Sarah asked evenly.

Alex nodded, but tears dripped off the end of her nose and splattered on the water bottle she was still gripping.

"There were two of them," she managed to say before she lost her nerve completely. "Twin brothers. They'd attacked a young girl, raped her and cut her, then left her for dead. We were almost at the end of our shift when we saw them. They ran, and I ended up following them into an alley. Jack—he was my partner—he was too far away to help me." She put her hand to her mouth, almost gagging at the remembered stench of garbage rotting in the stagnant heat. "They hit me, knocked me down, and dragged me into a building." Cold sweat made her shirt cling to her back, and she shuddered. Sarah didn't say anything, but just reached up to take Alex's hand from her mouth and held on to it tightly.

"I managed to kick out at one of them," Alex said, willing Sarah to understand how hard she had tried to get away, "but I was so scared. We'd all seen the photos of the kid they'd hurt. I felt—" She gulped convulsively for air. "They forced me to lie facedown and one of them lifted my shirt. I felt the knife and then he started to cut me. I screamed, but no one came. I didn't think anyone would find me in time."

"But they did," Sarah said. "Someone found you."

"They found me." Alex nodded and her breathing became less labored. "What happened between then and when I woke up in the hospital is pretty hazy, but I remember asking Jack what they'd done and the look on his face when he told me. I could feel the pain across my back, but mostly I just felt relief because…"

"Because that was all they'd done," Sarah finished.

"Yeah." Alex's throat closed on the word, but she forced herself to continue. "Because that was all they'd done."

Outside, somewhere above the shelter, an owl hooted twice. Grateful for the interruption, they both looked up, even though there was no way they would be able to see it. Alex took another sip of water and then carefully screwed the top back onto the bottle. She offered it to Sarah, who set it aside without drinking. She was studying Alex as if she knew there was worse to come.

"He didn't just cut me," Alex said, into the expectant stillness. "He carved the word *bitch* into my back. I spent a month in and out of the hospital. It took three skin grafts to cover the damage, but you can't really see what he did now." She saw Sarah's eyes open wide with horror and felt a slight pang of regret. There had been no real need to give so much detail, but somehow she felt compelled to tell her every last one of her secrets. "I went back to work, but everything was different. People looked at me with this weird tilt to their heads."

"Oh, this one?" Sarah gave her the exact faux-sympathetic, dewy-eyed look that Alex had grown so utterly weary of.

Despite herself, Alex laughed. "Fuck me, that's perfect," she said.

Sarah smiled with her. "It's the look that says 'you poor dear, it must be so awful, now please tell me all the gruesome shit so I can gossip about you on Facebook.'" Her tone held an edge so familiar that Alex was reminded, not for the first time, how much they had in common in terms of shitty experiences.

"Everyone tiptoed around me, waiting for me to break, and I guess I did," Alex admitted. "When I got the job out here, Jack told me I was running away." She averted her gaze, ashamed all over again, but Sarah cupped her chin and turned her face into the light.

"Sometimes you need to run away," Sarah said, tracing her finger across Alex's bottom lip.

Alex swallowed, her stomach suddenly flip-flopping with nervous anticipation. "Never know what you'll find when you do," she managed.

"No, you don't."

They met halfway, their lips brushing together in the barest of caresses. It sent a shock of sensation through Alex, and she tangled her fingers in Sarah's hair to pull her closer and kiss her properly. Sarah's lips parted, chapped skin giving way to warmth and softness, and Alex could taste the salt of tears and something earthier that was probably dirt. She smiled, slightly bewildered by everything that was happening to them. She felt Sarah smile with her, and when she pulled back, the green in Sarah's eyes seemed bright even in the dull light.

"Muck and chocolate granola," Sarah said with a grin. "How's that for romance?"

"At least it's original," Alex countered easily. "Hearts and flowers are such a cliché." She traced the contours of Sarah's face with her fingertips and sighed. "I hate to say this, but we should probably get some sleep."

She didn't want to sleep. She didn't want dawn to break and the reality of where they were and the danger they were in to come crashing back upon them. She wanted to stay in that warm, safe little shelter, cut off from the outside, spending hours learning every part of Sarah. She kissed her again, only pulling away when they both ran out of breath. This time, as they lay down there was no awkwardness between them, and Sarah slipped her arms beneath Alex's shirt to clasp her bare midriff.

"Just because it's warmer," she said innocently.

There was no way Alex was going to believe that, but then she certainly wasn't going to complain, either. She covered Sarah's hands with her own and, despite the longing that felt like a physical ache, she allowed her eyes to close.

❖

A rustle of cloth and a groan of revulsion were the first things to greet Sarah when she awoke. The shelter was still dark, with no sign of light peeking through the walls. She squinted at the green glow as she lit up her watch: 5:46 a.m. Although she knew they wouldn't be able to go anywhere until dawn at the earliest, there was no chance now of her going back to sleep. Alex also seemed to be wide-awake. She had moved closer to the entrance, and the beam from the flashlight was casting her shadow against the wall. Sarah rubbed her eyes and rolled over in time to see Alex screw her face up as she pulled her pants on.

"Ugh, that feels so gross," Alex muttered.

Sarah watched her stretch her legs and then rub at the material in an attempt to warm it. It was only when she bent low to reach her calves that Sarah reluctantly cleared her throat.

"Oh, hey," Alex said, not sounding the slightest bit self-conscious.

With an easy smile, she dropped to her knees and kissed Sarah. It felt like the most natural thing in the world, and it surprised Sarah that there was no awkwardness between them, none of the stiffness that sometimes plagues the morning after those first tentative moves that prospective couples make toward each other. When they finally broke apart, she kept Alex's face cupped in her hands.

"That feel better than your trousers?" she asked, teasing the soft skin at the corners of Alex's mouth with her thumbs. In lieu of an answer, Alex turned her head slightly and captured one of the thumbs between her lips. Sarah took a ragged breath; there was a promise in Alex's eyes that was doing very strange things to her knees. "Forgot about the spare pairs we pinched, didn't you?" she said.

"Shit." Alex looked toward their bags. "Yes, I did."

Back at the hut, not knowing how long it would be before they found help or help found them, Alex had decided to take all of Merrick's clothing. Now she pulled the pants out of the backpack and held them against herself.

"Bit long on me, so we might have to hack a couple of inches off for you," she said, and then her eyes closed with pleasure as she pulled on a clean, dry pair in place of the muddied ones she had been wearing. "Oh God, I think I'm in heaven."

Sarah fastened the zipper on her own pair and Alex opened her eyes to see what she was laughing at.

"Oh."

"Yeah, oh," Sarah said mournfully. "I think these might constitute a trip hazard." Her feet were nowhere to be seen, the material of each leg bunching on the floor of the shelter. Fastening her belt as tightly as it would go just about kept the pants on her hips.

Alex turned Sarah's wrist and lit up the dial on her watch to calculate how much time they had before they could leave. Her shoulders dropped as she relaxed slightly. "Right then. Let's see what we can do here." She held her pocketknife between her teeth as she adjusted the material and then used the blade to slice cleanly through the cloth. "Reckon you'll be a trendsetter soon as we get back. The distressed look is very now," she said, once she had cut both pants legs to a satisfactory length.

Sarah regarded her with what she hoped was an appropriate amount of skepticism, but Alex just stuck her tongue out at her and then turned the material up twice on each side for good measure.

"There. Perfect." She took the hand Sarah offered her and stood. "Last thing you need is anything else to trip over," she added with a sly grin, and ducked as Sarah swatted at her.

"I can't help having two left feet when it's dark and I'm knackered," Sarah protested.

Alex gave her a quick kiss on the cheek and then stooped to collect their water bottles. "You can give those two left feet of yours a rest if you want. I'll go find that stream you fell into, and you get everything packed up."

Sarah chewed nervously on the inside of her cheek as Alex straightened with the bottles in her hands. It was 5:51 a.m. Five minutes of grace was all they had allowed themselves, and those five minutes of pretending that everything was fine were now up.

"I'll be okay," Alex said, obviously noticing her hesitancy. "It was, what? Fifteen minutes in the dark, so probably less now that I can see. We could leave it and chance finding something this morning, but we know that stream was running fast enough to be clear."

Sarah murmured in assent; the last thing they needed was a stomach upset, and at the moment, they had no way of boiling the water prior to drinking it. They had run out of purification tablets two days ago.

"Take your knife," she said, aware that Alex's mind was already made up.

Alex patted the pocket of her jacket. "Already got it." She pushed aside one of the branches at the shelter's entrance and squeezed through the gap. "I'll put this back for you." She gave the shelter an appraising look. "You're pretty well camouflaged from out here. The light's not great yet."

Sarah looked at the sky, where deep shades of indigo were swallowing the stars one by one. "Be careful," she managed to say.

"I'll be as quick as I can, okay?" Alex blew her a kiss and then rearranged the branch into place.

Sarah stood stock-still in the middle of the shelter, listening to her footsteps fade away. For a few irrational seconds, she considered running after her and insisting that it really would be more sensible if she accompanied her to the stream. Instead, she forced herself to sit cross-legged on the cold floor and start rolling up their blankets. Alex was right; clean water was essential if they were to spend another day hiking, and it would be quicker this way. They would be able to set off sooner. As much as Sarah tried to persuade herself, though, her arguments still rang hollow. She wanted Alex back with her so badly it was making her gut hurt. She shoved the blankets into her pack and distracted herself by folding the wet clothing they had discarded that morning. Then she glanced at her watch. Only three minutes had passed. It felt like much longer. She was just about to begin an inventory of what little food they had left when one of the branches at the entrance was lifted away. Unable to disguise her relief, she looked up with a smile.

"Hey, that was quick. Did you find somewhere close…" Her voice trailed off, the smile falling from her face.

The figure crouching in the entrance was not Alex but Nathan Merrick, and the gun he held was pointing directly at Sarah's chest. He raised his other hand to his mouth and pressed one finger to his lips in a stark warning. She scrambled to her knees, snatched up a flashlight as a weapon and tried to push herself away, but there was nowhere for her to go. Merrick moved faster than she did, grabbing her wrist and twisting it until she dropped the flashlight, and then hauling her toward him.

"Just give me an excuse to fucking shoot you," he hissed.

She didn't answer him, her focus narrowed to the grinding sensation of his hand on her wrist. The pressure was so relentless she thought he meant to snap it, and when he suddenly released her, all she could do was bow her head and cradle her arm. The respite was short-lived, however. Just as abruptly, he shifted his hold to the collar of her jacket and forced her facedown at his feet.

"Shit, I might just go ahead and shoot you anyway." He was breathing hard, and she could feel his entire body trembling as he tried to rein in his anger. "Chasing you through the middle of fucking nowhere." With his hand bruising the back of her neck, he pushed until her cheek ground into the rough carpet of pine needles. "Where did he go?"

She barely heard him. Her breath coming in great, terrified gasps, she reached out to the flashlight he had kicked away, but the handle turned as her fingernails scratched on it, spinning it beyond her grasp. Merrick, apparently tired of being ignored, dragged her up to her knees and backhanded her across the face.

"Oh God." She put her hands out to steady herself as the walls of the shelter seemed to sway and multiply. Her cheek throbbed in time with her racing heart, and black spots drifted across her vision; she wondered whether he would kill her if she vomited on him. It took her longer than it should have to recognize that he was pressing the barrel of his gun against her forehead.

"Where did he go?" he repeated, enunciating each word as if she were stupid. Spittle flew from his mouth when he spoke, and she was on the verge of asking him what the hell he was talking about when she realized he was referring to Alex.

"Stream," she whispered, her throat feeling as if it were lined with broken glass. "He went to the stream. He won't be gone long." She saw no reason to correct Merrick's mistake. He had obviously been watching the shelter when Alex left; distance, poor light, and Alex's short hair conspiring to push him to the wrong conclusion. He seemed completely wrong-footed, and Sarah wasn't sure which had him so unnerved: the fact that she wasn't alone or the fact that her companion was supposedly male. Whichever it was, she just hoped it would be enough to make him cut his losses rather than risk trying to take them both on at once. She didn't know where that left her, but she didn't really care as long as Alex was safe.

"Keys and the GPS, now," he demanded. His eyes kept flitting to the walls of the shelter as if he might be able to spot Alex's approach through them. Sarah could feel the metal bruising her skin as he increased the pressure on the gun. She closed her eyes miserably when his finger twitched on the trigger. So much for keeping Alex out of this. As far as she knew, the keys were in Alex's jacket pocket, and Alex had taken the GPS to the stream with her too. A flood of adrenaline made Sarah's legs shake so hard that she had to sit back on her heels. She licked her dry lips.

"I don't have them." She looked up at Merrick as she spoke, determined not to let him see how frightened she was. "Alex took them with him." Defiance made her punctuate her declaration with a shrug. She vaguely detected a blur of movement and heard the gun rip into the skin of her forehead a split second before the pain hit her. The force of the blow made her head snap back. Too disorientated to steady herself, she slumped to the side as a familiar thick tang of copper filled the small shelter and blood began to run into her eyes. She tried to raise a hand to the injury, but her arm refused to cooperate and she had to let it drop back down. Her body jolted once as Merrick kicked her in the abdomen. His voice was tense and agitated and he was asking her something, something about Alex having a gun. Curling herself up as tightly as possible, she left him to rant and allowed the grayness to fold in on her.

CHAPTER ELEVEN

"Get up."

Although Sarah heard the snarled command, it seemed to come from within a thick fog. It brought more pain with it: an ache in her back that made her moan softly, betraying the fact that she was awake.

"Get the fuck up. I won't tell you again."

Her head hurt too. The pain dulled her senses and her understanding of what was happening to her, though she responded instinctively to the rage in his voice by attempting to stand. She tried to bring her hands in front of her to use as leverage, but it took another impatient kick to her back to shock her into realizing her hands were bound tightly behind her. Somehow, she managed to struggle onto her knees. The exertion all but knocked her down again, and she panted against the cloth that was fastened across her mouth. Her nostrils flared as she forced herself not to panic at the almost overwhelming sense of suffocation. She must have been breathing while she was unconscious, she reminded herself in an attempt to be rational, and if she panicked now, then the next time Merrick kicked out at her, she wouldn't be able to kick him back. It was this last point that gave her enough motivation to calm down, and when he dragged her to her feet she was able to stay upright.

She shivered as she stood there. A cold draft hit her torso and she looked down to find her jacket open and her shirt untucked. She had no recollection of Merrick searching her. The thought made her feel so sick that she staggered, only the wall of the shelter preventing her from falling. She rested her cheek against the chilled pine and willed herself to stop shaking. Through the gaps in the branches she could see that the light outside had barely altered; it appeared that only a few minutes had passed, but even in that brief time, Merrick had ransacked the shelter. He had Alex's backpack strapped across his shoulders. The food Sarah had been about to take stock of was gone, and she assumed that he had taken it. Although she knew she had left at least one of his bags behind at the rocks where she had witnessed him murder the prison guard, he did not seem to have brought any of his own kit with him. The rope Alex had used as a safety line was now cutting deeply into Sarah's wrists, and she had been gagged with a brightly colored bandana from Alex's pack. Merrick had obviously intended his mission to be a quick recovery of his stolen items; she doubted he had ever planned to leave her alive. Feeling strangely sanguine, she wondered where he had found the paper he was writing on and how she could take advantage of her stay of execution. A pounding headache wasn't conducive to intricate plotting, however, and she hadn't thought of anything even remotely constructive before he took hold of her arm and pushed her ahead of him.

Once outside the shelter, he turned her to face him. With one hand, he held her jaw to keep her still, and with the other, he wiped the paper across her forehead.

"Think he'll get the message?" he asked. He displayed the paper for her to see, obviously pleased with his own ingenuity. It bore one word: KEYS. Her blood was smeared across the last two letters. The cloth in her mouth precluded an actual answer, and she didn't deign to respond in any other way. He walked away from her with a cocksure laugh. Sweat trickled down her spine as she watched him anchor the paper to the forest floor with rocks. Then he struck a match and held it to the shelter until a piece of wood caught fire.

"I think he'll get the message," he said as flames began to lick at the branches and smoke drifted through the walls.

Sarah certainly got the message: he wasn't willing to risk encountering Alex without knowing whether she was armed or not.

He had taken or destroyed everything that would help her, and he was now going to try to drag her on some sadistic kind of hunt. Sarah scanned the forest, terrified that Alex would be close enough to see or hear the fire, but there was no sign of movement in the trees. Seeming to pick up on her fear, Merrick gestured with his gun.

"After you," he said with a thin smile.

She allowed herself to breathe a little more easily; they were heading in the opposite direction to the stream. All she could hope now was that Alex would decide to leave her to her fate and run.

❖

The acrid smell of smoke was the first out of place thing Alex noticed. It wasn't too obvious initially, just the slightest change in the scent of the air, but it instantly put her on her guard. She quickened her pace, jogging along the trail they had broken the previous night as the smell began to irritate the back of her throat and make her cough. By the time she could see the clouds of smoke, she was sprinting flat out. The water bottles fell to the ground as she ran into the clearing.

"Oh fucking…No. *Sarah?*" Caution forgotten, she screamed for Sarah over and over, her voice quickly growing hoarse. She took her jacket off, common sense deserting her as she approached the shelter fully intent on extinguishing whatever she could. She was less than a yard away when the roof of the shelter collapsed. The flames claimed it enthusiastically, and the rush of heat from the new fuel forced her back to a cooler patch of grass. She sank to her knees, sobbing and sick to her stomach. There was nothing left for her to salvage. The fallen tree was smoldering all along its trunk, and the walls she had constructed had been utterly destroyed. No one within could have survived.

She leaned forward and vomited until there was nothing left to come up. The bitter taste of bile made her retch again, and she wrapped both arms around her abdomen as if that might somehow ease the pain there. She couldn't look at the shelter, couldn't bear to risk a glimpse of anything that might confirm Sarah had been trapped in there as it burned. This wasn't an accident. She knew Merrick was involved somehow. There was no reason for Sarah to have lit a fire; all Alex could think was that Merrick had found her and hurt her and left her to burn.

Birds sang cheerfully overhead, the rising sun lifting their spirits and making the frosty clearing look beautiful. Alex covered her ears with her hands and closed her eyes to block it all out.

She wasn't sure how long she'd stayed like that. Her legs were cramped beneath her, and she was cold despite the fire and the sunshine. In front of her, the shelter had been reduced to ashes. Crumbling gray shapes stirred and floated upward as the breeze played over the top of the pile. She took hold of a solid-looking stick that lay nearby and climbed to her feet. She swayed, dizzy from a head rush and still feeling nauseous. Little needles of pain pricked her legs as their circulation was restored, and she had to use the stick to prop herself up until the discomfort had worn off. When she was confident she could move, she walked across the clearing.

Heat and smoke rose to greet her as she approached the ruins of the shelter. Her grip around the stick turned her knuckles white. She had searched for bodies before. Back on the force, she had witnessed many of the seemingly countless ways that there were to die, and the terrible indignities that could be suffered by people who had left their houses that morning without the faintest idea that their lives were to be cut short within hours. She had seen what heat or cold or trauma or the passage of time could do to a body, and she had gradually gotten to the point where she was inured to the emotions involved. None of that helped now. None of that prepared her in any way for what she was about to do.

With tears clogging her nose and the taste of bile still foul in her mouth, she pushed the stick into the ashes and began to pull the pile apart. Her arms felt leaden, as if her revulsion at her task had pervaded her muscles. The stick jarred and caught several times, but all it drew out were two metal buckles she recognized from the old backpack and a set of heat-warped cutlery. Although no expert in forensics, she knew the fire could not have been hot enough to destroy all evidence of a body, that she would have found bone fragments had Sarah been inside the shelter. She quickly turned to look across the clearing, as if staring at the ashes any longer might make that fact change. The stick suddenly felt too heavy to hold. She allowed it to slip from her fingers. A faint clack as the wood hit stone made her look down.

"What the hell?"

The sheet of paper had obviously been arranged for someone to find. A circle of stones secured it to the ground and stopped the wind from tearing it away. She snatched the paper up, confusion and hope combining to make her pulse pound in her ears. When she touched her fingertips to the blood on the paper, it was tacky, and she knew without a doubt that it was Sarah's. The one-word message Merrick had left coated with her blood was not the most subtle of gambits.

"Holy shit," Alex said, turning a slow three-sixty on the spot. She didn't think she had ever been happier to learn that someone she loved had been injured and taken hostage. But then no one she loved had ever—She gave a short laugh as her thought process stalled, recognizing for the first time exactly how much Sarah had come to mean to her.

"Just hold on," she whispered. She had no idea what she was doing. She had no plan, nothing but the clothes on her back, a small knife, a sturdy stick, and plenty of water. Her odds were horrendous, but—she spotted the downtrodden grass that led out to the far side of the clearing—at least she knew which way she was going.

❖

The noise from the helicopter was merely a distant drone, but it was enough to make Merrick force Sarah down into a crouch. She couldn't help but look up, searching the sky more with hope than genuine expectation. Nothing but a solitary bird interrupted the blue, but she drew comfort from the fact that people hadn't stopped looking for them. Even if she was a lost cause, Alex was still out there and in need of help.

A yard away from her, Merrick slurped noisily from a canteen he had unhooked from his belt. She tried not to watch him, but she couldn't close her ears, and the sound of the liquid was something akin to torture. She was so thirsty. Her tongue felt thick and swollen against the gag. She didn't know how far they had walked, but the latter section had been climbing steadily. Without the use of her hands to balance her, she had repeatedly slipped and fallen, and the constant barrage of abuse from Merrick had been even more wearing than the forced march. Despite her attempt to remain impassive, she cringed as he moved toward her.

"Here."

He pulled the gag roughly from her mouth and held the canteen to her lips. She coughed as she tried to gulp too quickly, half the water ending up down her chin, and long before she had had enough, he took it away and finished the remainder himself. She pulled her knees up and wiped her chin on the pants she had stolen from him. After a few moments, there was a rustle of plastic, followed by the sound of contented chewing. She licked her dry lips, her mouth watering as the smell of sweetened oats reached her. When her stomach rumbled, she muffled the sound behind her legs, trying not to draw his attention, but he seemed quite happy eating and in no hurry to gag her again.

"Who is he, then?" Merrick chewed as he spoke, pieces of trail bar falling onto his jacket. She looked at him in disgust. She didn't answer until he repeated the question and reinforced it by waving his gun in her direction.

"Nobody," she said, her voice scratchy with lack of use. "He's nobody. He was just lost like me." She swallowed hard, willing him not to sense the lie.

"Likely to fuck off and leave you, is he?"

"Yes," she said quickly. Her hands were shaking; she was relieved that they were out of Merrick's sight. "We were just trying to get out of here. He has a family back in Boston."

"Won't come running after you, then?" His tone told her he didn't believe her.

"No, probably not." She was trying to make her answers convincing, but her voice cracked and she leaned her aching forehead on her knees. Alex would come running, and fighting, and probably wielding a sharpened stick, and she would more than likely get herself killed in the process. Tears began to soak into the fabric of Sarah's pants. "How did you find us?" she whispered, trying to change the subject before she gave everything away.

"Heard you screaming in the night like a fucking banshee," Merrick said, screwing up his wrapper and throwing it into the bracken. "First thing you ever did to make my life easier." When he grinned at her she could see chocolate coating his teeth, but the grin faded within seconds. "Okay, I reckon that's enough show-and-tell." He refastened the gag so tightly she almost choked on it. Then he took out a folded knife. Her eyes widened as he flicked the blade straight. "Quieter than a bullet," he whispered, his lips brushing her ear. He pressed the cold metal against her neck. "Don't even fucking breathe while I do this."

Staring straight ahead, Sarah was already holding her breath. She watched water drip lazily from a leaf, sunlight catching the droplets and casting rainbows through them, as she felt him untie her hands. She ran out of air and had to take a breath, the blade nicking her throat as she inhaled. She heard him chuckle. He had left the rope wrapped around her right wrist and now brought it forward to retie her hands in front of her. He kept hold of the rope that remained.

"Might make you less of a clumsy bitch," he told her. He lowered the blade and wiped it clean on her jacket. She glared at him and he slapped her so hard that he knocked her onto her knees. "Or not," he said with a shrug and set off walking. The rope pulled taut, grinding into her wrists and dragging her forward. She used the momentum to stand. Then, with no other options open to her, she followed him further into the forest.

❖

Leaning on her stick, Alex took a minute to catch her breath. The stick creaked beneath her weight, but it didn't break, and she patted it in gratitude. Its lower half was gray and battered from her frantic search through the ashes, but she had held on to it like a talisman ever since leaving the clearing.

A flutter of movement and a flash of artificial color in the undergrowth caught her eye. Using her stick, she maneuvered a plastic wrapper from the bracken. She recognized the trail bar brand as one of her own selection, while the condition of the wrapper showed that it had been discarded recently. She tucked it into her pocket, not wanting to leave Merrick's garbage lying around. The wrapper was the first tangible piece of evidence she had found to confirm that she was on the right trail, but even so, his route had been easy to follow. Too easy. It was making her extremely nervous. Merrick seemed to have made no attempt to cover his tracks; two sets of footprints—a large pair of heavy boots and a smaller pair behind them—had frequently been left in the half-frozen mud. Now, as she paid more attention to where she stood, she could see the flattened areas of grass where he and Sarah had obviously rested. She had no idea where he was leading her or what kind of end game he was planning. She knew she was moving faster than they were; she had been all but jogging along the trail, and as she set off again, she forced herself to slow down. For the next fifty yards or so she could clearly see where Merrick had walked. Hoping against hope that she wasn't about to fuck everything up, she began to cut a wide arc above that path. She had no intention of playing the role of lamb to the slaughter, and there was no way in hell she was going to make this easy for him.

❖

Despite Merrick's threats, the last time Sarah had fallen it had taken her several minutes to get back up. She couldn't maintain his pace, no matter how hard he pulled on the rope, and eventually, he seemed to reach the conclusion that keeping his hostage conscious was in his best interests. At the next stream they came to, he stopped and looked pointedly toward the water.

"Don't make yourself puke," he said.

He dropped the rope but made no further effort to help her, and she watched him warily as she wrestled the gag from her mouth. Then she knelt beside the fastest part of the stream and for a long moment simply let the water cascade over her hands and wrists. It hurt at first, the cold and friction making the abraded skin beneath the ropes burn and sting, but a pleasant numbness followed shortly afterward, and she closed her eyes in relief. She cupped her hands as best she could and took careful sips of water. When nothing adverse happened, the liquid seeming to settle her stomach, she drank more deeply and then left her hands to dangle in the stream. Two quiet taps at her side made her look down. Merrick had tossed two glucose tablets into the mud for her. She didn't bother to wipe them clean but just crunched into the first one and then allowed herself to savor the second.

By the time he took up the rope again and forced her to start walking, her thoughts were clearer. He had left the gag hanging around her neck as if to goad her into crying out for help. She was moderately insulted that he would even bother with such a cheap trick. Every so often now, he stopped in his tracks and tilted his head to the side, listening for any sounds that might indicate they were being followed. On one of these occasions, she heard a scuffle as if someone or something had slipped. The sound came from only slightly behind them, and Merrick smiled at the same time Sarah shuddered.

"Don't think he's run off back to Boston," he said and then leered at her. "You fuckin' him? Is that it?"

Although revolted by his tone, she didn't shy away from him but held his gaze, and when she spoke her voice was as hard as steel.

"Fuck. Off."

His look of surprise that she had dared to speak to him in such a way was worth the punch that split her lip and made her nose bleed. She had seen the blow coming and braced herself in time, managing to stay on her feet and raise her hands to ward off most of its force. He reared back, his fist still clenched, her blood staining his knuckles, and she watched him struggle to contain the urge to beat her until she was no longer able to answer him back.

"Not here," he said, more to himself than to Sarah. His breath on her face was harsh and sour as he gagged her again.

She waited until he turned his back on her before she wiped the blood from her nose. The bleeding slowed but didn't stop, so she opened her mouth as wide as possible to allow herself to breathe. The trick worked and she smiled, slightly bemused by her own resilience. There was no question that she was scared, but her greatest fear was for Alex, and she knew that when the time came she would fight tooth and nail to try to keep Alex safe. A hard tug on her wrists made her grind her teeth into the cotton of the bandana. She battened down the temptation to pull back on the rope, to try to knock him off balance and just take her chances. She suspected he would shoot her before she was close enough even to try to throw a punch.

The next time she tripped, she made sure it was right beside a sharp-edged stone, and that the stone was already in her jacket pocket by the time Merrick strode over to her. She lowered her eyes as if cowed and he gave no indication he had seen what she had done. Blood from her nose dripped steadily down her jacket, occasional droplets splattering on the path like a gruesome breadcrumb trail. Although she couldn't stop Alex from following them, she had no intention of letting her take Merrick on alone.

❖

Alex slammed her stick into the shifting dirt and tried to do likewise with the toes of her boots. It was enough to stop her from slipping, but she sighed as she watched stones tumble down the slope. This was the exact type of hike they had been trying to avoid the previous day and with good reason; it was dangerous, hard work, and painfully slowgoing. She was also well aware by now that Merrick had doubled back on several occasions to lead her in a tortuous route. If he was doing so to try to wear her down and tire her out, his tactic was having the desired effect.

She sidestepped cautiously to a lower section where trees and undergrowth gave her something to grab on to and use for traction. From that level, Merrick's trail was just about visible, snapped branches and parted bracken showing her the way. She briefly contemplated following in his footsteps again, but realized that if he decided to wait for her somewhere along the path, she would walk straight into an ambush. Her boots dislodged more stones as she set off. She shook her head in exasperation. If she continued to make this much noise, she might as well walk on the trail. At the moment, however, sacrificing a silent approach in favor of an unpredictable one seemed to be the lesser of two evils.

❖

Sarah wasn't entirely sure what she had been expecting. In some of her darker moments during the hike, she had imagined a lair rigged with explosives and beset with devices of torture. Certainly at no point had she supposed Merrick would be dragging her toward a small yet civilized camp.

She let him steer her over to the side of a khaki two-person tent and sat when he pushed her down. Now that they had apparently reached their destination, a dreadful sense of anticipation had started to make her legs quake, and her stomach threatened to rebel against the water she had drunk. She waited nervously as he tied the end of the rope around the stump of a stout shrub, but he walked away as soon as he was satisfied that she was securely tethered. She took a deep, relieved breath. There was no sign of his girlfriend at the camp. Somehow she was sure that the gunshot she and Alex had heard had sealed the woman's fate. The pain in her wrists brought tears to her eyes as she drew her knees up and wrapped her arms around them, but there was something undeniably comforting about making herself as small a target as possible.

A heavy thud and a metallic clatter startled her. She looked up to find Merrick kneeling at the entrance of the tent. Once he was certain she was watching him, he unzipped a duffel bag identical to the one she had stolen and began to unpack it. She turned her head away from the sight of him lifting out an assortment of weapons, but not before she had seen him slap a clip into another handgun and angle the blade of a vicious-looking Bowie knife so that it flashed silver and then gold as it caught the sun. It took some time and concentration, but she managed to tune out the noises he was making and listen instead to the sounds of the forest around her. Water was rushing over rocks somewhere to her left, something small and energetic scratched through dried leaves at the base of a tree, and a bird of prey gave a shrill cry high overhead. There was nothing to suggest that Alex was nearby, for which Sarah was immeasurably grateful.

She heard Merrick strike a match, the sound quickly followed by a smell of burning. When she looked back, she saw him sitting cross-legged by a small fire. He was paying absolutely no attention to her, so she took the opportunity to move her hands behind her knees, enabling her to reach the stones in her pocket. Blindly, she ran her fingers over and along the various edges and surfaces, trying to find one that might be sharp enough to cut through the ropes at her wrists. She pulled out a likely candidate, manipulating it in her fingers to turn its sharpest edge against the first strand of rope. It took mere seconds for her to concede that her efforts were going to be in vain. It was a great idea in theory, but in practice her fingers were too stiff and too sore for the kind of fine dexterity the task demanded. The stone was nowhere near large enough or sharp enough, either, and the rope itself was so thick it would probably have stood up well to a serrated blade, never mind a little piece of granite.

"Bollocks."

She would have kicked herself for her own naive stupidity, had Merrick not already spent a large part of the morning kicking her. He stood up and she immediately closed her fist to conceal the rock, certain that her cursing had alerted him. Instead of coming across to her, however, he went into the tent. She heard rustling and banging as he searched for something. Keeping one eye on the tent's entrance, she brought the rope to her mouth and began to worry at the knot. The gag got in the way, making it difficult for her to breathe, and a musty, blood-tinged scent rushed into her nostrils. She didn't care. At least she was doing something. Even if it didn't work, at least she was doing something.

❖

For the second time that morning, Alex could smell smoke. She immediately stopped walking and wiped her sweaty palms on her pants. Her heart was beating so forcefully that she had an irrational fear Merrick might hear it. She crouched low, grasses prickling her chin, and tried to gauge her distance from the fire, but the strengthening breeze made it all but impossible. A sharp rip of pain at the base of her thumb prompted her to ease her grip on her stick. Instead, she took her anxiety and frustration out on a splinter that had worked its way beneath her skin, scratching at it roughly until the skin around it became red and heated. When she breathed in, smoke tickled at her throat and she had to keep her mouth shut to stop herself from coughing.

The fact that Merrick had stayed in one place long enough to light a fire suggested that he was finally ready for Alex to catch up with him. She closed her eyes against the implications of that; she didn't even want to consider what he had planned for Sarah. In the darkness, an all too familiar sense of helplessness threatened to overwhelm her. She couldn't do this. In spite of her earlier bravado, what could she honestly hope to achieve against an armed man who was holding an injured woman hostage? She would get herself killed, and worse than that, she would get Sarah killed.

The splinter suddenly came free and she stared at the small droplet of blood that formed in its wake. She automatically stuck her thumb into her mouth, a habit from childhood that was surprisingly soothing. She put her other hand into her pocket and her fingers touched the cool metal of the keys that had started this nightmare in the first place. Whatever those keys unlocked had been worth breaking Merrick from jail and sending him into the wilderness. It had made him murder indiscriminately and, after Sarah had unwittingly intervened, had made him chase her down with a single-minded relentlessness. Alex had never really had the time to consider the potential consequences of what might be hidden out here, but given Merrick's links to white supremacist groups, they became more frightening the more she thought about them.

The keys jangled lightly on their chain as she brought them out and set them on the palm of her hand. Merrick wasn't interested in a trade, she knew that as surely as she knew she didn't intend to offer him one. In which case, keeping the keys on her person would only work to his advantage if the likely odds played out and he killed her. She switched the GPS on and studied the coordinates of her current location. There was a memory function in the GPS's menu, but she didn't dare use it, and there was no way for her to write the coordinates down. Precious minutes ticked by as she tried to memorize the short sequence of numbers, but she persevered until she was confident that she knew them by heart. She looked around for some kind of landmark and spotted a bizarrely shaped tree just to her left that was bowed by the prevailing wind and stunted by vicious winters but that continued to thrive regardless. She bent down to tuck the keys beneath one of its gnarled roots.

"Good luck finding those, you fuck," she muttered.

A subtle darkening of the forest around her made her look up at the sky. Gray storm clouds had gathered overhead, blocking out the sun, and she wondered whether it was cold enough for snow to fall instead of rain. Either option might work to her advantage, reducing both the visibility and the likelihood that Merrick would hear her approach. Feeling slightly heartened, she cautiously set off walking again. A solitary droplet of sleet landed on her nose and she caught it with her tongue as it slid lower. Within seconds, the drizzle became a downpour and fallen leaves began to crackle as the heavy drops landed on them. She walked on with more confidence, heading into the encroaching mist for cover and continuing to plot a course around Merrick's original path. The smell of smoke became ranker as more sleet fell, the moisture presumably starting to extinguish the fire. She entertained the spiteful little hope that Merrick had been cooking himself a meal that would now be ruined. The thought made her smile grimly as she pulled her hood up and used the smoke to guide her through the storm.

CHAPTER TWELVE

The deterioration of the weather seemed to have messed up Merrick's game plan somewhat. Huddled with her back to the worst of the sleet, Sarah watched him pace the perimeter of the small clearing, obviously straining to hear Alex's approach. He was brandishing a handgun and she had seen him tuck a second one into the back of his pants. She used his distraction to continue working on the knot at her wrists. Although it was far from untied, she had managed to slacken it, twisting her right wrist until the rope was slick with blood. The blood made a decent lubricant, while the anesthetizing coldness of the sleet helped her to bear the discomfort. She could see a gap around her wrist now and was on the verge of attempting to wriggle it free completely when she heard Merrick's heavy tread coming toward her. She dropped her hands, terrified that he might have seen what she was doing, but he barely even looked at her. He stooped to unfasten the rope from the base of the shrub and pulled her up by the collar of her jacket.

"Time to find out how close your boyfriend is," he said, shaking her like a dog.

She had been cramped in one position for so long that her legs were too numb to hold her. He gave a snarl of anger before hauling her bodily into the center of the clearing. He pressed his arm across her throat, making her gasp for air, and she struggled to gain her footing even as she clawed at his sleeve. He slapped the side of her head with his gun, more as a warning to behave than anything else, but it still made her ears ring, and he had pulled her gag away by the time she could focus again.

"Scream for me and I won't hurt you," he said.

The soaked material of his jacket rubbed coarsely against her throat as she shook her head. "No fucking way," she managed to choke out.

"Suit yourself." His voice was calm and measured, and that alone was almost enough to make her obey him. She ground her teeth together and tasted blood where a cut on her lip had reopened. Before she could stop him, he kicked at her legs and she lurched forward onto her knees. He reached around and half-opened the zipper on her jacket, and then tugged at its collar until it gaped at the back. Sleet hit the skin he exposed and her teeth chattered uncontrollably as she felt the tip of a knife pricking at the side of her shoulder blade.

"You ready to scream for me now?" he asked, pressing the knife just hard enough to break the skin.

She sobbed once but shook her head again. She wouldn't willingly draw Alex into this; he would have to kill her before she did that. The knife moved, etching a tight line down her back, and she heard his breathing become harsher and faster. For a fleeting moment, she wondered what he had done, but then the pain hit her and everything slowly tilted sideways. She grasped at the wet earth for a few seconds before he righted her. Warmth and cold trickled beneath her shirt, and when she bit down this time, blood flooded into her mouth. Behind her, Merrick was waiting, his body shifting as he tried to scan every section of the clearing. Threads of mist twisted through the trees that surrounded them, playing tricks with perspective and muffling any sounds. As he looked to the left, a sudden flash of light on the opposite side of the clearing caught Sarah's eye. The light instantly vanished and she knew that Merrick hadn't seen it. With a sinking heart, she realized that Alex was close, closer than she had expected, close enough to do something stupid and impulsive unless Sarah acted first.

When Merrick bent her forward to cut her again, she forced herself to go limp. She slipped from his grasp and he cursed incoherently, fumbling to keep control of his gun, his knife, and his hostage. The blade skimmed a hair's breadth from her eye, but before he could get a firm hold on her collar with his other hand, she bit down on the one holding the knife.

Unlike Sarah, he did scream. She kept her teeth clamped on his skin until his fingers went into spasm and he let go of the knife. Then she threw herself back and slammed her head into his nose. Cartilage splintered as his nose gave way beneath the impact, but she was already falling forward again, too stunned to do anything else and struggling to remain conscious. She heard him speak but couldn't tell what he was saying, only that he sounded surprised. Something splashed beside her, landing in a puddle of mud and blood. She reached her fingers out to it and clasped them around cold metal. The pistol felt heavy in her hands, heavier than she would ever have supposed, and someone, a voice she recognized, was imploring her to shoot.

❖

Watching Merrick torture Sarah and not being able to do a thing to stop him had been the most awful experience of Alex's life. Poised at the edge of the clearing, she had forced herself to remain concealed as he sliced into Sarah's back. Even when he stopped cutting, he kept the knife at her throat, and there was no doubt in Alex's mind that he was prepared to kill Sarah at the slightest provocation. More than anything, she wanted Sarah to know that she was there, that Sarah wasn't alone in this. As soon as Merrick had his back turned to her position, she struck a match, but the storm snuffed out the flame before she had a chance to put it out herself, and she wondered whether Sarah had even seen it. What Sarah did next gave Alex her answer.

Alex was already running, her stick held high like a baseball bat, as Sarah bit into Merrick's hand. His scream was cut off by the impact of Sarah's head with his nose, but the ensuing struggle left her quiet and unmoving at his feet. Distraught, Alex wavered for a second, but despite the blood pouring from his nose, Merrick was far from disabled. He had picked up the knife again and he was dangerously close to Sarah. His head whipped around when he heard Alex's footsteps, but at her appearance he seemed to falter as if shocked, and he lowered his gun arm a fraction.

The words "Who the fuck are you?" had barely crossed his lips before she took advantage of his confusion by rushing at him, swinging her stick. The wood cracked into the top of his cheek, making him stagger to the side, and she followed up with a second hit that landed squarely on his forearm. The gun flew from his grasp, landing close to where Sarah lay, but she barely seemed to realize what it was.

"Sarah!" Alex yelled, bringing her arm up to try to ward off a wild slash from Merrick's knife. He was trying to free something from the back of his pants, but a probable fracture to his arm was making his attempts uncoordinated and ineffective.

"Sarah, get the gun!"

There was no answer, no indication that Sarah had even heard her. The stick snapped in two when Alex smashed it against Merrick's torso.

"Oh shit," she whispered.

He stepped closer to her, the knife slicing through her jacket and drawing blood from her arm.

"Sarah, please. Fucking shoot him, please."

She was tiring and he pressed his advantage, opening a cut on the back of her hand, a grin slowly forming on his face. Her feet skidded in the wet grass and his grin widened. When he raised his arm, blood dripped from the blade and coated his fingers. He never noticed Sarah dragging herself upright, and the first time he saw the gun that she threw across to Alex was when Alex pointed it at his chest. As he gave a roar of pure rage and stabbed down with the knife, she fired instinctively, two shots that tore into his torso and sent him flying backward. He landed in a tangled heap by Sarah's side and Alex saw her recoil and scramble away.

"Stay still, Sarah. I got him." She barely managed to sound the words out, but Sarah made a small noise of understanding regardless, and she seemed calmer as Alex took the three steps to Merrick's side. With her gun still pointing unwaveringly at him, she flipped him onto his back and pressed her fingers into his neck. His eyes stared straight ahead, blood frothing at his lips as he took uneven, irregular breaths. She found a pulse but it was too fast to count and she could feel its strength slipping as he continued to hemorrhage. Within seconds, the throbbing beneath her fingertips had slowed dramatically, and then she lost it altogether. The breaths he was taking became a terrible rattle that stopped and started without warning. Realizing that there was no danger of his getting up again, she left the knife in his slack fingers, wary of tampering with what would become a crime scene. His breathing stopped completely and she turned away from him, her entire body beginning to shake. When she sagged to her knees, Sarah met her halfway and flung her bound arms around Alex's neck. She was crying, great, racking sobs, and she pushed against Alex as if she never meant to let her go.

"Hey, hey, it's okay," Alex murmured into her hair, unsure whether she was trying to convince Sarah or herself. Sleet continued to fall steadily and they were both soaked as well as covered in blood by the time Sarah's cries tapered off. She hesitantly lifted her arms, the ropes at her wrists hampering her movement.

"Hey," Alex said softly.

"Hey." Sarah touched the tips of her fingers to Alex's cheeks. "You shouldn't have come," she said. "You shouldn't have come."

"Yeah, well." Alex kissed her hands gently and then lowered them and began to untie the knot securing her wrists. "I only just found you. I wasn't going to lose you again so damn fast." She winced as she peeled the rope from Sarah's skin. "Son of a bitch."

Sarah had almost managed to wrench her right wrist free, removing a large portion of skin in the process. Bruises marred her face, and blood was still trickling down her chin from a split in her bottom lip. Alex glanced at Merrick's body, saw the deep crimson staining the puddles it was lying in, and felt nothing but hatred for what he had put Sarah through.

"Come over here," she said, guiding her to sit in the shelter of the tent.

Sarah balanced her elbows on her knees and held her hands up as if she couldn't bear to risk anything touching the raw skin that encircled her wrists.

Alex bent down to her eye level. "You okay?"

"I'm fine," Sarah replied, a little too quickly. "Just sore." This time she managed to smile wryly at her own understatement.

"Are you still bleeding?" Alex nodded toward Sarah's back. Sarah had pulled her jacket straight, fastening the zipper to the hilt and concealing what Merrick had done to her.

"I don't think so. It wasn't deep. I'm okay, Alex. Really."

"Yeah, yeah," Alex said quietly, but she understood the unspoken request that she allow Sarah time to regain her composure. She touched her hand briefly to Sarah's cheek, and then flicked Merrick's flashlight on and cast the beam around the tent. She found her own backpack, stuffed with the remnants of their food stocks, and two more bags that were half unpacked. One held nothing but weapons, and she pushed it as far away from them as she could, concealing it in the darkest corner of the tent. The second contained a small quantity of food, a map, two blankets, and a first aid kit. While all of those would be invaluable, they didn't include the one thing she needed the most. She peered through the sleet to where the mist was curling over and around Merrick's body. Going out there and searching him was the last thing she wanted to do, but ultimately practicality won out. She wrapped one of the blankets around Sarah, pulling it up under her chin.

"I'll be right back," she said.

Sarah was already trying to stand. "No, I'll come with you."

"He's dead, Sarah."

Sarah shook her head, common sense temporarily abandoning her, and Alex had to grasp her shoulders to keep her sitting down. "He's dead," she said again, with absolute finality.

Sarah looked up at her with wide eyes. "I can still smell him," she whispered. Her face was so pale that Alex wondered whether she was going to pass out. The tent stank of stale sweat and gun oil. She started to retch, and Alex maneuvered her closer to the entrance.

"That better?"

Alex watched her lift her face to the sky and close her eyes. The sleet was tapering off, leaving thin, diluted trails of blood and tears on her skin. The fresher air seemed to settle her. Once Alex was certain that Sarah wasn't going to faint, she kissed the top of her head and then walked across the clearing. Merrick's half-lidded eyes seemed to gauge her approach. Undeterred, she returned the stare. She had long ago lost count of the number of corpses she had seen, many of which had suffered a violent death. She knew the stink of clotted blood and loosened bowels, and the frozen look of horrified recognition on the faces of those more accustomed to meting out pain than being on the receiving end of it. Merrick was the first man she had ever shot, though, and the first she had ever killed. She knelt unsteadily in the slick grass and began to search his body.

She found what she was looking for clipped onto his belt. A small green LED was flashing on top of the radio and the display on its front indicated that its battery was half-full. A handgun fell loose when she tugged the radio free, and it was only then that she realized what he had been struggling to reach just before she shot him, and exactly how close he had come to getting hold of it. She left the gun lying impotently in the filth and blood of its owner and hurried back to Sarah.

❖

The sun was doing its best to break through the storm clouds. It was nowhere near enough to warm Sarah or dry her clothing, but it made her smile all the same. Alex was also looking a lot happier as she jogged toward the tent, a small black radio clasped in her hand. Sarah felt a relief so profound it made her sway on the spot.

"Does it work?" she asked, as Alex sat beside her.

"Only one way to find out." Alex was already turning the dial, trying to establish the radio's frequency and channel. She shook her head in frustration. "Can't remember the goddamn channel mine was set to." She chose one, seemingly at random, but when she voiced a call for assistance there was no answer. "Shit."

Sarah set a hand on her thigh in silent encouragement and Alex continued, dialing through the numbers sequentially as she kept one wary eye on the battery strength. Feeling cold in the intermittent sunlight, Sarah reached for the blanket before nestling into the crook of Alex's arm. It was only when she felt her body jerk that she realized she had been dozing. She came awake instantly when she heard a man's voice in animated conversation with Alex.

"No, no. We're over the other side. Hang on, hang on. Oh shit, I have this GPS." The GPS sounded its welcome tone as Alex switched it on. She gave Sarah a thumbs-up with a smile that stretched from ear to ear.

"Take your time, honey," the disembodied voice said patiently. "We've come in by the East Fork Creek, so I guess we're not too far from you."

"Okay, I got it." Alex passed the coordinates over the radio.

Sarah unfolded Merrick's map and spotted the river that the man had mentioned. She indicated it to Alex, who let out a whoop as she finally identified where they were in relation to it.

"Oh, we're close! You could be with us by tomorrow."

"I got you," the man said, his accent soft and reassuring. "You guys be okay out here for another night?"

"We're good. Tell Walt we're fine. He with you?"

"Walt?" The man hesitated and conferred with someone in the background. "Naw, he's leading the search over by Ross. I'll try and get a message to him, though."

"That'd be great, thanks."

"No problem. You need shelter tonight. Walk a couple of miles due east and you'll pick up the creek. Another half mile or so, there's a cave formation. Be a good place to stay, and we can rendezvous with you there."

Sarah nodded enthusiastically as Alex looked to her for confirmation. She really didn't want to spend the night in Merrick's tent if they had any other options.

"Sounds like a plan," Alex said. Static began to eat into the reception and the man's reply was lost beneath it. The connection cut out abruptly. She carefully set the radio down and then gathered Sarah into her arms.

Sarah tucked her face into Alex's neck and kissed the soft skin of her throat. "You taking me home?" Sarah murmured, and kissed her again when she laughed.

❖

Their bags were heavier with the tent and the extra gear in them, but despite the prospect of rescue, they were reluctant to leave supplies behind. Sarah had continued to insist that her injuries could wait to be treated, and Alex had taken one look at the set of her jaw and chosen not to push the issue. There had been two bedding rolls in the tent, neither of which they could bear to take with them. Without speaking, Alex chose the larger of the two and carried it across to Merrick's body. Together, she and Sarah unfolded the roll, draped it over him, and weighed the cloth down with rocks. She had already noted the position of the camp in order to pass the information on to the authorities. She felt Sarah take hold of her hand and squeeze it gently.

"You okay?" Sarah asked.

"Yeah." Alex tore her eyes away from the makeshift grave. They had allowed him more dignity than he deserved. "Yeah, I am."

"He didn't give you a choice, Alex."

"No, I know that." She traced her fingers around a darkening contusion on Sarah's cheek. Seeing the absolute trust on Sarah's face, she immediately felt calmer, reassured by the knowledge that if placed in exactly the same circumstances, she would make exactly the same decision all over again.

They left the clearing without looking back, a circular smudge of ashes, a duffel bag, and a dead man beneath a blanket the only evidence remaining of what had occurred there. As soon as they were back in the trees, Sarah took a deep breath of freshly dampened pine and heard Alex do likewise. Two and a half miles, she told herself. That was all they had to walk. Then there would be a cave for shelter, close to a river for a ready supply of fresh water. They could have a fire, a hot meal, and a decent night's sleep before the rescue party arrived in the morning.

"I bet there's a bloody bear in the cave," she said morosely.

Alex stared at her before starting to laugh at her serious expression. "Probably," she agreed sagely as soon as she had enough breath to speak. "Or at the very least a big ol' troll."

"Probably a bear *and* a troll," Sarah said, but she lost the battle to keep her face straight.

Alex took hold of her hand. "Got guns now."

"Yes, we have," Sarah said, then corrected herself. "Well, you have."

Alex had selected two of Merrick's handguns, both of which she was carrying, since Sarah had declined to take one. They had left the bag containing the rest of the weapons by the fire pit. The odds of anyone happening upon them before the authorities got there were slim to none.

Alex stopped walking and the puzzled expression on her face slowly altered as something that had obviously been niggling at her became clear at last. "Oh hell, is that why you threw the gun to me back there?"

Sarah sheepishly dug the toe of her boot into the leaf litter. "I've never fired a gun. That was the first time I'd ever held one," she admitted. "I don't even know how to, you know…" She pantomimed clicking the safety off and aiming. "More likely to shoot my own bloody foot off."

Alex took the gun from where she had tucked it into her belt. "Well, this is a Glock, so there's no safety on it," she said. "It's basically ready to go as soon as it's loaded."

"Oh." Sarah regarded the weapon as if it had the potential to leap out of Alex's hand and kill her where she stood. Alex altered her hold on the Glock, shifting to a two-handed grip that Sarah recognized from every cop show she had ever watched on television.

"Finger off the trigger until you're ready to fire," Alex said, tapping her trigger finger against the side of the gun to emphasize her point. "Focus on the front sight, to the point where the back sight and the target are a little blurry, then pull the trigger all the way back. You have to pull it like you mean it to counteract the inbuilt safety mechanisms."

Sarah nodded, not really understanding a word of what Alex was telling her. "Or just chuck the gun across to you," she said with a self-deprecating smile.

"Good thing you throw like a Major League pitcher," Alex said. "Baseball reference," she clarified, when Sarah continued to look blankly at her.

"Oh. Sorry, more of a footie fan."

"NFL?"

"No, *football* football." Sarah rolled her eyes. "The one where they don't pick the ball up and run with it, hence *foot*ball."

"That's soccer."

"Unless you live in the rest of the world, in which case it's football."

Alex shrugged as she tucked the Glock back into her belt. "The rest of the world is wrong."

Sarah nudged her sharply and sent her stumbling into a puddle. "Sorry, don't know my own strength," she said, in a tone that implied she wasn't sorry at all.

Alex made a show of shaking water off her boots. "You could cook supper as penance," she suggested craftily.

After a pause for careful deliberation, Sarah nodded her agreement. "Probably the safest option anyway. If we're going to come up against bears and…trolls?" She looked to Alex to confirm she had the right nemesis. "Then the last thing we need is a bout of listeria as well."

Alex feigned being cut to the quick for a moment. A second later, Sarah had to sidestep a blatant attempt to elbow her into the next puddle. It felt so good to be laughing again and even better to be back with Alex. Sarah had missed her more than she would have thought possible. Despite the aches and pains, and the horror of what they had just been through, she felt happier than she could remember being in a long time.

❖

The river proved impossible to miss. They had been able to hear it long before they reached it: a foaming mass of white water that crashed over rocks and cast cold spray into their faces as they walked along its banks. Here and there, small placid pools had formed where channels diverted away from the main course. Sarah eyed them longingly. For hours now, she had been plagued by a crawling sensation that went deeper than the dirt and dried blood that coated her skin. She wondered whether a plunge into the icy-cold water would cleanse away the memory of Merrick's hands on her. It surely wouldn't make her feel any worse than she did at the moment. She glanced at Alex, who was walking quietly beside her. The earlier euphoria had burned off, and she could tell Alex was teetering along the same fine edge of near collapse that she was. She put her hand out to steady Alex as she weaved dangerously close to the water.

"Sorry," Alex muttered.

"Shouldn't be much farther."

"I'm good."

"I know you are," Sarah said gently. She tugged on Alex's sleeve and brought her to a stop, but when Alex looked at her expectantly, she found herself unsure of what to say. Then she realized that it really all came down to two words. "Thank you," she said.

Thank you for not leaving me, and for not giving up on me, and for saving my life. But before she could voice any of those, Alex had taken hold of her hands and pulled her closer. Sarah drew in a breath to speak, but Alex cut her off with a kiss.

"Thank me later." She formed the words against Sarah's mouth, only the slightest sound passing between them, and Sarah felt a thrill that fluttered in her stomach and then bolted lower, rendering her speechless. She nodded helplessly, somehow resisting the urge to drop her bag and thank Alex there and then.

CHAPTER THIRTEEN

"No bears." Alex stepped purposefully around the small cave. Her flashlight beam picked out a jagged rock ceiling that sloped into pitch-black as it met the far wall. Closer to the entrance there was ample space for them both to sleep, and they could safely stand up without risking a concussion.

"No trolls either," Sarah said. With her hands on her hips, she looked around the shelter and nodded her approval. "If we sleep over this side, we should be dry enough."

The western wall dripped water steadily. A tiny pool had formed over the years, and when Alex dipped her hand in, her fingers seemed to disappear into the inky depths.

"Don't fall into this," she warned Sarah, even though the pool was barely six inches in diameter. "I might lose you forever."

Sarah narrowed her eyes in response, but something in her expression must have given her away because she could see Alex studying her carefully.

"You okay?" Alex said, wiping her hand dry on her pants.

"No." Sarah folded her arms, wincing as the abraded skin on her wrists snagged on her jacket. "I need to get clean," she said, and then shook her head when Alex gestured to the pool. "No, all of me. I just…I need to get him off me."

"Jesus…" Alex's voice trailed into nothing, and she stared at Sarah with a look of horror. "Did Merrick—"

"No! Shit, no." Too late, Sarah realized how what she had said must have sounded, but she could barely bring herself to articulate what she did mean. She took a breath and looked at Alex, who nodded reassuringly at her. "He had his hands on me," she said, her voice so quiet Alex had to step closer in order to hear her. "And one time, he hit me." She touched her fingers to the tender laceration on her forehead. "And he must have knocked me out for a minute or so. When I came round, he'd opened my jacket and my shirt was all untucked."

Water dripped like a metronome, ten tiny splashes falling into silence, and then Alex picked up the bag that contained most of their clothes.

"Let's go for a swim," she said and led Sarah out toward the river.

❖

Sarah's toes began to tingle as soon as she stepped into the water. Her bare feet slipped across the stones on the riverbed, her skin already turning numb and bright pink. Behind her, she heard Alex squeak and then curse fluently enough to make a sailor blush. The pool they had chosen was as clear as glass and dropped sharply a foot from where Sarah was standing. Silver flashed against the green-gray of the stones as fish swiftly disappeared into the murkier waters beyond the ledge. She tucked her T-shirt into her boxer shorts, closed her eyes, and dove in.

The shock of the cold hitting her face seemed to make everything slow down for an instant. She caught her breath instinctively but was careful not to panic or allow her breathing to fall out of synch; taking a sudden gasp and ending up with a lungful of water was a fast track to drowning. Forcing herself to move, she swam the width of the pool. The pain that Merrick had left her with gradually faded as the water chilled sensation away. She turned onto her back to see Alex tentatively crouching at the edge of the water, giving herself a hurried wash. Alex shook her head in disbelief and then even more vehemently in refusal as Sarah beckoned her to go in farther.

"You're mad!" Alex yelled above the noise of the river.

Sarah waved in cheerful acceptance and then dove beneath the water again. She wouldn't be able to stay in more than two or three minutes, but already she felt better, cleaner, and lighter as if a great burden had been lifted from her shoulders. She swam back to the shallows and took the cloth that Alex offered her.

"Fire," Alex managed to say through chattering teeth. "I need a fire. A really big fire."

"If you'd put more than your big toe in, you'd be a whole lot warmer by now," Sarah said. She scrubbed her arms with the cloth, careful to give her wrists a wide berth.

"I put both my feet in, see?" Alex wriggled her toes but then grimaced as water splashed onto her legs. "Right, that's it. I'm outta here."

"I'm done." Sarah squeezed her dripping ponytail. Every inch of her skin felt energized, but she knew that a bone-deep cold would soon creep in and that Alex was right about the fire.

Wrapped in blankets, they ran back to the cave, pausing every now and again to collect fallen branches to use as firewood. They dropped their bundles, quickly dried themselves, and then redressed in the cleanest clothes they could find. Alex was the first to finish, and she already had a fire flickering in a shallow pit by the time Sarah had gotten the knots out of her hair.

Holding her hands out to the flames, Alex flexed her fingers as prickles of heat gradually chased away the cold. She looked up to see Sarah walking haltingly toward the fire, both hands busy behind her head as she tried to tie her hair back.

"Oh bugger it," Sarah growled in frustration.

Alex caught a glimpse of the snarled-up catastrophe at the back of her head. "Sit down," she said, patting the crinkly plastic bag she had laid out to cover the wet ground and waiting until Sarah complied before moving to kneel behind her. "This isn't exactly my strong suit," she said as she wrestled the elastic tie free.

"Can't be any worse than my efforts," Sarah said. "My hands aren't really working very well."

Alex made no comment, unsure if it was the cold water or Sarah's injuries that were crippling her, and not wanting to force an explanation. "My mom would've given her right arm for me to have had hair like this," she said.

"She would?" Either the warmth or Alex's ministrations seemed to be having a soporific effect on Sarah, and there was a drowsiness creeping into her voice. "But yours is perfect as it is," she murmured. "It suits your face."

Halfway through twisting the tie, Alex hesitated. "It does? My mom always said it made me look like a guy."

"Then your mum is officially ridiculous."

Alex couldn't help but snort in agreement. "Oh, you've met her." Never having been comfortable with accepting compliments, she set about her task with renewed vigor.

Sarah reached behind herself, though, and fumbled blindly for Alex's fingers. "I think you're beautiful," she said softly.

Unsure how to respond and almost certain that nothing would come out if she tried, Alex just nodded.

Sarah's smile broadened. "And now I've made you blush."

Alex contemplated an attempt at denial but thought better of it when she felt the heat rising in her cheeks. "Yeah, a little," she conceded.

Sarah grinned. "That's cute too." She quickly ducked her head back down, giving Alex the opportunity to collect herself.

The tie pinged loose as Alex did everything utterly wrong. By the time she had fashioned what looked to be a passable ponytail, Sarah's shoulders had slumped; Alex wondered whether she had actually managed to fall asleep sitting up.

"Sarah?"

"Still here." She made no objection when Alex flipped the lid from the first aid kit.

"You warm enough for me to do this?" Alex said, gesturing at Sarah's back.

"Just about." Sarah edged nearer to the fire. She shrugged out of her jacket and pulled the rest of her clothing off over her head.

Alex laid Sarah's clothing by the fire and then turned her slightly to position her in the best available light. The wavering flames made the incision stretching down her back look ghastly.

"Fucking asshole," Alex muttered emphatically. The wound had reopened as Sarah undressed. Alex fumbled for something she could use to stop the bleeding. The fire flared and crackled around the empty gauze wrapper she tossed into it but she still heard Sarah's low moan when she pressed the wad of gauze against the incision.

"It's not too bad," she said, only partially succeeding in keeping the anger from her voice. Merrick had cut shallowly, intent only on causing pain, but the wound ran from the top of Sarah's shoulder blade to the base of her rib cage. It tapered off the lower it went, as if he had struggled to reach that far beneath her clothing. Toward the top, where he had dug in deeper, Alex kept the gauze in place until she was sure that the bleeding had stopped.

"Getting good at this." She deftly placed butterfly bandages across the wound. "Wish you'd stop giving me quite so much practice though." Beneath her hands, Sarah's shoulders twitched slightly as she gave a short, apologetic laugh.

Alex sealed down a dressing before moving around to face her. "Now, where else?" She tipped Sarah's chin in her hand to appraise the cut on her forehead. The swim in the river had cleaned the dried blood from her face. It had also made the bruises more apparent, but there was nothing that required Alex's ad hoc brand of emergency first aid. "That looks okay as it is," she said, and then sighed. "Fucked up your wrists though, didn't he?"

With obvious trepidation, Sarah nodded, offering Alex her hands.

"Damn." Alex had always prided herself on having a strong stomach, but looking at the ravaged skin on Sarah's wrists made her feel queasy. Deep, bloodied furrows encircled Sarah's left wrist, and on her right she had multiple injuries extending up onto her forearm where she had come so close to getting herself untied. Despite the plunge in the pool, shreds of hemp were still embedded in the wounds.

"Tell me something about yourself that I don't know," Alex said, by way of distraction, as she soaked a cloth in water and eased it onto Sarah's left wrist.

Sarah screwed her eyes shut for a couple of seconds, obviously waiting for the pain to settle to a reasonable level. "Ah, that stings a bit," she said, opening one eye in time to see Alex start to peel strands of rope from a patch of abraded skin. "Something you don't know? Hmm, like what?"

"Like anything. Favorite color, favorite place in all the world, first kiss…" Alex winked suggestively, making Sarah chuckle.

"Okay, well, I like blue. That classic china blue that looks so pretty against white. Not for clothes, but if I had a house to decorate, I would choose that for my bedroom."

"Sounds nice." Alex waited for Sarah to nod her consent and then gently reapplied the cloth. "I used to like red, but now I mostly like anything that doesn't show dirt."

"Any color so long as it's khaki?"

"Yeah, that sounds about right." Satisfied that Sarah's wrist was clean, she dabbed antiseptic around it and wrapped it in a bandage. "One down…" She held her hand out for Sarah's right wrist and stroked her fingers in sympathy. "One to go. You ready for this, honey?"

"Ready."

"So, favorite place in the world?" The cloth went back on and she watched Sarah's face pale, beads of sweat breaking out on her forehead. "You gonna pass out on me?"

"No."

"Puke on me?"

"Maybe."

She shrugged. "Least you're honest."

Sarah managed a thin smile. "The Bernese Oberland," she said.

"Gesundheit."

This time Sarah's smile reached her eyes. "My favorite place in the world. The Bernese Oberland in Switzerland."

"Fabulous chocolate," Alex offered. "Beyond that and those stupid clocks, I don't know much about the country."

"It's an amazing place." Sarah's voice was wistful and she didn't seem to notice when Alex began to tease the debris from her wrist. "There's this little village right at the foot of the Eiger. The mountains sweep up from the valley floor, and it's just the most stunning view. I went with my mum before she married Richard and went back for two weeks earlier in my travels this year." She smiled, remembering. “The glaciers were a lot smaller, but the cows still had bells around their necks.”

“They really do that?” Alex turned Sarah’s wrist and started on its underside.

“Yep, they really do that. Must be like having permanent tinnitus for the poor buggers.”

“The very height of cow cruelty,” Alex concurred. “You still have one question left, missy.”

Sarah feigned forgetfulness but then relented when Alex started to make sloppy kissing noises at her.

“Okay, okay. Sophie Threadbetter. We were six years old. Under a coat in the school playground.”

Alex let out a mock gasp of horror. “Six years old?” She shook her head sorrowfully. “And already a lesbian.”

“Yeah, there was never any hope for me,” Sarah said cheerfully. “Sophie, on the other hand, is now married with four kids. I used to see her when I was back at my mum’s. She always looked so tired… Ow!” She jumped as Alex tackled a particularly stubborn thread.

“Sorry, sorry. That’s the last of it.”

Alex wrapped Sarah’s wrist in a clean bandage, and then watched her open and close her fist experimentally.

“Thank you,” Sarah said.

“Not too tight?”

“No, it’s fine.”

“Hiding anything else?”

“No. Are you?” Sarah asked pointedly.

“I’m okay.”

“You’re favoring your right arm.”

“Damn, don’t miss much, do you?” Alex rolled her sleeve back to reveal the nasty slice Merrick had given her. “You could kiss it better,” she suggested, and then laughed when Sarah bent her head and did just that.

“Want an actual dressing to go with that kiss?” Sarah said.

“Probably advisable.” Alex couldn’t help but stare at her as she concentrated on tending to the wound. The sun had set, leaving them only the firelight, and Sarah’s face came in and out of the shadows as she moved. She looked lovely, the orange glow tempering the pallor and the lines of weariness. When she ducked her head low to tape the bandage in place, Alex ran her fingers through the wisps of loose hair that curtained Sarah's face.

Sarah was smiling as she met her gaze. "I'll make supper," she said, her voice slightly hoarse. "You make the bed."

The bed. One bed. Alex swallowed dryly and nodded, not quite trusting herself to speak. She wavered sideways as she stood, and Sarah reached out an arm to steady her.

"You gonna pass out on me?" The firelight made her eyes dance with mischief as she reiterated Alex's earlier question.

"Don't think so." The giddiness eased and Alex blew her breath out. "Okay. Bed. Supper." She turned to go one way as Sarah turned to go the other. Chancing a look back, she caught Sarah watching her. They grinned like children caught with their hands in the cookie jar, before averting their eyes and making a show of focusing on their given tasks. It was only when Alex spread their blankets in front of the fire to dry that she realized she had never been so nervous in her life.

❖

Alex sprinkled a packet of crackers on top of her portion of thick vegetable broth. She cradled the mug in both hands, blowing on the soup to cool it. Sarah's herbs and spices had apparently survived her ordeal at Merrick's hands; the rich aroma drifting up to Alex was far removed from that of any freeze-dried soup to which she had ever added water. Her stomach rumbled in anticipation, but the soup was too hot to gulp down quickly. She glanced at Sarah, only to see that Sarah's mug was already half-empty.

"How the hell?"

Sarah shrugged as she swallowed another mouthful. "Years of drinking piping hot tea, probably. I can't bear the stuff if it's gone even slightly tepid."

Alex took a chance and captured a floating cracker between her teeth. Steam gusted out as she breathed. "Oh that's really good."

"It's reconstituted veggie broth."

"Yeah, but you've reconstituted it perfectly," Alex countered, braving the heat to risk a sip.

"The crackers are a large part of its charm." Sarah examined their plastic packet. "Not something I'd put with soup, normally. Soup's more of a toast or bread roll thing where I come from."

"My parents went over to Britain once. Did the usual tour: London, Stonehenge, Stratford-upon-Avon, Edinburgh…"

"They didn't take you?" Sarah sounded both surprised and saddened.

"They didn't take us anywhere. We'd either stay with our nanny or get packed off to summer school. I've never left the U.S."

"Never?"

"Never." She set her mug down and turned to face Sarah. "I always wanted to travel. I was trying to save up, but a cop's salary doesn't stretch very far, and then suddenly I wasn't a cop anymore."

"Your parents…" Sarah's question trailed off; Alex was already shaking her head.

"They never offered and I never asked."

Sarah stroked her fingers down Alex's cheek. "Lot of world out there, Alex."

"Yes, there is." She turned her head and kissed the palm of Sarah's hand. "Maybe one day, huh?"

Sarah closed her eyes, her lips parting slightly as Alex moved her mouth to Sarah's throat. "Definitely one day," Sarah said. Her voice was breathy and her cheeks were pink in the warmth of the fire. Alex kissed her gently and then with more urgency when she moaned her encouragement.

Without any kind of prompting, they sat up together on their nest of blankets. Alex raised her hand to the zipper of Sarah's jacket, feeling strangely hesitant and uncertain until Sarah took hold of her fingers and placed them against the metal clasp. The repetitive click of the zipper opening sounded unbelievably loud. It snagged at the bottom and Alex struggled to work it free with hands that had abruptly lost their dexterity. When it finally came loose, she pushed the jacket back off Sarah's shoulders and then paused. She studied

Sarah so intently that Sarah, evidently having figured out the reason for her consternation, began to giggle.

"How many?" Alex asked despairingly.

"Five."

"Five!"

Sarah could hardly confirm the number for laughing. "I was cold!"

"Gonna take me all fucking night," Alex muttered. "How the hell am I supposed to erotically remove five layers of clothing?"

"Well, how many are *you* wearing?"

"Are we including bras?"

"No."

"Four."

Sarah shrugged. "We could just do our own," she suggested.

"Would certainly be quicker," Alex said with a grin. "You mind?"

Sarah had already thrown her jacket off and her sweater was halfway over her head. "Not at all," she mumbled through the thick wool.

It took them less than a minute to strip down to their underwear, and a good few seconds of that were spent rescuing a T-shirt that Sarah had overenthusiastically launched into the embers of the fire.

Alex had seen Sarah half-naked before, but not like this, not with a flush of excitement coloring her skin, her chest rising and falling rapidly. Goose bumps covered her bare arms, but when Alex touched her, she wasn't cold. Alex drew her onto her lap and she went willingly, wrapping her legs around Alex's waist. She smiled shyly and then kissed Alex in a way that didn't feel shy at all.

Alex moved her hands lower, playing her fingers around the soft cotton of the bra Sarah was still wearing, before unfastening it and dropping it. Salt and wood smoke combined on the tip of her tongue as she traced it across Sarah's skin. Apparently somewhat distracted, Sarah took two attempts, accompanied by some very creative cursing, to undo the clasp on Alex's bra, and when she finally had it in her hand, she tossed it over her shoulder.

"That better not be on the fire," Alex said, trying not to laugh. "It's the only one I've got."

"It's not on the fire." Sarah ran her tongue between Alex's breasts. "Might be in the pool," she said, edging toward a nipple, "but it's not on the fire."

Her lips closed, sucking eagerly, and Alex instantly forgot what might have been in the pool. She slipped her fingers beneath the elastic of Sarah's boxer shorts, sliding them down into slick heat, and Sarah's mouth fell open, small gasps escaping her as her back arched. She smiled at the same time Alex did and then began to move with her in an easy rhythm.

"This mean we're dating then?" Alex asked innocently, before giving a not so innocent twist of her fingers.

"Oh God…" Sarah nodded helplessly, her hands gripping Alex's shoulders for leverage. "At least I cooked you dinner first." She started to laugh and buried her face in Alex's neck.

"Hell of a first date," Alex said. She swirled her thumb, making Sarah bite down on the side of her throat, and suddenly neither of them had breath left to speak.

❖

At some time during the night, Alex must have put fresh wood on the fire. It was the only explanation for the fire still being alight when Sarah awoke, but she had no memory of Alex ever having moved. Lying on her back, feeling languid and content, she considered the way in which she and Alex had celebrated their reunion and wasn't entirely surprised that she had slept so soundly. The brightness of the daylight filtering into the cave made her check her watch and she raised an eyebrow at the time; at this rate they would be late for their own rescue.

"Hey," she whispered, close to Alex's ear. The sound made Alex mumble a little, but she stubbornly remained asleep. "Alex." Sarah kissed her ear and then the corner of her jaw. By the time she reached the lips, she caught Alex smiling. "Faker," she said, kissing her anyway. Alex returned the kiss, making up in enthusiasm what she lacked in coordination.

"I think we need to get up." Sarah's tone was utterly lacking in conviction, largely thanks to Alex's hands having found their way beneath the layers of clothing she had put back on before going to sleep. "Oh, don't do that." She shook her head in a halfhearted protest. "Rescue party, Alex…"

Alex nodded sagely, her fingers deft on the button at the top of Sarah's pants.

"They'll be here soon," Sarah continued weakly, finding herself unable to care about, or even really remember, why she was trying to call a halt to this.

"I can be quick," Alex said. Her hand edged into the space she had made in Sarah's clothing. "Can you be quick?"

"Jesus fucking Christ," Sarah whimpered.

Alex smiled. "I'm going to take that as a yes…"

❖

Although Sarah was by no means frivolous with their dwindling supplies, she risked cooking an entire packet of grits for breakfast and treated them both to a bag of trail mix she had found buried at the bottom of Alex's pack. She didn't bother trying to split the last packet of cocoa; it went into a mug for them to share.

Heavy clouds had gathered overnight and showers of sleet had alternated with snow to coat the ground in thick slush. Fortunately, Alex's diligence through the night meant that the fire had been established enough to stay alight. They huddled in front of it, taking turns sipping the cocoa while it was still hot. The camp was neatly packed up, their bags stowed in the shelter of the cave. Every few minutes, Alex turned the radio on, but there was no response from the channel she had hailed the rescue team on the previous day.

"Probably the weather messing up the signal," she said, turning the radio off for the fourth time. "Don't look so worried."

"I'm not worried." Sarah tried to smile, but even she wasn't convinced by her efforts. A nagging ache in her side had been making her restless since she sat down. Among her many other aches, she had almost forgotten about the bullet wound, but it had started to hurt again this morning. She tucked herself closer to Alex and felt Alex take hold of her hand. The mere contact was enough to make her shiver pleasantly. If the previous night's exertions were the reason for her discomfort, it was a price she was more than willing to pay.

"So what happens when we get back?" Alex kept her voice to a low murmur, as if she were afraid to hear the answer but couldn't stop herself from asking the question.

"Bubble bath and a warm bed," Sarah said lightly, but Alex's body remained tense, pressed against her.

"And then?"

Sarah met her gaze. "And then, I don't know," she admitted. She ran her thumb across the back of Alex's hand. "I've read that it's gorgeous here in the summer."

Alex kissed her forehead. "And I don't mind getting rained on in England."

"Well," Sarah said, "I guess we're not going to have a problem, then." She felt her mood lighten, relief and happiness coursing through her.

Alex was sitting up straighter now, and when she spoke again it was without her earlier trepidation. "We could travel…"

"Yes, we could. I could show you those cows with bells—"

"Alex!"

The man's voice cut into Sarah's and she looked at Alex to reassure herself that it wasn't just a trick of the wind. He shouted again, the call clearer this time. Although he still sounded some distance away, they scrambled up and ran out into the sleet.

"Over here!" Alex yelled. "Hey, we're over here!" She waved her arms as if afraid that their cries and the light from the fire wouldn't be enough to guide the rescue team to the right place.

In less than a minute, three men were visible, walking quickly along the side of the river. Two of the men carried a large pack each, while the third—who appeared to be older—bore a smaller load. He moved ahead of his companions with a broad smile on his face. Alex and Sarah walked through their small campsite to meet him halfway.

"So which one of you's Alex?" he said, his hand outstretched in greeting.

Alex raised hers in acknowledgment. She didn't recognize the man, but his accent told her he was the one she had spoken to on the radio.

"Good to meet you, sir." She shook his hand firmly.

With his free hand he waved away the formalities as the men he had traveled with caught up to him. "No need to stand on ceremony with me," he told her. "I'm Nicholas, Nicholas Deakin."

He still had hold of her hand. Without warning, he pulled her off balance, wrapping his arm across her throat when she stumbled and pressing her tightly against him. Too stunned to try to fight, she saw Sarah start to move toward them, but at the same time she heard the swish of metal against leather as the men behind her both pulled weapons from holsters.

"Sarah, no!" Her warning was choked off as Deakin jerked his arm, but Sarah stopped, her eyes wide with terror. When Deakin beckoned her to come closer, she looked at Alex for guidance. Alex shook her head once and seconds later felt the prick of a blade on the soft skin just beneath her ear.

"No, no! Wait, don't!" Sarah's words tumbled together. She instantly held her hands up in supplication and walked across to Deakin.

Everything seemed to fall utterly still then, and all Alex heard was that soft Southern accent as the knife drew blood in a stark warning. "I believe you have something that belongs to me."

CHAPTER FOURTEEN

Sarah's pale face and wretched expression made Alex feel like crying. It was either that or fight, but the blood running under the collar of her sweater told her the latter wasn't an option. Neither was giving Deakin what he wanted, because she had hidden the keys in the middle of the fucking forest and in all the excitement since then she had forgotten to let Sarah in on that fact. She caught Sarah's gaze and hoped to hell that Sarah would follow her lead.

"We don't have the keys," she said, even though the mere act of speaking made her bleeding worse.

Sarah blinked in confusion but made no comment, obviously waiting to see what else Alex would say.

"You better be lying to me." Deakin kept his tone low and controlled, but the point of the knife twisted and Alex gasped in pain.

"I'm not lying." She thought it would be in their best interests to sound remorseful, despite knowing that she and Sarah would be dead by now had she kept the keys with her. "We knew Merrick was looking for us, that he'd kill us the minute he got what he needed, so we hid them." She tried to move her head to ease the pressure of the blade but Deakin's hold on her was unyielding. "We hid them," she insisted. Panic was muddling her thoughts. She didn't know who the men were, but Deakin's demands strongly implied that he and Merrick had been working together somehow. Taking a deep breath, she glanced at Sarah, who gave her a barely perceptible nod of encouragement. The trust she saw in Sarah's eyes calmed her enough to let her think logically. She needed to buy time, and if she told the truth about where the keys were, Deakin would find them in a matter of hours. The lie came easily to her. "We left them back at the hut. They're under a rock by a little stream."

She couldn't see Deakin, but she felt him incline his head and watched with horror as one of the men walked toward Sarah. Without saying a word, the man pressed his pistol against Sarah's forehead and forced her to her knees. The click of the safety made Alex jump and she shook her head violently, no longer caring about the knife or the mess it was making of her neck.

"Tell me again, Alex," Deakin said, his voice sweet and sickly as if he were cajoling a child. "Tell me again where the keys are."

"At the hut," she said, sobbing now and so close to giving him exactly what he wanted. She dug her fingernails into her palms and willed herself not to break. "They're at the hut. I can show you on the map. We hid them under a rock by the stream. Please, *please*, I'm telling the truth."

Sarah had her eyes closed and Alex could see her trembling, as if this latest twist had just been too cruel for her to cope with. Deakin nodded once and Alex felt her knees give way, his arm the only thing holding her up. The man standing next to Sarah slowly lowered his gun, and Sarah opened her eyes just before he smashed the gun into the side of her face. She slumped into the mud without making a sound.

"Son of a bitch!" Alex screamed. She kicked back, her hands clawing at Deakin's arm. He sighed as if inconvenienced and waited until she had worn herself out.

"This is how it's going to work," he said calmly, as soon as she had capitulated and sagged against him. "We will search you both and go through your gear. If the keys are not here, Aaron will return to the hut. If the keys are not where you say they are, things will get very unpleasant for you both. Think on that, Alex." He lowered his arm, and without waiting for permission, she ran to Sarah, who was slowly pushing herself up.

"No, just stay still for a minute, sweetheart," she said.

Ignoring the advice, Sarah managed to sit up straight, but that was as far as she got before she collapsed into Alex's arms.

"You're okay," Alex said quickly. A large welt was already forming on Sarah's jaw and a cut in the center of it splattered blood onto the snow. "You're okay, I've got you."

"Get her up." Deakin made an impatient gesture from where he stood conferring with his men.

"Might've been easier before that prick gave her a concussion," Alex yelled back, her fury overriding her caution. Then, more quietly, so that only Sarah could hear her, "Can you stand?"

Sarah nodded against Alex's cheek, her breathing rapid and uneven. It was a trick Alex recognized; Sarah was trying not to throw up.

"Hey, if you're gonna puke, do it on Deakin's fancy leather boots, okay?" she muttered.

"I'll do my best." Sarah gave her a small smile but then screwed her eyes shut as she stood. "Oh fuck." She swayed alarmingly. "Where're his boots?"

Alex somehow kept her upright as Deakin and one of the men approached. The man who had hit Sarah had already gone to the cave, presumably to search and collect their gear.

"Arms out," Deakin said without preamble.

Alex glared at him. "You want to pick her up again?"

If her tone irritated him, he didn't let it show on his face. Instead, he roughly spun Sarah around so that she faced Alex; instinctively she clasped her arms around Alex's neck. At a quiet command from him, the other man stepped forward, and Alex felt Sarah stiffen as he began to search her. He patted and pressed around her torso and down her legs, but she remained stoic despite the indignity, and even managed a shrug when he pulled two stones from the pocket of her jacket. By the time he was finished with her, she was able to stand unaided while he searched Alex. He found nothing but her pocketknife, Merrick's GPS, and a handful of matches. The guns she had taken from Merrick were still in the cave. At no point had she ever contemplated this scenario, ever thought of arming herself before going to meet their supposed rescuers. She ground her teeth together as Sarah caught her hand in a death grip. If her naivety got Sarah killed, she would never be able to forgive herself.

Snatches of conversation between the three men filtered through to her and Sarah as they stood hand-in-hand with the sleet pelting their faces. Aaron was getting ready to leave, and Deakin, aware that the caves made an obvious shelter, was intent on moving to a location less likely to be targeted as a priority by genuine rescue teams. While the other men began to rearrange their packs to accommodate their extra supplies, he brought a map and his own GPS over to Alex.

"Is this the hut?"

She took time to consider the map, although she had immediately recognized the hut as the correct one. If he was eager to leave the caves, it might mean that search parties were a little too close for his comfort. It was only when he tapped his gun against the map in an unsubtle hint that she nodded her confirmation.

"Yes, that's the one." She was so disoriented now that she couldn't work out how far away the hut was. They had spent three nights out in the open since leaving it, but an entire day had been lost chasing down Merrick, and Aaron would no doubt cover the ground more quickly than she and Sarah had. All three of the men had radios clipped to their belts. One call from the hut to report the fruitless mission was all Deakin would need to act upon his earlier threats.

A sharp jab in the middle of her back prompted her to follow Deakin as he walked out of the clearing in the direction of the river. Aaron took a left and was swiftly swallowed up by the forest.

"We don't have long, do we?" Sarah murmured. Her eyes were still tracking the path Aaron had taken.

"No, we don't," Alex said, unable to put a falsely positive spin on anything and certain that Sarah wouldn't want her to.

They walked as slowly as they dared, one man in front of them, one man behind. Although the huge trees and scruffy undergrowth would make life difficult for anyone attempting to find them, Alex knew that Deakin had been in too much of a hurry to bother concealing the remnants of their campsite. Bearing that in mind, she deliberately stumbled and fell to one knee, slamming her hands hard upon a rock. It flipped over, its lichen-coated upper half turning to the side. She pushed down on it when she stood, leaving it at a noticeably odd angle. The man bringing up the rear shoved her to keep her walking, but Sarah caught her eye and gave her a quick nod. Fifty yards farther along, Sarah slid in a puddle of slush and snapped an overhanging branch as she grabbed hold of it. The branch hung low, the green wood of the fresh break obvious to anyone who might know what to look for. It wasn't much, Alex was well aware of that, but right at that moment, it was all they had.

❖

Dusk brought snow with it. Thick flakes the size of Sarah's palm drifted down, melting upon contact with the wet ground at first but then beginning to settle as the flurry developed into a more persistent fall. The gentle rustle of snow on the pine needles had an almost hypnotic effect on Sarah, enabling her to block out the throbbing in her jaw and the hot ache that was gradually worsening in her side. The din of the river seemed to lessen, and the occasional burst of static from Deakin's radio no longer set her pulse racing. She stuck her tongue out as she walked along, not catching enough flakes to quell her thirst but feeling better just for the soothing chill of the ice melting against her parched throat. All too soon, the clouds broke apart, the snow tapered off, and then stopped altogether. She sighed and watched their boots churning mud into the pure white layer that covered the path.

"We'll have to stop soon," Alex said in an undertone, as if sensing the change in Sarah's mood. "Gonna lose the light."

Sarah nodded, her mouth suddenly dry again. Although she felt utterly worn out, continuing to walk in the dark seemed preferable to stopping. The men had largely ignored them while they were hiking, but recent experience had taught her that things were likely to change for the worse as soon as they stopped to camp. She stared at Deakin's back as he marched ahead of her. He didn't seem in the least affected by the strenuous nature of the pace he was setting, or by the path he was breaking. He rarely allowed them to rest, and when he did it was mere minutes before he ordered them to move again. His demeanor betrayed nothing. He had yet to raise his voice above a level she had to strain to hear, yet the man walking behind them obeyed him without question and deferred to him with the utmost respect. In the hours since leaving the caves, he had barely touched her, but she was more terrified of him than she had ever been of Merrick.

"Hey."

Alex's voice made Sarah jump. She was unable to guard her expression quickly enough, and Alex wrapped an arm around her, pulling her into an embrace. Sarah clenched the material of Alex's jacket in her fists and struggled to stay silent when all she really wanted to do was sob and scream and tell her how scared she was. She stayed there, breathing in the familiar smell of sweat and damp hair, until the man behind her pushed her so hard that her teeth clashed together. Alex dropped her arms away and they walked on without saying a word.

❖

Alex obediently handed over the pack she had been carrying and then took the opportunity to study the site Deakin had chosen as a camp. The small patch of grass and gravel was in an excellent strategic position. On one side it opened out to the river, allowing easy access to water. Tall boulders surrounded the rest of it, providing shelter from the wind and concealing it completely from view. Anyone who might have noticed their trail and managed to track them up river would still have difficulty spotting this location.

Unlike Alex, Sarah didn't appear to be analyzing the layout of the terrain; her attention was fixed on the tent that Deakin's companion was laying out.

"It's too small," she said.

"The tent?" Alex frowned, confused, but Sarah shook her head.

"No, the clearing." She crossed her arms tightly, trying to stop herself from shivering, and Alex slowly realized what she meant.

Deakin had forced Alex to bear the weight of Merrick's tent for the entire day, but she could see now that the site had only enough flat ground for them to pitch one. It didn't take a genius to figure out whose would take priority. Her suspicions were confirmed when Deakin dropped a filthy tarp and two blankets at her feet.

"Don't go any farther than those two rocks over there," he said, indicating an overhanging slab of granite that nestled snugly against a smaller boulder. "Tanner will be building a fire. I suggest you stay as close to that as possible." He made his instructions sound entirely reasonable, as if they were all out for a weekend excursion and he was trying to make everything run smoothly.

There were plenty of ways in which she would have liked to respond. None of them were polite, most of them involved profanities, and any of them would have earned her, or most probably Sarah, some kind of punishment. Thinking better of it, she said nothing but merely picked up the tarp and waited until Deakin walked away. Before Alex could stop her, Sarah stooped low and gathered up their blankets. She grimaced as she stood, attempting to conceal the support she was giving her right side by covering her hand with the thick wool. The wound there had obviously been troubling her throughout the afternoon, but she had made no complaint and seemed determined not to make any now.

"Just a twinge," she said through gritted teeth. "Don't worry."

Alex nodded, deciding not to push the issue, since they had been set a task that needed completing in what little daylight remained.

It took them several attempts to spread and anchor the tarp, arranging it over the gap between two rocks so that it formed a roof but also hung with enough left over for them to sit on. Lying down would leave them partly exposed to the elements, but it was the best they could muster, given what little they had to work with. Sarah didn't appear to care. Wrapped in a blanket, she sat in the darkest corner of the tiny shelter, rested her head back, and closed her eyes. Alex inched down beside her, and for a while there was nothing but the rush of the river and the splatter of sleet falling onto the canvas above their heads. A hint of orange light from outside the tarp gradually increased in intensity and Alex felt a feeble warmth begin to ease the numbness in her hands and face.

With her eyes still closed, Sarah stretched her hands toward the opening of the shelter as if that alone would be enough to make her comfortable. She shuffled down until her head rested on Alex's thigh. Her legs were sticking out into the sleet, but it didn't seem to trouble her, and within minutes, the cadence of her breathing told Alex she was asleep. Sitting in the darkness, Alex tried to ignore the low conversation of the two men beyond the shelter, men whom she and Sarah would somehow have to outwit and overcome if they were to have any chance of surviving. Beneath her palm, Sarah's forehead felt unusually warm. She shook her head in dismay. Not only were they running out of time, they had long since run out of luck.

❖

Sarah jolted awake when the beam of a flashlight hit her face. She blinked rapidly, shielding her eyes from the worst of the glare. The glow from the fire had barely changed, suggesting that only minutes had elapsed since she dozed off. Alex's hand was on her shoulder, the grip harder than Alex probably intended as she tensed in anticipation. Something heavy thudded onto the canvas. Half-blind and still stupefied from sleep, Sarah couldn't immediately distinguish the object, but the hitch in Alex's breath was enough of a warning.

"You." It was Tanner's voice. He flicked the light toward Alex. "Tie her."

Without the light obscuring her vision, Sarah saw that he had thrown down two lengths of rope. She had expected this, but even so, the prospect of being bound again made sweat break out on her hairline. Alex reached for the rope, misery etched on her face.

"Hands behind, then her feet," he said. "No fucking around, unless you want me to do it."

Not wanting Alex to have to tell her, Sarah turned her back and brought her wrists together. That mild pressure was enough to make her feel faint, but she managed to stay compliant as Alex secured the rope over the dressings.

"Tie it tighter. If you make me do it, she'll lose her fingers," Tanner warned her, and Sarah heard Alex smother a curse. A moment later, the bindings dug into her flayed skin, the severity of the pain knocking her off-balance so that Alex's hand on the back of her jacket was the only thing that stopped her from pitching headfirst into the rock.

"Do her legs," Tanner said.

"Give her a fucking minute, you asshole." Alex somehow managed to keep her voice from rising, but the sound of flesh striking flesh told Sarah that he had slapped her.

"Sarah, you okay?" Alex murmured.

Sarah nodded quickly. "Are you?"

"I'm fine. He hits like a girl." Alex projected the insult over her shoulder, having apparently abandoned their earlier plan of keeping a low profile.

Sarah turned around and winced at the blood dripping from a cut just below Alex's eye. "You're going to have a right shiner," she said, trying to distract herself from the sensation of the rope cutting into her wrists.

"Huh?" Partway through binding Sarah's legs, Alex paused.

"Black eye," Sarah clarified.

"Oh." Alex touched her fingers to her cheek and frowned at the blood. "Damn. His ring caught me."

Impatient at the delay, Tanner shoved her aside and finished the knot at Sarah's ankles. When he was satisfied she was secure, he grabbed hold of Alex's right arm and wrenched it awkwardly behind her back, using it to push her to the ground. She heard him fumble with his belt and tried not to hyperventilate when seconds later she felt the cold bracelet of a handcuff cinch around her wrist. She surrendered her free hand without protest, but that didn't make him go any easier on her. The metal drew blood as soon as she tried to test the limits of the connecting chain. He lashed her ankles together with his belt and left her lying facedown, her entire body trembling with remembered and fresh terror. Dizzy from breathing too rapidly, she turned her cheek onto the cold canvas and closed her eyes.

"He's gone, Alex." The canvas rustled as Sarah edged across to her. "Are you okay?"

"Yeah." It took almost all her remaining strength to push herself onto her knees. The rock felt reassuringly solid when she leaned against it, and she managed to straighten her legs and sit reasonably comfortably. Unable to control her movements effectively, Sarah swayed into Alex as she attempted to adopt the same position. A series of bangs sounded from the clearing, and they startled before Alex shook her head in recognition.

"He's pitching the tent." She kept her lips a hair's breadth from Sarah's ear, keen to take advantage of the noise Tanner was making. "I'm sorry," she whispered.

"This isn't your fault, Alex." The volume of Sarah's reply was just as guarded.

"No, I mean about hiding the keys. I'm sorry I didn't tell you. I meant to and then it just got lost in everything else."

Footsteps came close to the shelter and they both froze, instantly falling silent. When the footsteps had faded, Alex could still feel her pulse hammering in her chest.

Sarah took a deep, steadying breath. "We're in quite a lot of shit, aren't we?"

"Yeah, we are."

"Do you think Merrick was working for these guys?" She pushed herself even closer to Alex, her words hissing directly into Alex's ear. "That these are the ones who broke him out of jail?"

"I guess so," Alex said. The day's forced march had given them no chance to discuss what was going on, but she had drawn the same conclusions as Sarah.

"So this is what white supremacist pillocks look like," Sarah muttered with unfettered disgust, apparently not too concerned about the men overhearing that one.

Alex wasn't sure what a pillock was, but it sounded like a good enough insult, and she nodded in agreement. It seemed like a lifetime since she had told Sarah about Merrick's links to the groups; given

Sarah's condition at the time, Alex was amazed she had managed to retain the information.

"How long till Aaron gets to the hut and figures out that you lied?" Sarah whispered as the banging started up again.

Alex jerked her head around, but then wondered exactly why she was surprised that Sarah had been able to read her so well. "I bet your life on that lie," she said, the words almost choking her.

"You *saved* both of our lives with that lie," Sarah told her without a hint of recrimination. "There was nothing else you could do."

"I guess not." Reassured, Alex leaned against the rough granite and tried to think like a cop instead of a frightened, half-starved, exhausted hostage. "We probably have another thirty hours or so before he reaches the hut," she said at length. "And that's being optimistic. He's in much better shape than we are."

"All he'll need to do then is radio through to Deakin." Despite being barely audible, Sarah's voice was tight with fear.

"I know. I don't think we should wait till the last minute. If we're gonna do something, we need to do it soon."

There was a shuffling noise as Sarah turned onto her left side. Alex lifted the blanket with her teeth and tried with only partial success to rearrange it over her.

"Any bright ideas?" Sarah said, already sounding half-asleep.

"Rest. The state we're in right now, we can't do anything." Alex kissed Sarah's forehead, tears filling her eyes when she thought of the last time she had done that and how different the circumstances had been. "Might be easier if we lull them into believing we're going to behave ourselves."

"And then we misbehave?" Sarah asked.

"Yeah." Alex chuckled at the drowsy enthusiasm Sarah had managed to muster. "Then we—" She cut her reply off as footsteps approached. They sounded quicker and more purposeful than the last time, and without even thinking, she pushed herself slightly in front of Sarah just as Tanner's large form blocked out the light from the fire. He bent low and unsnapped the belt at Alex's ankles before dragging her up by the collar of her jacket.

"Move," he said, not giving her the opportunity to protest.

Smoke and warm air caught in her throat as he propelled her beyond the shelter. The momentum made her lose her balance; unable to right herself in time, she skidded onto her knees.

"Alex!" Sarah's attempts to follow them were abruptly cut off when Tanner kicked her squarely in her chest.

"Bastard," Alex spat, "you fucking bastard." Rage had left her beyond caring about her own safety, and all she felt was gratitude when Tanner turned his back on Sarah and pulled her up again. He spun her around to face the tent. Deakin was sitting on the far side of a blazing fire, eating from a tin plate, and the flames illuminated the satisfied nod he gave Tanner. Thick, cold fingers brushed Alex's as Tanner gripped the chain at her wrists. He raised his arm deliberately, slowly lifting both of hers and forcing her to her knees in an effort to prevent her shoulders from dislocating.

"You kneel," he said, his voice shaking with barely suppressed violence. When he tugged viciously on the chain, she moaned and then hated herself for giving him the satisfaction. "You kneel in front of him, you fucking dyke."

"Fuck you," she whispered, with all the vehemence she could muster. His fist clouted the back of her head, jolting her arms upward, and she retched without warning, dry heaving against her empty stomach.

"Thank you, Tanner." Deakin's intervention had an instant effect. The pressure on Alex's arms ceased, and she heard Tanner's boots tread heavily in the mud as he stepped back. "Watch the other one," Deakin told him curtly.

She scrambled around, trying to see where Tanner was going, and took a shaky breath when she saw him stop just in front of the shelter.

"He won't touch her," Deakin said, and Alex turned back to face him. He chewed a mouthful of food deliberately. "Not like that. He has a wife and a child. He is given to God and would not debase himself with one given to deviance."

She bit her lip so hard she tasted blood. She had no response to Deakin's statement, no response that wouldn't earn her a bullet between the eyes, at least; and if their vile ideology kept Sarah safe then she wasn't about to start arguing the finer points.

He continued to eat, ignoring her as he scraped his plate clean. He set it aside with his knife and fork arranged neatly on top, and reached for a steaming mug. For several minutes, he did nothing but take careful sips. His gamesmanship gave Alex her first opportunity to look at him properly—not that there was much to note. In appearance, he was the archetype of everyone's favorite uncle, the one who would buy you candy and not say a word if you sneaked a piece before dinner. His age was difficult to determine, but she estimated that he was somewhere in his mid-fifties. He was lean and athletic in build, with muscles bulging beneath the sweater he wore. The outdoor life seemed to agree with him, but the hands wrapped around his mug were clean and well-manicured, as if somehow symbolic of a man who had any number of devotees willing to do his dirty work. She knew from her time on the force that the police rarely managed to tie men like Deakin to their crimes. They would invariably slither free without a stain on their character, leaving some unfortunate lackey to do the time on their behalf. That Deakin was out here, taking such a massive risk by directly involving himself, made her even more afraid of whatever it was that he was searching for.

He turned to refill his mug and she shuddered before she could stop herself. The firelight had picked out a small black swastika tattooed on his scalp. It was an insignia he could easily have covered by letting his hair grow, but out here he seemed entirely comfortable with it being on display. Although by no means conclusive, it gave further credence to the theory that he was linked to Merrick; not that being right about that made her feel any better.

"Did you kill my niece, Alex?"

She jumped at his voice, and when she met his eyes, she suspected he had been studying her for some time.

"No," she said. She didn't know who his niece was, but the only person she had ever killed was Merrick.

Deakin leaned forward, watching her intently. "Is Nathan Merrick dead?"

"Yes."

Her answer seemed to provide him with some semblance of satisfaction, and she belatedly realized that his niece was most likely the woman Sarah had seen with Merrick.

"He took Sarah," she said by way of explanation. "But before that, we'd heard a gunshot…" She left the implication hanging. There was nothing she could do to make him believe her version of events, but she didn't think she had anything to lose by giving him the information.

He stared at her for a long moment before raising his mug in her direction. "Then I guess you did me a favor," he said in a tone that suggested she shouldn't expect one in return.

"How did you find us?" she asked, careful not to sound as if she was demanding an answer. It was something she had been unable to work out. Although it was true that they had arranged to rendezvous at the caves with him, Deakin had obviously been right on their tail before then.

He grinned at her, baring his teeth, and patted the radio on his belt.

"Nathan Merrick would have sold his own sister if there was a profit in it," he said. "That back-stabbing son of a bitch stored something in the park for us but neglected to tell us exactly where he'd hidden the keys to the store." The grin had disappeared and a vein throbbed at Deakin's temple. His face was red with anger. "We went to a lot of trouble to arrange for him to come out here and complete his side of our contract. My niece Bethany was assigned to him." He didn't seem concerned by the double-standards implicit in whoring out his niece to further his own business deals. "The radio we issued to her had a tracker implanted in it. We intended to monitor Merrick's location." He arched an eyebrow at Alex. "Imagine my surprise when I heard your voice."

Fresh blood burned against her freezing fingers as she wrenched her wrists against the cuffs. She didn't need another reminder of the threat Deakin posed, but when she thought of his organization and the technology he had access to, the hairs stood up on the back of her neck.

Apparently finished with his interrogation, he clicked his fingers at Tanner, who came and escorted her none too gently back to the shelter. The whites of Sarah's eyes were the first thing she saw, staring up at her. As Tanner retied her ankles, she nodded to let Sarah know she was okay. Then, from the gap at the front of the shelter, she watched him walk back to Deakin. The two men spoke briefly before Deakin retired into the tent and left Tanner sitting by the fire. There was no point in Tanner keeping watch from anywhere else, since any escape attempt would have to pass straight through the clearing, alerting him immediately.

When Alex turned around, Sarah was close enough to touch her. Unable to use her hands, she did the next best thing and pushed up against Alex's chest.

"You're all right," she said, relief stark in her voice. Her hair was wet beneath Alex's chin and Alex realized she had risked antagonizing Tanner by watching all that had transpired between herself and Deakin. It gave her an idea.

"Tanner's by the fire," she whispered. "Is there any way you can watch him without letting him see you?"

"Should be able to. The canvas hangs down in a flap. It gives pretty decent cover." Sarah frowned. "Why?"

"Watch him. Let me know if he moves an inch."

Although obviously perplexed, Sarah did as she asked, maneuvering close to the shelter's entrance on her belly and signaling with her bound hands when she was in position.

Alex, meanwhile, had tucked herself as far into the shelter as she could possibly go. The chain at her wrists was short, but one time on a night shift—fueled by caffeine, a sugar rush, and plenty of bets against her—she had succeeded with a chain that had been a few links shorter. Her jaw set with concentration, she stretched the chain to its limits, pushed her shackled hands down, and wriggled them beneath her bottom. It hurt more than she could have imagined, placing stress on shoulder joints that already ached deep in the bones, but she persevered, keeping one eye on Sarah for any kind of warning. Blood made her fingers tacky, and perspiration dripped off her nose as she inched her wrists to the top of her thighs and then rolled onto her side. Back on that night shift, she had won the money without breaking a sweat, but then she hadn't just endured days of punishing hikes, and her limbs hadn't been covered with bruises that overlapped to the point where she would have difficulty finding an unmarred patch of skin. Now her legs complained bitterly as she scrunched them up and strained to pass her chained wrists over them. Agonizing seconds ticked by before she felt the soles of her boots scrape across the metal.

When she dared to look up, Sarah hadn't moved. Lying with sleet glistening in her hair and her eyes fixed on the fire, she gave no indication that anyone beyond the shelter was aware of what Alex had done. Alex curled into a ball and pressed her bleeding wrists to her chest. Every part of her seemed to be throbbing in unison and the exertion had made her head spin, but at least they now had a chance.

CHAPTER FIFTEEN

The water tasted faintly of moss and blood but Sarah didn't care. She pressed her lips to Alex's cupped hands and drank until there was nothing left but cold skin. Patiently, Alex repositioned her hands at the juncture where melted sleet dripped down the canvas, and allowed the water to pool in her palms again. They were taking advantage of the water while it continued to run into the shelter, but collecting it was a slow process, and what little Sarah had drunk had barely quenched her thirst. Alex offered her hands again, but Sarah shook her head.

"You," she whispered, careful to keep her words to a minimum. The sleet had just stopped, and the only noises to break the stillness of the forest were the background drone of the river and the faint crackling of the fire. As Alex drank her share, Sarah spoke directly into her ear.

"Top pocket." She nudged her chin toward the one she meant.

Alex dried her hands on her pants and unzipped the pocket. She grimaced at the rasp of the zipper even though there was no realistic chance of the noise carrying beyond the canvas. A faint rustle of plastic packaging told Sarah she had remembered correctly, and she smiled as Alex manipulated the remnant of the Kendal Mint Cake from its wrapper. It snapped cleanly in two and Sarah stopped Alex when she made as if to break it again; there was so little left that it was pointless trying to ration it. Keen to savor the candy, Sarah tried to let her piece dissolve on her tongue. Her attempt failed dismally and she ended up chewing and swallowing it greedily. Her stomach rumbled, eager for more, but she shook her head vehemently when Alex offered her the tiny piece that remained of her own portion.

Sarah's body felt reenergized after even this tiny amount of fuel, and she made no complaint as Alex repositioned herself to resume their task. Over an hour had passed since Alex had first wrestled her wrists from behind her back. They had quickly discussed their strategy and decided that dividing the men was the obvious tactic. Sarah had shrugged, pointing out in a whisper that their captors would have to let them go and pee at some point. And that—such as it was—was currently their plan. They were working to get Sarah to the point where she would appear bound but be able to slip free if an opportunity presented itself. The probability that Tanner would check on them increased the longer they took, and she knew that Alex would have to return her own hands to their original position sooner rather than later.

With her chin resting on her knees and her eyes squeezed shut, she counted to three hundred to take her mind away from the discomfort. When she reached her target, she rotated her wrists against their bindings to check whether Alex had yet managed to loosen them. The dressings beneath the rope shifted, exposing her torn skin, but the rope stayed firmly secured and she shook her head to let Alex know she needed to keep trying. She restarted her count and had reached two hundred and fifty-six when Alex paused. "Try now." Alex mouthed the words against Sarah's ear, the rush of air feathering the hair that had come loose from Sarah's ponytail.

Sarah took a breath to steel herself. The rope felt different somehow, and there was more room for her to move her hands. Pain burned up and down her forearms as the dressing on her left wrist gradually unraveled. Alex pulled it away completely, giving Sarah even more room with which to work. The instant she was certain she could wriggle her hands free, she nodded urgently.

"Done."

It was the only cue Alex needed. They changed places without speaking; Sarah lying at the shelter's entrance and Alex pushed into its darkest recesses. A faint draft of warm air tickled over Sarah's face as Tanner stoked the fire and the wind changed direction. Embers flew into the air, and a fresh log caught quickly, throwing up more sparks. Behind her, she heard Alex grunt once and then a clack of metal that didn't even make Tanner raise his head. She pushed back beneath the canvas when Alex gently nudged her foot.

"Sleep," Alex whispered.

Sarah hunched up against her gratefully, even though she was too wired to close her eyes. The tiny space filled with the smell of musty damp wool as they spread out the blankets. After so many days, there was something comforting about its familiarity and she found herself yawning. She felt Alex kiss her cheek and then her forehead, the chapped skin of Alex's lips lingering there as if checking for a fever. She wanted so much to stay awake, to mark these hours as precious, if they were to be some of their last, but weariness was rapidly taking the place of fading adrenaline. As the tips of Alex's fingers brushed against hers, she allowed herself to give in, and closed her eyes.

❖

Sarah woke to find her teeth chattering so hard they were making her jaw ache. Despite a chill that seemed to reach down into her very core, her cheeks felt hot, and sweat had plastered her hair to her forehead.

"Bugger." She mouthed the curse, trying not to disturb Alex, and dried her hair by rubbing it on the knees of her pants. She knew she had an infection; she could feel the pulsating heat centered on the bullet wound in her side, and straightening her legs made something thick and wet seep onto the dressing that covered her sutures. She was already feeling sick, and the oozing sensation was almost enough to tip her over the edge. She breathed raggedly through her nose, keeping her mouth firmly shut and waiting for the queasiness to pass. As soon as it had, a series of violent shivers racked her and, unable to reach the blanket, she curled in on herself instead. When she was finally able to look up, she found that Alex was awake and watching her intently.

"Jesus," Alex whispered. Repeating her gesture of the previous night, she put her lips to Sarah's forehead. It made Sarah wonder exactly how long Alex had known she was sick.

"How bad?" Sarah wasn't sure she wanted an answer.

"Bad enough," Alex said.

"So we need to do this now, before it gets any worse." Sarah pushed with her feet, moving her bottom along the canvas.

"No." Alex automatically reached out to her, but the handcuff chain snapped taut and her effort fell well short. She rocked backward in anguish. "Sarah, no."

Sarah shook her head, unable to meet Alex's eyes as she continued to shuffle toward the entrance of the shelter. She saw Tanner walking back from the river with a pot of water, and called out to him before she lost her nerve or Alex had a chance to stop her.

"Excuse me!"

Behind her, Alex made a noise like a wounded animal but didn't attempt to intervene. They both knew that this was their best shot and that, with her hands as good as untied, only Sarah would have the element of surprise in her favor.

Sarah tried again. "Excuse me!"

Tanner placed the pot down on the ground and walked over to her.

"What?"

"I'm sorry, sir." She did her best to appear embarrassed. "I need to go."

"Too fucking bad." He turned to leave. "You're not going anywhere."

She somehow managed not to roll her eyes. Did he actually think she was asking to go home? "No, I need to *go*."

This time he seemed to grasp her meaning. She realized he was probably punch-drunk from lack of sleep; Deakin was nowhere to be seen, and she doubted there had been a fair division of guard duties through the night.

"Right. Uh…" Obviously not keen to make a decision on his own, Tanner looked at the closed flap of the tent and then across the clearing to a thick patch of trees. Sarah bowed her head and sniffled miserably, looking as weak and helpless as possible. She tensed when she felt his hand tighten around her bicep. "Come on then," he said.

She fell down as soon as he pulled her up. "My legs," she gasped, instinctively shrinking back, expecting a blow. "They're tied."

He didn't hit her, but just swore softly and snatched at the knot binding her ankles, giving her the chance to recover from the head rush that had all but incapacitated her when she stood. The second time around, she was able to walk alongside him as he marched her over to the clump of trees that stood about fifty yards from the tent, beyond the rocks that delineated the boundary of the clearing. It was darker beneath the trees; she blinked, trying to adjust to the gloom. Exertion and fear combined to make her heart thrum rapidly in her chest, but Tanner's pace was slowing. He gauged the terrain and then pushed her in the direction of a broad thicket of undergrowth that would be tall enough to shield her from view. She hesitated and he gestured impatiently. The movement pulled his jacket open and she tried not to stare at the gun she could see tucked into the waistband of his pants.

"What the fuck you waiting for?"

Sarah licked her lips. Her mouth was dry, and this time she didn't know if she could stop herself from being sick. "I can't," she said, so quietly that he had to come closer to hear her. "My hands…Please." Her terror might have been feigned earlier, but as he stopped right in front of her, it was real enough.

"Turn around," he said, casting a nervous glance in the direction of the clearing.

She knew she wasn't going to get a better opportunity. Before he could look back at her, she had ripped her hands free of the rope. Its bloodied strands slapped against her arms as she grabbed for the gun and then shoved him with all the strength she could muster. He stumbled, stepping awkwardly to one side, but the force had been nowhere near enough to push him over. He turned to face her, a sneer curling his lip as he realized what she had done.

"Stay right there," she said. Her arms shook as she pointed the gun at him, her finger poised on the trigger. She couldn't be certain, but it looked like the gun Alex had taken from Merrick. Pull the trigger all the way back, Alex had told her. Pull it like you mean it.

Sarah widened her stance in readiness. She was gasping for breath and sweating so much that the gun slid in her grip.

"Lie down, facedown," she hissed. Tanner didn't move, didn't make any indication that he had even heard her. "*Now*." She took a step back, sure that she wasn't safe even though she was holding him at gunpoint.

She was right. He raised his arms as if in surrender and then lunged for the gun. She pulled the trigger, yanking it as hard as she could and sending him lurching away from her even as the recoil knocked her into the dirt. She sat there stunned, with nothing but a buzzing in her ears, and the reek of cordite making her cough until her eyes watered. As she struggled to stand, the buzzing noise was slowly replaced by the agonized shrieking coming from Tanner.

"You fucking bitch. You filthy fucking bitch." He was still on the ground, holding his left thigh with both hands. Blood spilled between his fingers at an alarming rate, and began to pool beneath him. "You broke my fucking leg."

Good, Sarah thought, but she didn't have the breath left to say it. His jaw moved as if to issue further threats, but he threw up on himself instead and lost consciousness seconds later.

"Oh God." Sarah felt her legs buckle and she slammed onto her knees. Wisps of gray drifted into her vision. "No, no." She couldn't faint. Deakin would have heard the gunshot. She had to get back to Alex. "No, fucking, *no*."

When she stood up, her stolen pants slipped down her hips in such a ludicrous way that she almost laughed, before starting to cry instead. With one hand hitching them up so they wouldn't trip her and the other hand clasped around the gun, she ran back toward the clearing.

❖

Alex was leaning forward on her hands, panting from the effort of bringing them from behind her back and trying not to panic, when she heard the gunshot.

"Shit." She scrambled up as footsteps rapidly closed in on the shelter. With no time to second-guess herself and no way of knowing what had happened to Sarah, she ran straight at Deakin, barreling into him so that they both fell to the ground. They tumbled over each other and she heard him grunt as her elbow collided with his ribs. Taking advantage of his disorientation, she clubbed her fists into his face, blood and saliva slick on her knuckles as his lip burst open. Her advantage lasted only seconds. From the corner of her eye she saw him raise his hand to her collar, and with one flick of his wrist, he threw her off him as casually as he might swat a fly. She skidded through the mud, the roar of the river suddenly overwhelming as she slid closer to its banks. The side of her head struck a rock, snapping her neck backward and making her vision blur and then darken.

When she opened her eyes, everything had shifted.

She was upright, Deakin's arm crushing her throat, and her feet scrabbling for purchase as he pressed a gun against the side of her head. Sarah stood in front of them, holding a gun so tightly that her arms were quivering with fatigue. She gave a choked sob when she saw that Alex was awake, and Alex felt a grief so complete that it nearly knocked her out again.

"What are you thinking, girl?" Deakin asked Sarah. "Thinking you might be able to shoot me in the head?" He spat a thick clot of blood into the mud. "You haven't got a hope in hell."

She looked at Alex, her eyes begging for advice. Alex shook her aching head, fully aware that Deakin was more right than he would ever know, that this was the first time Sarah had even held a gun.

"Please, just let her go." The raw agony in Sarah's voice cut through Alex like a blade. They weren't both going to get out of this, that much seemed perfectly clear, and accepting it as a fact made her decision easier.

"Sarah." She raised her voice above the volume of the river, ignoring the crack Deakin gave her with the butt of his gun. "Find a radio. You'll be fine, sweetheart."

Sarah shook her head, clearly not understanding what Alex meant, yet seeming to sense that something awful was about to happen.

Alex closed her eyes; she couldn't bear to look at Sarah and still do this. Bracing herself with her feet apart, she quickly began to push backward. She felt Deakin's arm slip slightly just before he fired a shot that deafened her. The shot flew wild and wide, the bullet pinging harmlessly off a rock as Deakin lost his footing. She kept pushing, steadily gaining momentum and forcing him along with her, until the crumbling bank of the river gave way beneath her feet. There was a strange, free-falling sensation that cut off abruptly as they crashed into the water.

❖

"*Alex?*"

Sarah's legs felt like they were moving through molasses. Nothing seemed to be working properly, and she could hear someone screaming, but by the time she reached the river only seconds had passed. Her jacket was already in her hands, her boots loose enough to be kicked off. The remnants of the bank were steep and unstable, the water deep when she lowered herself into it. Still clinging onto the bank, she tried to breathe through the shock of the cold. She saw Deakin's arms flailing just beyond her reach, but then they fell motionless as his head collided with a massive boulder. His skull cracked like a cantaloupe, and thick gouts of crimson swirled through the rapids. The current twisted him around, snapping at his limp body before dragging him deeper and out of sight.

"*Alex?*"

She ducked her head beneath the water, trying to see through the foam and the silt churned up by the collapse of the riverbank. A brief flash of color appeared in the murk, and when she surfaced again, she spotted Alex ten yards away, her chained hands clasped weakly around a small piece of wood. Unable to do anything but keep her head up, she was drifting dangerously close to the current that had overcome Deakin.

Sarah took a huge breath and then dove and struck out toward her, forcing herself to keep swimming even when her lungs burned and her muscles threatened to cramp and seize up. She turned her back as a wave rose up, feeling her skin scrape across the submerged rock that had caused the turbulence. Alex was almost close enough to touch now, but she disappeared beneath the water again. Sarah reached out frantically, kicking against the rock for extra leverage, and felt thick, heavy material brush against her fingers. She snatched at it, clamping it in her fist and flipping over onto her back so she could haul Alex properly into her grip. With her hand cupping Alex's chin, she began to turn, aiming for the shore and trying not to think about how limp Alex felt or how far from the camp they might have drifted. She was tiring, her thoughts muddled by a deadly combination of exhaustion and hypothermia. Something slammed into her shoulder, tipping them both sideways, and she gulped a mouthful of water before she could stop herself. She coughed, simultaneously hacking water up through her nose and mouth and nearly losing her hold on Alex in the process.

"Fuck this!" She screamed her defiance to anything that might have been listening. The yell cleared her lungs. She gave one final push toward a small channel she could see leading into a calmer pool of water. Away from the main tumult of the rapids, it immediately became easier for her to kick, and she was able to steer a course with more accuracy. Smaller rocks began to knock against her legs, and when she experimentally lowered her feet, the tips of her toes brushed against the bottom. She gave a cry of relief, falling forward and grappling for the riverbank, one arm now wrapped bodily around Alex. When her fingers got a proper hold on the grassy ledge, all she could do was gasp for breath and try to keep Alex's head above the water. The ledge at that point was too steep for her to pull herself up, let alone drag Alex out as well. Treading water, she scanned the riverbank for a shallower incline. With one hand intermittently gripping the bank to guide her along, she dragged Alex another ten yards downriver to a sloping beach. Silt and pebbles dislodged beneath her knees as she approached the beach, and she realized belatedly that the water was shallow enough to stand up in, although her legs collapsed beneath her when she tried. Functioning largely on autopilot, she managed to crawl onto the beach and drag Alex from the water.

"Alex?" She turned her onto her back and unzipped her jacket with numb fingers. "Don't you fucking dare…" she whispered. She pressed her hand and then her ear to Alex's chest to feel for breathing. The pulse at Alex's throat was beating strongly, but her breaths were labored and rattling against the water in her lungs.

Trying to remember the lifeguard training from her job at the swimming pool, Sarah positioned Alex on her side, tilted her jaw to open her airway, and improvised by slapping her on the back.

"Cough," she said fiercely. "Come on, cough, Alex. Come on, love. You'll feel better, I promise." She yelped when she felt Alex's hand twitch. Encouraged, she hit her harder, prompting a fit of coughing so violent that it ended in Alex vomiting a large amount of dirty water onto the gravel.

Alex groaned, still coughing convulsively. Keeping her in the recovery position, Sarah wiped her mouth clear of secretions. It made a mess of Sarah's sweater sleeve, but she didn't care. She didn't care about anything other than the fact that Alex had just opened her eyes.

"That was a fucking stupid thing to do." Sarah tried to yell it, but the words came out broken by sobs.

Alex mouthed the word "sorry," but any sound she might have made was silenced beneath another fit of coughing that left her limp and blue around the lips.

"Shit." Sarah looked up, trying to gauge where they were in relation to the camp. They were still on the same side of the river, and although it felt like they'd been in the water for hours, realistically, they couldn't have traveled very far from the clearing. Still, there was no way Alex was in any condition to walk back.

The sand Alex lay on was sodden, the weight of her body sinking slowly into it as water lapped at her toes. Beyond the scattering of stones and driftwood that delineated the beach, Sarah could see a patch of grassy undergrowth ringed by trees. She hooked her arms beneath Alex's and interlaced her fingers to strengthen her hold.

"Give me a push, Alex," she said, more in hope than expectation.

Alex tried, her legs scuffling ineffectually in the sand as Sarah lugged her onto the grass inch by laborious inch. The grass was long enough to conceal Alex if she remained lying down, and even though Sarah was certain there was no one left to harm them, it made her feel less anxious about what she had to do next.

Bending low, she rested her hand on the clammy skin of Alex's forehead.

"I love you," she whispered, as tears tracked twin lines of heat down her cheeks. "Stay right here, okay? I'll be back as soon as I can."

❖

"Radio, blankets, clothes, food, matches, handcuff keys." Sarah chanted the list of essentials as she ran, her addled brain skipping items and rearranging their order on each repetition. "Gun," she added, trying to make a mental note to pick hers up from where she had dropped it alongside her boots and jacket. "Oh, boots and jacket." As if to emphasize her oversight, something crunched into the sole of her left foot, hard enough that it would almost certainly be painful just as soon as her extremities regained sensation. At least the numbness was one thing in her favor, the second being the apparent fever-reducing effect of the cold water she had been immersed in. Neither of those was likely to last for much longer, however, and she was relieved beyond measure when she finally picked up the faint smell of smoke. She had been running flat-out for five minutes by then, and as soon as she slowed to a walk, her legs began to fold.

"Just keep going," she muttered, her memory jumping back unbidden to a set of parallel bars with Ash waving chocolate at one end and Isaac's gentle encouragement behind her. "Gun, boots, jacket, cuff keys. Radio, *radio*."

The possibility that Tanner would have somehow made it to the clearing had plagued her until she had distracted herself with the lists. As the fire came into view, she surveyed the area furtively, but there was no sign of him. Even so, she picked up the Glock first, the weight of it strangely reassuring in her hand as she pushed her feet back into her boots.

The tent was well stocked with food, equipment, and dry clothes. She swiftly changed out of her soaked layers and set aside a spare set of clothing for Alex. Sitting in full sight on top of a cozy-looking sleeping bag was a radio that she grabbed and turned on, willing the battery to be full so that she would not have to go and search Tanner for his. The light flashed green, and static hummed when she thumbed the talk button.

"Hello? Can anyone hear me?" She waited for an answer, to no avail. After a careful switch to the next possible channel, she repeated her message. Her stomach twisted with fear: fear that no one would answer her and fear that, if someone did, it would be Aaron, or another of Deakin's cronies waiting to play the same trick all over again.

"Hello? Can anyone hear me? Please come in."

A click cut into the static. Then a voice, female and familiar, and tremulous with hope.

"Sarah? Is that you, honey?"

A rush of adrenaline made Sarah drop the radio. She snatched it up again as Marilyn, obviously afraid that she had misheard the hail, repeated her question.

"I'm here," Sarah managed to say, and then stronger, "I'm here. Please, *please* don't go."

"I'm not going anywhere," Marilyn said slowly and carefully, as if she were negotiating a hostage crisis. "We have teams out looking for you all over the area. Can you tell me where you are?"

Deakin's GPS lay abandoned beside his radio. When Sarah flicked it on, she found it required no passcode, and she squinted at the coordinates it provided, her vision doubling intermittently. She read the numbers out, stumbling over the second set and repeating them all in response to Marilyn's patient prompting. She remembered Deakin calling the river the East Fork Creek, so she told Marilyn that as well.

"Good, that's real good," Marilyn said. "I got you."

"I've got to get back to Alex," Sarah muttered, already halfway through shoving supplies into a backpack.

"Alex?" Marilyn's voice rose an octave and there was a sudden babble of voices in the background. "Alex is with you?"

"Yes. Well, no." Sarah stuffed a sleeping bag into the pack. She had upended everything but still hadn't found the keys to Alex's handcuffs. "I'm going back to her now. She's a little way down the river. Shit." She shook her head in an attempt to clear it. "Those coordinates, that's the camp, but we were in the river." Tears of frustration made her vision even more blurred. None of this was coming out right. "I ran for five minutes," she said, taking care to sound all the words out. "We're five minutes' run downriver from the camp."

"I got it, Sarah," Marilyn said. "I'm gonna pass that on to our closest team. Don't worry."

"Thank you," Sarah mumbled, busy sealing the pack up and hoisting it onto her back. "I have to go now."

"Sarah?"

"Yes."

"Take the radio with you, okay? Leave it on this channel."

"I will." Sarah stared at the radio, paralyzed by an irrational but overwhelming fear. "Marilyn?" she said.

"Go ahead."

"Where did you sign my permit for?"

Marilyn answered without hesitation. "Desolation Peak with a camp at Ross Lake."

"Thank you," Sarah whispered fervently, any lingering doubts about Marilyn's identity completely eradicated. "Oh God, thank you."

CHAPTER SIXTEEN

The weight of the pack had slowed Sarah considerably. Unable to tolerate it on her back for long, she had swapped to carrying it in her arms before ultimately lowering it to the ground and dragging it by a strap for the remainder of the distance. She was beginning to worry she had taken the wrong route when she heard Alex's hacking cough just ahead of her.

Alex was pretty much where Sarah had left her, except that she had managed to sit herself up slightly by leaning against a fallen tree. She didn't look comfortable, and her wheezing was audible from several yards away, but she raised her bound hands in greeting as Sarah ran across to her.

"Hey." Sarah cradled Alex's face and kissed her cold lips.

"Hey." Alex's voice was hoarse and even that short reply came out fractured by coughing and squeaking. "You okay?"

"Fine. I'm fine." Sarah had thrown open the backpack and was rifling through it. "I spoke to Marilyn. There's a team on the way," she said, pulling out a sweater and pants, and chasing down a pair of socks that had flitted into the grass when she unraveled the sleeping bag. She held up the clothes. "You going to help me out here?"

"You got a key?" Alex rattled the handcuffs to emphasize her point.

"No." It was the one thing Sarah hadn't been able to find; Deakin had probably taken it to the bottom of the river with him. She opened the side pocket of the pack. "No, but I've got a knife…"

Deakin may have been a white supremacist with a deplorable worldview, but he knew how to maintain his weapons and his Bowie knife sliced through Alex's outer layers of clothing as if they were butter. The fresh sweater trapped her arms beneath it when Sarah tugged it over her head, but the elated expression on her face suggested it was preferable to being soaked. With her hands bound, though, she didn't seem to have the strength or coordination to help Sarah with her pants, and in desperation Sarah took the knife to those as well, apologizing profusely when she accidentally nicked her knee. The spare pants had probably belonged to Tanner. They were large and loose, and Alex managed to stay awake long enough to wriggle into them. By the time Sarah tucked her into the sleeping bag, her eyes were heavy-lidded and her head was drooping.

"You sleep, okay?" Sarah told her, propping her up against the pack that was now stuffed with her shredded clothes. "They'll be here soon."

Alex nodded and closed her eyes. Sarah, too drained to do anything else, was content just to sit beside her for a while and watch her breathe.

❖

The shriek of an eagle circling above the cliff on the opposite side of the river startled Sarah from an uneasy doze. Silently berating herself for having fallen asleep, she turned to check on Alex, a movement that caused a sharp stab of pain in her abdomen and reminded her that she wasn't exactly in the best shape either.

Alex didn't stir when Sarah put a hand on her cheek. The skies had cleared through the morning, but the sunshine only emphasized how pale she was and made the dusky tinge to her lips more apparent. She was shivering intermittently. Sarah looked around the unkempt patch of grass and bracken surrounding them. There was plenty of wood from deadfalls scattered on the ground, more than enough for a fire. All she had to do was stand up and collect it, but her stomach roiled at the thought of moving, and even as she sat there, her legs felt like jelly. She opened Deakin's first aid kit and looked at the packets of painkillers. The trade names were mostly unfamiliar to her, but she knew that Tylenol was for pain and fever, and the advice leaflet in the box of Advil said similar. She dry-swallowed two of each, gagging on the taste and hoping they would stay down long enough to give her some respite.

Supporting her side with her hand, she slowly gathered as much wood as she could and—keen to get all her activities completed in one go—filled a pot with water. The fire lit on her third attempt, smoldering at first before sparking properly into life as one of the larger logs caught. Sarah was watching the water slowly beginning to simmer when the harsh tone of the radio cut through the relative calm. She stared at the small black handset, eager to speak to Marilyn but assailed by the familiar dread that it would be one of Deakin's men on the other end. The tone seemed to grow more insistent, echoing through the clearing and bouncing back off the river. She blocked it out, working to convince herself that even if it was Aaron, he would be miles away at the hut by now and couldn't hurt her from there. The thought gave her the confidence to pick the radio up, the tone ceasing immediately as she pressed the talk button.

"Hello?"

"Sarah?" Marilyn sounded barely on the right side of frantic. "Are you both okay?"

Sarah glanced at Alex, who had inclined her head slightly at the disturbance but had yet to open her eyes.

"Not really," she said, trying not to allow Marilyn's panic to bleed into her. "Alex isn't breathing properly. She took some water into her lungs and I don't know what else I can do to help her."

"Is she conscious?"

"Now and again."

"Okay. There are medics on their way to you. The team has given an ETA of three hours. Let me try and get ahold of them..." Her voice trailed off and Sarah heard her hold a rapid discussion with two different men, another radio buzzing faintly in the background. Sarah found Deakin's GPS and worked out their exact location while Marilyn conferred with the rescue team. She turned her attention back to the radio as Marilyn addressed her again.

"The medics say you should try and keep Alex awake," Marilyn told her. "When she's able to drink, push fluids, the sweeter the better, and keep her warm."

Sarah nodded, relieved that she had inadvertently followed most of this advice already. "I got her changed and into a sleeping bag but I can't get the handcuffs off her," she said, and heard what sounded like a muffled gasp from the other end of the connection. When Marilyn replied, it was with obvious difficulty.

"You've done real good, Sarah. Three hours, that's all, and they'll be with you."

"Okay. Oh…" Slowly but surely, Sarah pulled together the mention of the handcuffs with the need to tell Marilyn about Tanner. She rubbed a hand on her forehead and her fingers came away wet with sweat. "There's a man in the woods, close to the camp I told you about. He worked with Deakin. I shot him in the leg. I didn't have time to tie him up, but his leg was broken and he was bleeding a lot."

Marilyn let out a surprised laugh as Sarah paused for a breath. "Shouldn't give my guys too much of a problem then?" she said.

"He was unconscious when I left him," Sarah conceded. She didn't want to acknowledge that she might have killed him, but the thought wormed its way into her head regardless.

"I'm sure you did what you had to do, Sarah. The medics will take care of him too."

Sarah thumbed the talk button but released it again without responding. For a couple of seconds, there was silence from both sides, then: "Marilyn?"

"Go ahead."

"Tanner might have a key," Sarah said quietly. "For Alex. He was the one who cuffed her." The logic of that had escaped her when she had returned to the camp; all she had wanted to do was collect the supplies and take them back to Alex. "I have our coordinates for the rescue team, if that'll help." She read out the numbers as they appeared on the screen, hoping they made more sense to Marilyn than they did to her.

"That will definitely help," Marilyn said, once she had read them back for her to confirm. "I'll pass all the information on."

Sarah nodded, feeling calmer now that she had remembered everything she needed to say. "I'm going to make Alex a drink."

"Good girl. You do that and call me if you need me."

"I will." She cut the connection and set the radio down. She wrapped a scrap of T-shirt around her hand to protect it, and reached for the pot of hot water.

❖

"Drink this. No, don't spit it out." Sarah held the cup of sweetened tea to Alex's lips. "Drink it. That's right."

It was the third time she had tried to follow Marilyn's advice to "push fluids," and as usual, Alex was not being the most compliant of patients.

"Look, it's not my fault Deakin packed this stuff instead of cocoa. It's only fruit tea. I don't see why you're pulling your face." Sarah took a sip to prove her point and only just refrained from spitting it back into the cup. "Shit, that tastes like cat piss. What flavor is it supposed to be?" She checked the packet. "Pampering pomegranate and goji berry." The grass steamed as she emptied the cup onto it. "Well, I suppose it must be very stressful being the leader of a bunch of skinheads," she muttered.

The smug expression on Alex's face was ruined when she began to cough. Sarah helped her lean forward and supported her until the worst of it seemed to have passed.

"Better?" she asked, guiding Alex back against the pack.

"Yeah, thanks."

"How's about vanilla, chamomile, and honey, instead?"

Alex nodded, her body still jerking with coughs she was trying to suppress. Sarah poured more water and stirred the tea slowly as it steeped.

"I'm sorry," Alex said, so quietly that Sarah barely heard her above the tapping of the spoon on the metal cup.

"About the tea?"

"No, about the river." She coughed again and Sarah tried to brace her, but she moaned in pain regardless. "So stupid. Shoulda left me in there."

"Like that was ever an option." Sarah ruffled Alex's hair. "Just don't do it again, okay?"

"No fucking chance of that," Alex said fervently. "Drowning hurts like a bitch."

Sarah smiled, holding the cup for her to sip from. "So did hauling your arse out of the water."

Alex's eyes had closed, and when Sarah nudged her, it seemed to take an awful lot of determination for her to open them again. "Thank you for hauling my 'arse' out of the water," she mumbled.

"My pleasure." Intent on keeping her awake, Sarah persevered with the cup. "It's a nice arse," she added as an afterthought.

Alex's shoulders began to shake as she laughed, which set her off coughing and made Sarah instantly apologetic.

"Shit. Sorry. Here, try the tea."

Alex choked a mouthful down and then took a second more comfortably.

"What happened to Deakin?" She was looking around now, as if fractured pieces of the past few hours were only just returning to her.

"He hit his head and the current took him under." The cloying smell of the tea combined with the memory of his skull splitting into the water made Sarah's stomach churn, and she moved the cup farther away from her. "He's dead, Alex," she said, wondering whether she would ever think of the man with anything other than loathing. "And Tanner's in the woods with a bullet in his leg. I don't know if he's…" She shook her head. "I don't know if he's still alive. I could've checked when I went to the camp, but I was so tired." The words came out like a confession, and Alex must have picked up on her distress because she leaned her head on Sarah's shoulder. "I just wanted to get back to you," Sarah whispered, as guilt and sorrow and stress drained her anger away.

She felt Alex kiss her cheek and moved her head a fraction so that the next kiss touched her lips.

"So much of this I would want to change," she said. "But if it meant not meeting you, I wouldn't change a thing." Abashed, she wiped her face dry before she dripped tears into the tea, and then reached over to wipe Alex's face for her. "And that's about as mushy as I'll ever get."

"You could blame it on your fever," Alex suggested.

Sarah winced. "Yeah, I was hoping you'd forgotten about that."

"Kinda hard to forget when I just burned my lips on you."

"Oh."

"How long till they get here?"

Sarah studied her watch, struggling with the simple calculations. "About an hour and a half."

"Got time for more tea."

"Yup, got plenty of time for that."

"What do we have left?"

There were three bags remaining in the packet. Sarah tried to keep her face straight as she read them out. "Tangerine Temptress, Blueberry and Banana Burst, or Buttercup Sage." Alex stared at her in disbelief and Sarah shrugged. "Or we could just drink water."

"I vote for that," Alex said quickly. "I feel crappy enough as it is without choking on a cup of Buttercup Sage."

Sarah tossed the packets into the fire, crinkling her nose at the pungent smell that rose up. "Bloody hell, as if we needed further proof that Deakin was a psychopath."

Alex was attempting to bury her nose beneath the neck of her sweater. "God, I need my hands." She smiled when Sarah leaned across and held her nose for her. "Oh honey, if that's not a sign of true love," she said, her voice sounding as if she was impersonating a duck, "then I really don't know what is."

❖

The soft clink of the handcuffs was muffled by Alex's sweater, so that she could continue to twist her hands against the metal without disturbing Sarah. She didn't like to think what damage she was doing to her wrists, but the pain in them was the only thing keeping her alert. She couldn't ever remember feeling so tired. Not even after working a week of night shifts in the middle of a Los Angeles summer, the heat baking her as she tried in vain to sleep through the day. This was a different kind of tired altogether, an almost irresistible yearning to give in, to stop having to fight so damn hard for every breath she took, and simply to close her eyes instead.

The metal bit into her skin when she deliberately pulled her wrists apart, the renewed agony jolting her awake. She knew there was a very strong possibility that if she closed her eyes, she wouldn't be opening them again. Her chest whined like a decrepit set of bagpipes as she breathed. It felt as if she were trying to draw air in through a wet sock, and it made something grate at the base of her lungs. There was still fluid in her chest; she could hear it when she coughed, and she occasionally ended up with a mouthful of dirty water. Not often enough to clear it, though, and the relentless coughing combined with the matted laceration at her temple had given her a throbbing headache.

There was a restless whimper from where Sarah lay with her head cushioned on Alex's thigh, and Alex murmured softly to settle her. She had fallen asleep about twenty minutes ago, wrapped so tightly in a blanket that barely any of her remained visible. The Glock lay in front of her, still loaded and within easy reach. Once bitten, twice shy, Alex thought. She didn't care if Sarah had been in contact with Marilyn; there was no way they were meeting this rescue team without being armed.

A rustling in the undergrowth instantly made her look up. Sarah had obviously heard it too, because she was struggling to unwind herself from the blanket. Her eyes were glassy and unfocused when she glanced at Alex, but she snatched hold of the gun and pointed it in the direction of the noise.

"Easy," Alex said, not liking the barely contained panic evident in Sarah's reaction. "Take it easy."

Sarah ignored her, one hand swiping hair from her face, the other still clasped around the gun.

"Two hands, Sarah," Alex said, and Sarah nodded nervously, moving her free hand into a rough approximation of the correct position.

The noise was closer now but scatter shot as if something was darting from side to side. It sounded nothing like the tread of a person. Alex shook her head, relaxing slightly. "Probably an animal," she whispered.

Sarah muttered what sounded like agreement, but didn't move an inch. The long grass edging the clearing began to shift as it was disturbed. Then it parted wide, to allow a large black and tan dog to run straight toward them. Sarah let out a yell, her finger twitching on the trigger just as Alex called a warning.

"Sarah, no!"

The dog barked in excitement, completely oblivious to the chaos he had wrought, and bolted over to lick Alex's face.

"Hey, Kip," she spluttered, unable to do anything to curtail his enthusiastic greeting. "Sarah, meet Kip," she said as Sarah carefully lowered the gun. "I think there's a damn good chance we're about to be rescued."

CHAPTER SEVENTEEN

As if sensing how cold Sarah felt, Kip had wriggled as far onto her lap as he could and allowed her to wrap her arms around him. She shivered into his coat, half-convinced that he would disappear like a mirage if she risked letting him go. Neither she nor Alex had been able to raise their voices sufficiently for any useful response to the faint cries of the rescue team, and she was hoping Kip's barking had been loud enough to guide them in. The fire was all but extinguished, and a cold fog rolled off the river as sleet began to fall again. She and Alex had pushed themselves as far as they could possibly go. Now all they had the strength to do was wait.

Kip's ears tickled her cheek as they pricked up and his tail began to thump against her thigh. He bounced off her knee and darted back the way he had come, his barks fading but still audible, letting them know he hadn't gone far. She couldn't help but place her hand on the gun, but she stopped short of picking it up.

"Are you sure?" she asked Alex.

"I'm sure," Alex told her with absolute certainty. "I can hear Walt now."

When Kip returned, he was walking sedately at the heels of a man whose smile immediately put Sarah at ease. The man's tanned face was dirt-streaked and weary, but he gave a shrill whistle to alert his companions and hurried across to crouch beside the fire. He set a large shotgun by the Glock before kneeling down properly.

"Hey, Walt," Alex said, but then shook her head, unable to continue.

"Damn, Alex." The concern in Walt's voice brought tears to Sarah's eyes. Without saying another word, he unzipped the sleeping bag, quickly figured out where Alex's hands were tucked, and lifted her sweater just enough to uncover them. He fished in the pocket of his jacket and took out a small key. "Found this on the man in the woods," he said, a hardening to his tone showing what he thought of Tanner. With a gentleness that belied his gnarled hands, he eased the handcuffs from her wrists. "Got medics on the way." He dropped the cuffs out of sight. "Have you both fixed up and out of here in no time."

Alex murmured her thanks and took hold of Sarah's hand as Walt turned to speak to Sarah.

"You the one been getting Alex into mischief, then?" His face crinkled like tissue paper as he smiled at her.

She tried to reply, but emotion clogged her throat. When she nodded in lieu of an answer, Walt patted her hand in tacit understanding.

A clamor of voices and the clomping of boots heralded the remainder of the rescue team. Walt met them halfway, directing two medics toward Sarah and Alex before conferring urgently with a middle-aged man in a park ranger uniform. The buzz of radios overlapped as three more men—heavily armed and wearing navy blue jackets emblazoned with *FBI*—took up strategic positions to keep a wary eye on the perimeter of the clearing.

After so long with only Alex for company, the activity was too much for Sarah, who instinctively shrank away, pushing herself closer to Alex. She flinched when one of the medics—the only woman in the team—knelt beside her and touched her wrist.

"Shit, sorry," the woman said, immediately withdrawing her hand. "I should've…" Flustered, she shook her head. "I guess you've had a pretty rough week, huh?"

Sarah arched an eyebrow and the woman smiled in recognition of the understatement.

"My name's Renee, and my colleague there is Theo. We need to take a look at you both, if that's okay?"

Sarah's reply was cut off when Alex started to cough. Within seconds, the attack had become so ferocious that she was making a terrible whooping sound as she tried to draw air into her lungs.

"Jesus," Sarah whispered. She watched, frozen in terror, as Alex's eyes bulged with distress.

Renee had already moved to help Theo, who passed her an oxygen cylinder as he hooked Alex up to a monitor and set a probe on her finger.

"Sats are only eighty-four percent. Tachy at one thirty-eight. Chest sounds like crap." He turned to Sarah. "How long was she in the water?"

Oxygen hissed from the tank. Renee waited impatiently as the reservoir bag on the oxygen mask inflated, and then she secured the mask over Alex's nose and mouth.

"About six, maybe seven minutes," Sarah said, peering over to try to see the numbers on the monitor. She knew from her time in the ICU that eighty-four percent was a dangerously low reading.

"Was she breathing when you got her out?" Renee asked gently, her fingers slapping at a vein on the inside of Alex's elbow.

"Yes." Sarah watched the needle slide beneath Alex's skin. "But not very well, and she's been wheezing ever since."

"I'll try her with an albuterol neb," Theo said. He glanced at the monitor. "Pressure's pretty low."

"Already on it," Renee muttered, concentrating on the IV she was setting up. "ETA on the chopper?"

"Not sure, Walt was dealing." He swapped the mask for one with a plastic chamber fixed beneath it. A white mist formed as the medication in the chamber mixed with oxygen. "Here you go. This should make things a little easier," he said to Alex, but she didn't seem to hear him. Her eyes were fixed on Sarah, the fear in them fading as her breathing gradually became less labored.

The numbers crept up to ninety-five percent and refused to go beyond, but the medics appeared to relax somewhat, and that was good enough for Sarah. They seemed even happier when the park ranger ran over to report that a rescue chopper was en route with an ETA of fifty minutes.

"We should let Harborview know about the pulmonary edema. She might need CPAP," Renee said, her fingers pressing down Alex's neck and spine. "Anything hurt back here, Alex?"

Alex shook her head before Renee could tell her not to.

"Think you might be happier if we don't strap you onto a long board, huh?" The look Alex gave her must have been answer enough because Renee patted her arm and smiled. "You gonna behave yourself for Theo while I have a look at Sarah here?"

Alex gave her a weary thumbs-up and offered her wrists to Theo as he set down dressings and antiseptic.

"Now, where were we?" Renee said. Placing a hand on Sarah's forehead, she frowned and used her free hand to pull her kit bag closer. "Dammit. Theo, have you got the tympanic?"

The thermometer beeped three times in Sarah's ear. Sarah studied the ground intently as she waited for the verdict, which came with a low whistle of dismay.

"One-oh-one point eight."

"Is that bad?" she asked, already certain that it was far from good.

"I'm guessing you've felt better," Renee said evasively, beginning to select IV supplies from her kit. "Marilyn told us you got shot. That was a few days ago now?"

"Yes." Sarah had no idea precisely how many days. She lifted her sweater away from the bandage on her side. "Alex had to stitch me up."

A look of unguarded horror flitted across Renee's face before she swiftly buried it beneath a mask of professionalism. She gestured to the stained dressing. "Okay if I take this off?"

Dirt filled Sarah's fingernails as she gripped hold of the ground, but she nodded slowly. She could see now where the inflamed skin was bulging beyond the dressing, and the draft of cool air passing across it was enough pressure to make the pain nearly unbearable. She tensed when Renee's gloved fingers touched her abdomen.

Renee quickly rolled a blanket to place behind her. "I think you better lie down for this," she said. She helped her lean back onto the pillow and wrapped a cuff around her upper arm. "That's gonna go tight for a minute." She watched the monitor as the numbers calculated. "You been dizzy? Sick?"

"Yes," Sarah said, feeling a combination of both as she answered. "It comes and goes. I could look after Alex okay for a while and then it'd hit me."

"Certainly hitting you at the moment," Renee muttered, unsheathing a needle that bore an uncanny resemblance to a drainage pipe. "Your blood pressure's way low."

"Mmm." Clouds scudded across the sky, fading and sharpening as Sarah stared at them. Cold fingers prodded hard, just above the tattered skin on her left wrist, and she heard Renee warn her about a "sharp stick." She nodded in sympathy; she had stood on a lot of sharp sticks when she had been running around without her boots on. The sympathy lasted right up until she felt Renee dig the needle deeply into her arm.

"God." She moaned and tried to pull away, but hands gripped her shoulders, keeping her in place. Instead of struggling, she just started to cry quietly. "Please don't," she whispered, as someone began to unpeel the tape around the dressing on her side. "Please don't do that."

"Start her with five," Renee said, somewhere beyond her line of sight. "She must be hurting like hell, the poor kid."

There was a warm flush of liquid in Sarah's arm, and a man's voice telling her that she would feel better soon, and then everything turned soft and melted away.

❖

"*Sarah*?" Alex kicked her blankets loose and, in defiance of all common sense, tried to move across to where Sarah lay.

"She's okay, Alex." Theo put out a hand to stop her, but she weakly slapped it away.

Sarah clearly wasn't okay. She wasn't moving, wasn't reacting as Renee lifted the dressing from her side. Her chest rose and fell far too quickly, condensation building up on the oxygen mask that now obscured her face. The IV bag hanging from a tree branch above her head was already half-empty, the liquid entering the chamber in a rapid stream rather than the sedate, steady drip so beloved of all the movies.

"She has an infection," Theo said. He shifted his hands to Alex's shoulders; it took barely any pressure for him to persuade her to stay where she was. "I need to help Renee get her cleaned up and start her on some antibiotics. The morphine I've just given her should keep her comfortable while we do that." He straightened Alex's oxygen mask and rearranged the blanket she had thrown off, pulling it up beneath her chin. The foil inner layer crinkled as he tucked it in. "Just sit tight," he told her. Then, seeming to realize she might need more incentive, he added, "I can't help her if I'm worrying about you."

His point hit home. She sagged back, watching as he connected a smaller IV bag to Sarah's line. He moved closer to Sarah, blocking Alex's view completely, and she thumped the ground with her fist in an impotent gesture of exasperation.

"Gotta let them do their job, Alex." Walt's voice came from behind her. For an old man with a rheumy eye, he missed very little.

"I know," she admitted quietly.

"Twenty minutes on the chopper," he said, taking the plastic lid from one of the medic's kits and using it to perch upon. "You warm enough?" With the ranger's help, he had rekindled the fire and rigged a canvas shelter that was protecting them from the worst of the sleet.

"Yes, thank you."

He ran a hand over his chin and then gestured beyond the shelter to where one of the FBI agents stood watching them expectantly. "Feds wondered whether you felt up to answering a couple of questions."

She pulled her oxygen mask down and nodded with some reluctance; even a rudimentary debriefing would take energy she didn't have to spare. Still, she was moderately surprised they had waited this long to ask to speak to her. Walt beckoned to the agent and then brought a steaming cup to Alex's lips.

"Figured you might need this first."

She took a cautious sip and closed her eyes in sheer pleasure. The coffee was hot, rich, and deliciously sweet. Walt chuckled, keeping her hands steady when she lifted them to cradle the cup.

"Not too fast," he said.

The liquid tracked warmth down into her stomach, but she heeded his advice and set the cup aside as the agent ducked into the shelter.

"Hi, Alex. I'm Agent Castillo." He introduced himself with a firm handshake and sat on the lid Walt had vacated. If the six foot three federal agent found it incongruous to be cramped up on the floor of a makeshift field hospital, he showed no indication of it in his expression.

"This won't take long," he said. "I'll come by and speak to you and Sarah properly once you're safely at Harborview."

Alex nodded, appreciating his consideration. She looked beyond him, trying to think past the tightness in her chest and the gathering fluid that was about to make her cough. Three numbers, there were three numbers she had memorized days ago, numbers this man would undoubtedly need—

The cough exploded out of her, pitching her forward, and she heard someone swear somewhere off to her right. The mask went back on, accompanied by a stern glare from Theo. She sucked in the mist, which initially made her cough even harder before gradually easing the narrowing and congestion in her airways. The numbers on the monitor skipped between ninety-three and ninety-five, and she gave a small smile of recognition.

"Thirty-seven. Fifty-one. Zero ninety-three," she said, as soon as she was confident she could speak. "There's a tree all weird and stunted at those coordinates. The keys to whatever Deakin was looking for are hidden under its roots."

Castillo's eyes widened; she had obviously pre-empted one of his most pressing concerns. He tapped the small radio on his lapel and spoke rapidly into it.

"Do you know where Deakin was ultimately heading?" he asked her.

"We plotted it on a map when we were at the hut," she said, having difficulty thinking that far back. "I might be able to remember…" Realizing that was doubtful, she shook her head and tried another approach, working it through slowly as she spoke. "Deakin didn't trust Merrick not to double-cross him. That's why he came to the park. His people packed Merrick's supplies and they included a GPS, so Deakin must have known the location of whatever Merrick had stored for him. All he needed from Merrick was the keys." She paused to take a couple of rasping breaths, uncertain how long she could continue not only to speak but to make sense. "We have Deakin's GPS. If it's anything like Merrick's, the coordinates to whatever was hidden out here will be programmed into it somewhere."

She licked her dry lips. The oxygen was making her mouth parched, and it was hard to make herself heard with the mask on. With a conspiratorial wink, Castillo unfastened the mask and handed her the cup of coffee.

"The keys were Merrick's get-out-of-jail-free card," he confirmed. "If he'd given those up to Deakin along with the coordinates, he'd still be cooling his heels in a cell." He waited until she looked at him over the rim of the cup. "So how exactly did you two get involved in all this?"

"Sarah stole Merrick's bag, ended up with the keys and his GPS."

"Oh." Castillo raised an eyebrow. "Yeah, that would do it." He gave a short laugh, but all traces of humor quickly left his face. "We picked Tanner up by the camp. He's in no condition to talk, and something tells me that even when he is, he won't be willing to rat out the rest of the organization. These bastards are nothing if not loyal to the cause."

Alex lowered the cup, relieved for Sarah's sake that Tanner was still alive. Her hand shook, upending what remained of the coffee into the grass.

"Did you find Merrick's body?" she asked quietly.

"No, not yet. But one of our teams fished Deakin's body out the river about two miles from here and a second team apprehended an unidentified male as he approached an abandoned logger's hut."

"Aaron," she said. "His name is Aaron. He's one of Deakin's men. I lied, told Deakin I'd hidden the keys at the hut." The coffee seemed to roil in her guts, and she put her hands out to steady herself. Was that it? Was it really over? Could she and Sarah finally get some rest now?

Castillo seemed to read her mind, since he secured her mask again before standing. The low canopy forced him to stoop awkwardly as he laid a hand on her shoulder.

"Soon as we're back in civilization and you're able, I'm going to need a positive ID on Aaron. Somewhat predictably, he is being less than forthcoming." He sighed. "He claims to be an innocent victim of the bad weather, although the Aryan fist tattoo covering his back would suggest otherwise. I'd have a mug shot to show you now, if this goddamn piece of shit had a signal."

His colorful language and obvious disdain for his smartphone made her splutter in amusement.

He squeezed her shoulder, careful not to apply too much pressure, obviously mindful of what she had been through. "The agency has been watching Nicholas Deakin and his group for almost ten years now," he said, going some way toward explaining the sheer scale of the FBI's involvement in the search and rescue operation. "This is going to break the case against them wide open. You did a great job, Officer Pascal."

She shook her head. "It's just Alex now," she said.

"Yeah, I know." He shrugged. "Damn shame, if you ask me."

He walked away then, leaving her to stare into the sleet and snow as it distorted the yellow lettering on his jacket, an effect that reminded her of watching interference on a television set. She looked toward Sarah instead. The medics seemed to have finished whatever they had been doing to her; she lay still and pale beneath a mass of thick blankets.

Theo noticed Alex watching them. "She's just sleeping, Alex," he said, wadding up a pair of soiled gloves and drying his hands so that he could put on a fresh pair. "She'll need surgery to clean the bullet wound out properly, but she'll start to feel better as soon as that's done and the antibiotics kick in."

"Did I…" Alex felt sick again. "With the sutures. Did I cause that?"

"I don't think so," he said gently. He pressed a button on Alex's monitor, and the blood pressure cuff on her upper arm began to inflate. "Bullet wounds carry a massive risk of infection. If you hadn't helped her, she would probably have bled out long before she ended up septic." Whatever he saw on the monitor was reflected in his troubled expression. He quickly exchanged her IV for a new bag and adjusted its flow. "How're you feeling?"

"Like hammered shit." There didn't seem to be any reason to lie to him. She was aware that her breathing was too shallow; her lungs felt like they were filling up with glue, and she couldn't seem to do a thing to stop it.

His reply was cut off by a sudden draft of air that made the canvas above their heads billow upward and shook its supporting poles. It took Alex another few seconds to distinguish the repetitive thrum of the helicopter from the turmoil it had created on the ground.

"Just in time," Theo yelled, a smile brightening his face.

Alex turned to Sarah, who, disturbed by the commotion, was blinking in confusion. She relaxed visibly when she saw Alex and wriggled a hand free from her blanket for Alex to grip hold of. The noise lessened as the helicopter regained altitude, a flash of red against the gray sky indicating it was circling for another approach.

Sarah watched its retreat apprehensively. "Did I ever tell you how much I hate flying?" she asked, her voice muffled by her oxygen mask.

Alex stroked her thumb across the back of Sarah's hand. "Even if there's a warm bed and a bath at the end of it?"

Sarah tilted her head to one side, giving the question careful consideration despite being half-doped on morphine. "Will you be there?" she said at length.

"Hell yes." Alex's heart rate skipped faster on the monitor as she smiled. "I wouldn't miss it for the world."

CHAPTER EIGHTEEN

Nothing smelled like pine. That was Alex's first indication that she might somehow have missed a fairly significant development. The constant white noise of the river had been replaced by the hiss of gas tickling her nose. The bed she lay on no longer squelched beneath her, and her feet were warm. Breathing didn't seem to be too much of an ordeal, and Sarah was holding her hand.

Sarah was holding her hand. Even in her semi-conscious state, that conclusion seemed so natural to Alex. She knew the touch of Sarah's fingers, the way Sarah would curl them around her own, and the gentle back and forth of Sarah's thumb skimming across her skin. She felt herself relaxing, giving in to the pull of sedative-soaked sleep, and then realized there was one thing that she didn't know: what the hell Sarah was doing out of bed.

Alex opened her eyes to the muted light of a hospital room. At first, she couldn't distinguish much beyond the drapes that surrounded her bed and the lumps in the blankets where her feet were sticking up. As soon as her vision sharpened, she turned her head to look at Sarah. Her neck felt stiff and tender, but the smile Sarah gave her was more than worth the discomfort.

"Welcome back," Sarah said. She raised Alex's hand and pressed her lips against it.

"Where'd I go?" Confused, Alex coughed dryly, shocked by the croak to which her voice had been reduced and by the pain that reverberated through her throat.

"Ouch." Sarah winced sympathetically. "Here, try this." She held a glass of water close enough for Alex to catch its straw. Ice rattled as their combined efforts made the glass shake. Alex restricted herself to a couple of sips as an unwelcome yet familiar queasiness told her that she had recently been given an anesthetic.

"What happened?" she whispered when Sarah lowered the glass. Sarah looked terrible. Her face was ashen beneath the layers of bruising, and she seemed to be keeping herself in the chair by force of will alone. All Alex could remember was a strange sensation of floating in midair, swiftly followed by a crushing darkness. With hindsight, she suspected the crushing darkness had not been a positive sign.

"You got too lazy to breathe for yourself." Sarah tried to keep her voice light, but gave herself away by shivering and pulling her blanket more tightly around her shoulders. "They had to put you on a ventilator. I slept through it all and sort of hit the roof when I found out."

"Oh," Alex said. "Shit." That went a long way toward explaining the haunted look in Sarah's eyes. "I'm sorry I scared you."

"You really did. We'd managed to get through everything and then to see you like that—" She squeezed Alex's hand. "You scared the shit out of me."

"Naw, no way." Alex smiled. "I've seen you in action. You don't scare that easily."

"I might have yelled at my doctor a little bit," Sarah said sheepishly.

"And now you've gone and gotten yourself out of bed." Alex could see a plastic tube leading from the bullet wound on Sarah's side, which strongly suggested she should not have been keeping her impromptu vigil.

"Yeah, I don't think she'll approve, somehow." Sarah didn't sound overly concerned. "But I'm not worrying about you so much, now I'm sitting here, so surely that's better for my recovery."

"Not sure your doc is going to see it quite like that."

"No, probably not."

Alex studied her carefully, mentally cataloging the injuries that seemed to stand out all the more for having been cleaned and dressed. Sarah sat patiently and made no comment despite obviously being conscious of Alex's scrutiny.

"How you doing?" Alex asked at length.

"I'm okay." Sarah's standard response came quickly, but she seemed to sense Alex's desire for honesty. She met and held her gaze. "I'm better than I was," she said. "I had surgery to get rid of all the gunk in here." Her hand hovered just above the tube in her abdomen. "And I seem to have acquired a new fashion accessory."

Alex nodded in appreciation. "Very bling."

Tilting her head to one side, Sarah considered the fluid the drain had collected. She grimaced. "I'm not convinced it's going to be a hit on the catwalks."

"No, possibly not. It is kinda gross, Sarah."

Sarah stuck her tongue out and Alex smiled hugely. She felt as if someone had just lifted a ton weight from her shoulders. She could barely believe that they were sitting safely in the hospital, undoubtedly scathed but already healing, having survived an ordeal that most people would have difficulty comprehending.

"I can't…" She shook her head, unable to articulate the thought.

"I know," Sarah said simply, and something in her tone made Alex certain she had been thinking along the same lines. "We're going to be fine, Alex."

"Yes, we are," Alex murmured. The words seemed to run together as tiredness finally began to overwhelm her. Apparently, with the release from days of tension came a need to catch up on days of lost sleep. She yawned, struggling to keep her eyes open. The yawn quickly morphed into a cough, but it didn't hurt nearly as badly as it had before their rescue.

"You going back to sleep, sweetheart?" Sarah smoothed Alex's blanket down and tucked in a loose corner.

"Mm, I think so. You should too."

"I will. Have sweet dreams."

Alex smiled, wanting to reply, but the soft sounds of the room were already fading out.

❖

Agent Castillo had used Alex's overbed table to lay out two FBI case files and his laptop. One of the files was dog-eared and straining at the seams, the second thinner and looking as if it pertained to a more recent investigation. Reading upside down, Sarah could only make out the title of the larger file: *Church of the Aryan Resistance, 2003—*

Castillo took the cap from his pen and then seemed to change his mind and put it back on. He cleared his throat again, something that seemed to be an unconscious habit when he thought what he was about to tell them would be distressing. Sarah felt Alex inch closer to her.

"Following the directions you'd given, a team recovered the body of the missing prison guard early this morning," he said.

Sarah shuddered, goose bumps rising on her arms as if someone had walked over her grave. "Do his family know?" The question seemed to stick in her throat. She took a sip from Alex's glass of water.

"They were informed shortly afterward." Castillo looked directly at her. "They were relieved to be able to bring him home, Sarah. His wife asked the agency to pass on her thanks to you."

There was nothing Sarah could say to that, so she nodded dumbly instead. She didn't feel deserving of gratitude, not when a small part of her still believed she should have been able to prevent the man's death, no matter how illogical that belief was.

"Stop it," Alex said in an undertone. "Stop blaming yourself."

"I'm with Alex on this one." Castillo opened the slim file and took out the first page. "The guard died instantly from a point-blank head shot. You said in your statement that you'd"—he used his finger to skim through Sarah's account—"'picked up a rock to throw, hoping to cause a distraction.' Knowing Merrick's history of shooting first and asking questions later, he wouldn't have wasted time looking for you before making that shot. The guard's fate was sealed the minute Merrick forced him to kneel at the edge of that cliff."

Sarah's mouth was dry; she swallowed more water. "Could you please pass on my condolences to his family?"

"Of course."

"Just one left out there now," Alex said quietly. "Unless you found the niece already?"

"No, not yet."

The information provided by Alex's statement had made Merrick's body easy to locate but, although no one expected to find Deakin's niece alive, the whereabouts of her remains were still a mystery. Castillo thumbed to a separate marker in the file and pulled out two color photographs.

"We did find this, however." He set the photographs in front of them.

The images were practically identical. Sarah moved one closer and saw Alex do likewise with the other. The camera had focused upon a dirt-covered metal box, carefully positioned on a white trestle table. In the background was a canvas awning, as if the photograph had been taken at a field camp. An unidentifiable figure wearing a full Hazmat suit stood close by.

"Jesus," Alex whispered. "What the hell was in it?"

"Anthrax." Castillo let his answer drop like a stone into the silence. Then he gave them another series of photographs: more Hazmat-suited figures, microscopes, and containment facilities. "Preliminary analysis identified the Ames strain."

"That was the strain used in 2001, wasn't it?" Alex sat up straighter, the cop in her obviously thriving on pulling the information together.

"Correct." Castillo seemed to notice Sarah's lack of comprehension and elaborated for her sake. "Shortly after the nine eleven attacks, Ames spores were mailed to several news media outlets and two Democratic senators. Five people were killed and seventeen infected."

"Bloody hell." Sarah could only imagine what a group like Deakin's might have planned to do with their cache.

Alex gestured toward the image. "Is this contained?"

"Yes. Soil analysis from the area shows no evidence of contagion. The team will be there for a while yet, but if nothing else, Merrick knew how to store the spores safely. We're still trying to trace back and identify his supplier. Explosives specialists on scene reported that the box was rigged to release the spores if anyone tried to force the locks, a fact I'm guessing Merrick made Deakin aware of."

"Do you know what Deakin's intentions were?" Sarah tucked her hands into the overlong sleeves on her sweatshirt, but even that wasn't enough to ease the chill from her body.

"Raids on his central compound and all of his registered properties provided us with quite a few clues," Castillo said. "We found blueprints and addresses for two mosques in NYC, the addresses of several community centers in areas largely populated by African Americans, and"—he shifted uncomfortably—"details of three support groups for gay teens."

There was no anger left in Sarah, only sadness that people could hate as blindly as Deakin and his followers. She unclenched Alex's fist and held on to her hand tightly.

"The intel we have indicates he had been plotting this for years." Castillo took the images back and returned them to the file. "I think it's safe to say that you both saved a lot of lives." Despite the somber mood in the room, an unexpected smile brightened his face. "Which leads me quite neatly to this…" He turned the laptop around, displaying two FBI appeals. One offered a reward for information leading to the recapture of Nathan Merrick. The second appeal appeared to be older, the typeface slightly more antiquated, and the reward it offered was far more substantial. Its target was Nicholas Deakin.

"I think the informal term is 'dead or alive,'" Castillo said dryly.

Alex seemed to decipher his cryptic comment before Sarah did. "No fucking way."

"What?" Sarah looked at one and then the other for an explanation.

"The FBI would like to offer its sincere gratitude for the part you played in the apprehension of both parties," Castillo said, as if he were reading from the official script. "The reward money is yours to share."

Sarah drained the water in the glass in one swallow.

"Holy shit," Alex whispered.

The reward money on the bulletins came to just over half a million dollars.

❖

"Oh my." Sarah opened the door of the hotel room wider, enabling Alex to join her on the threshold.

"Wow."

When Castillo had described the hotel as "exclusive," he hadn't been exaggerating. The room he had booked for them was beautifully appointed, with elegant furnishings and massive floor-to-ceiling windows providing panoramic views of the city skyline and across to Elliott Bay. Afraid she was going to make a mess of the plush carpet, Sarah stopped at the door to kick her sneakers off before venturing any farther. Alex was already busy exploring and her delighted shriek prompted Sarah to follow.

"Bloody hellfire." Standing with her chin propped on Alex's shoulder, Sarah gaped at the en suite bathroom. "That's big enough to do a few lengths in."

Alex ran a hand along the side of the extremely generous bathtub. "Wasn't thinking about swimming in it," she murmured. Her hand was cool from the porcelain when she reached back to touch Sarah's cheek.

The sound of a man uneasily clearing his throat made them both jump. "Sorry. Um, where would you like these?" The bellhop's arms were laden with shopping bags, but the beetroot-red coloring to his face and the lack of eye contact implied that something other than his burden was the cause of his discomfiture.

"Here, let me." Sarah moved to help him. After an awkward, fumbling handover that left some of the bags spilling their contents onto the floor, she ushered him from the room with a generous tip clutched in his fist. She shut the door behind him, leaned back against it, and started to laugh.

"I think we embarrassed that poor man," she said.

"Whatever gave you that idea?" Alex had delved into one of the bags and now spoke around a long piece of strawberry licorice. "Was it the stutter he suddenly developed or the way he tripped over his feet as he ran out the door?"

Sarah knelt and took a bite from the licorice dangling from Alex's mouth. She wound the remainder around her finger, using it to pull Alex closer.

"I seem to remember that I owe you a fancy dinner."

Confusion flitted across Alex's face before she managed to place the reference. "Clean pair of socks," she said quietly.

"Mmhm." Sarah gave the candy a gentle tug. "Did you want me to make good on my debt?"

Alex shook her head. "Not right now."

"Did you want me to fill up that bathtub?"

A vigorous nod this time, and Sarah heard the catch in Alex's breathing.

"Hold that thought." She kissed the tip of Alex's nose and headed into the bathroom.

❖

Alex emptied another shopping bag onto the floor, searching through the clothes they had bought earlier that day. There were only three bags left; she resigned herself to what she needed being in the last of them.

"Alex, it'll go cold!" Sarah's voice was slightly muffled by the bathroom door.

"I doubt that," Alex called back. "Half the lights in Seattle dimmed when you drew that bath."

There was a pause for a spell of splashing before Sarah's indignant reply. "I didn't draw it, I turned the taps on and ran it."

"You turned the *faucet* on and *drew* it," Alex corrected her, busy unfurling a pair of combat pants. She mouthed a silent "finally" as a small package dropped out and landed on the floor.

"Yeah, yeah." Sarah sounded as if she had her head under the water. She surfaced as Alex pushed the door open. "You're wearing far too many clothes," she said.

Alex untied the sash around the complimentary bathrobe and let the robe fall to the floor. "How's that?"

Sarah swallowed visibly. "Perfect," she whispered.

The water was deep and hot, and Alex sank into it with a long sigh. Bubbles popped against her chin as the heat worked its way into her muscles, encouraging them to relax. She searched blindly for Sarah's hand, then closed her eyes and carefully inched her head beneath the water. She only stayed under long enough to wet her hair, but still it felt like an achievement. Sarah kept a firm grip on her hand as she sat back up.

"You're very brave," Sarah said, beaming at her.

"It's only a bath."

"It's a pretty big one, though. And you did sort of drown less than two weeks ago."

"Yeah, I guess." Alex shrugged, feeling both abashed and absurdly proud. She reached a hand out of the tub, her fingers patting the floor until they touched the edge of the bag she had left there. "Got you a present," she said.

"You did? When?"

"When I lied and told you I had a craving for Tootsie Pops. I fucking hate those things." She grinned and held out her gift. The bar of Cadbury Dairy Milk had not been easy to find, and she had resorted to enlisting an over-enthusiastic sales assistant in the candy store to help her track one down.

"You really ate a Tootsie Pop just for me?" Sarah eased herself across the bath to straddle Alex.

"Just for you." Alex had actually eaten two and then felt queasy for an hour. The expression on Sarah's face, however, made all the effort worthwhile.

"Anyone ever tell you you're adorable?" Sarah said. Her skin was warm and soap-slick as she looped her arms around Alex's neck.

"No," Alex answered honestly. "I think you're my first." She whimpered as Sarah moved her hands lower, her fingers drawing a pattern in the bubbles covering Alex's breasts.

"Bath or bed?" Sarah asked, her hands disappearing beneath the foam.

Alex let her head fall back against the towels piled on the side of the bath as Sarah's fingers eased inside her.

"Or both," Sarah said with a nonchalant shrug, and reached for the chocolate with her free hand.

❖

They hadn't bothered to get dressed. The clothing they had bought remained untouched in its packaging at the foot of the bed. Outside, rain poured down the windows, the top of the Space Needle hidden beneath a pall of thick cloud. Alex licked melted chocolate from her fingers, and then leafed through one of the many travel brochures Sarah had covered the bed with.

"I'm making a list," Sarah said, chewing thoughtfully on a pen. Her hair, still damp from the bath, hung loose and tangled. There was a pencil tucked behind her ear, and with the pad of paper in her hand, she looked vaguely efficient, like a slightly absent-minded secretary who had turned up to work wearing nothing but a white robe and a sated expression.

"So, where are we going?"

Sarah handed the paper over. "It might need some work," she admitted, with what Alex soon realized was considerable understatement.

"'Somewhere warm. Cows with bells. England.'" Alex turned the page searching for more. When she looked up, Sarah was hiding her face behind her hands.

"You've been doing this all night." Alex tried to sound serious.

"Not all night! You distracted me. You did that thing with the thing!" Sarah made a gesture that would've had a priest dragging her into confession for a month, prompting Alex to double over laughing.

"Come here," Alex said, once she had the breath to speak. She unfastened the sash on Sarah's robe and then picked up Sarah's hairbrush. "Lie down."

Sarah didn't need to be told twice. She shrugged out of the robe completely and lay on her front with her head pillowed on her arms, then tried not to squirm impatiently as Alex began to comb the knots from her hair.

"Are you done yet?"

"No."

"Could you do it quicker?"

"Nope."

"Are you trying to drive me insane?"

Alex's laughter rumbled through Sarah, her naked thighs rocking against Sarah's back. "Possibly."

Sarah ran a hand over the sheets, attempting to distract herself. "Think these are genuine Egyptian cotton?" She heard the quiet tap as Alex set the brush down.

"Hell if I know," Alex said, her lips moving on the sensitive skin at the nape of Sarah's neck. "Turn over."

All consideration of thread count instantly forgotten, Sarah readily complied. She held her breath, studying Alex in the soft glow of the bedside lamp. Fading bruises created a patchwork of color on Alex's skin. Earlier, Sarah had kissed every one of the wounds, staking her own claim and occasionally leaving her own mark. She shuddered now as Alex began to do the same, her mouth and tongue easing across Sarah's torso until she reached the older scars, the ones that were never going to fade away. Her fingers sketched the lines, her touch simultaneously bold and gentle.

"We're a matched pair," she said, following her fingers with the softest of kisses.

Sarah blinked back tears. "I know." She felt Alex part her thighs, felt the heat of her mouth move lower still. "Oh God, I know," she whispered, and closed her eyes.

The End

About the Author

Cari Hunter lives in the northwest of England with her partner, two cats, and a pond full of frogs. She works as a paramedic and dreams up stories in her spare time.

Cari enjoys long, wind-swept, muddy walks in her beloved Peak District and forces herself to go jogging regularly. In the summer she can usually be found sitting in the garden with her feet up, scribbling in her writing pad. She also loves hiking in the Swiss Alps and playing around online. Although she doesn't like to boast, she will admit that she makes a very fine Bakewell Tart. She can be contacted at: carihunter@rocketmail.com.

Books Available from Bold Strokes Books

Desolation Point by Cari Hunter. When a storm strands Sarah Kent in the North Cascades, Alex Pascal is determined to find her. Neither imagines the dangers they will face when a ruthless criminal begins to hunt them down. (978-1-60282-865-0)

I Remember by Julie Cannon. What happens when you can never forget the first kiss, the first touch, the first taste of lips on skin? What happens when you know you will remember every single detail of a mysterious woman? (978-1-60282-866-7)

The Gemini Deception by Kim Baldwin and Xenia Alexiou. The truth, the whole truth, and nothing but lies. Book six in the Elite Operatives series. (978-1-60282-867-4)

Scarlet Revenge by Sheri Lewis Wohl. When faith alone isn't enough, will the love of one woman be strong enough to save a vampire from damnation? (978-1-60282-868-1)

Ghost Trio by Lillian Q. Irwin. When Lee Howe hears the voice of her dead lover singing to her, is it a hallucination, a ghost, or something more sinister? (978-1-60282-869-8)

The Princess Affair by Nell Stark. Rhodes Scholar Kerry Donovan arrives at Oxford ready to focus on her studies, but her life and her priorities are thrown into chaos when she catches the eye of Her Royal Highness Princess Sasha. (978-1-60282-858-2)

The Chase by Jesse J. Thoma. When Isabelle Rochat's life is threatened, she receives the unwelcome protection and attention of bounty hunter Holt Lasher who vows to keep Isabelle safe at all costs. (978-1-60282-859-9)

The Lone Hunt by L.L. Raand. In a world where humans and praeterns conspire for the ultimate power, violence is a way of life… and death. A Midnight Hunters novel. (978-1-60282-860-5)

The Supernatural Detective by Crin Claxton. Tony Carson sees dead people. With a drag queen for a spirit guide and a devastatingly attractive herbalist for a client, she's about to discover the spirit world can be a very dangerous world indeed. (978-1-60282-861-2)

Beloved Gomorrah by Justine Saracen. Undersea artists creating their own City on the Plain uncover the truth about Sodom and Gomorrah, whose "one righteous man" is a murderer, rapist, and conspirator in genocide. (978-1-60282-862-9)

Cut to the Chase by Lisa Girolami. Careful and methodical author Paige Cornish falls for brash and wild Hollywood actress, Avalon Randolph, but can these opposites find a happy middle ground in a town that never lives in the middle? (978-1-60282-783-7)

More Than Friends by Erin Dutton. Evelyn Fisher thinks she has the perfect role model for a long-term relationship, until her best friends, Kendall and Melanie, split up and all three women must reevaluate their lives and their relationships. (978-1-60282-784-4)

Every Second Counts by D. Jackson Leigh. Every second counts in Bridgette LeRoy's desperate mission to protect her heart and stop Marc Ryder's suicidal return to riding rodeo bulls. (978-1-60282-785-1)

Dirty Money by Ashley Bartlett. Vivian Cooper and Reese DiGiovanni just found out that falling in love is hard. It's even harder when you're running for your life. (978-1-60282-786-8)

Sea Glass Inn by Karis Walsh. When Melinda Andrews commissions a series of mosaics by Pamela Whitford for her new inn, she doesn't expect to be more captivated by the artist than by the paintings. (978-1-60282-771-4)

The Awakening: A Sisters of Spirits novel by Yvonne Heidt. Sunny Skye has interacted with spirits her entire life, but when she runs into Officer Jordan Lawson during a ghost investigation, she discovers more than just facts in a missing girl's cold case file. (978-1-60282-772-1)

Murphy's Law by Yolanda Wallace. No matter how high you climb, you can't escape your past. (978-1-60282-773-8)

Blacker Than Blue by Rebekah Weatherspoon. Threatened with losing her first love to a powerful demon, vampire Cleo Jones is willing to break the ultimate law of the undead to rebuild the family she has lost. (978-1-60282-774-5)

Silver Collar by Gill McKnight. Werewolf Luc Garoul is outlawed and out of control, but can her family track her down before a sinister predator gets there first? Fourth in the Garoul series. (978-1-60282-764-6)

The Dragon Tree Legacy by Ali Vali. For Aubrey Tarver time hasn't dulled the pain of losing her first love Wiley Gremillion, but she has to set that aside when her choices put her life and her family's lives in real danger. (978-1-60282-765-3)

The Midnight Room by Ronica Black. After a chance encounter with the mysterious and brooding Lillian Gray in the "midnight room" of The Griffin, a local lesbian bar, confident and gorgeous Audrey McCarthy learns that her bad-girl behavior isn't bulletproof. (978-1-60282-766-0)

Dirty Sex by Ashley Bartlett. Vivian Cooper and twins Reese and Ryan DiGiovanni stole a lot of money and the guy they took it from wants it back. Like now. (978-1-60282-767-7)

The Storm by Shelley Thrasher. Rural East Texas. 1918. War-weary Jaq Bergeron and marriage-scarred musician Molly Russell try to salvage love from the devastation of the war abroad and natural disasters at home. (978-1-60282-780-6)

Crossroads by Radclyffe. Dr. Hollis Monroe specializes in short-term relationships but when she meets pregnant mother-to-be Annie Colfax, fate brings them together at a crossroads that will change their lives forever. (978-1-60282-756-1)

Beyond Innocence by Carsen Taite. When a life is on the line, love has to wait. Doesn't it? (978-1-60282-757-8)

Heart Block by Melissa Brayden. Socialite Emory Owen and struggling single mom Sarah Matamoros are perfectly suited for each other but face a difficult time when trying to merge their contrasting worlds and the people in them. If love truly exists, can it find a way? (978-1-60282-758-5)

Pride and Joy by M.L. Rice. Perfect Bryce Montgomery is her parents' pride and joy, but when they discover that their daughter is a lesbian, her world changes forever. (978-1-60282-759-2)

Ladyfish by Andrea Bramhall. Finn's escape to the Florida Keys leads her straight into the arms of scuba diving instructor Oz as she fights for her freedom, their blossoming love…and her life! (978-1-60282-747-9)

Spanish Heart by Rachel Spangler. While on a mission to find herself in Spain, Ren Molson runs the risk of losing her heart to her tour guide, Lina Montero. (978-1-60282-748-6)

Love Match by Ali Vali. When Parker "Kong" King, the number one tennis player in the world, meets commercial pilot Captain Sydney Parish, sparks fly—but not from attraction. They have the summer to see if they have a love match. (978-1-60282-749-3)

One Touch by L.T. Marie. A romance writer and a travel agent come together at their high school reunion, only to find out that the memory of that one touch never fades. (978-1-60282-750-9)

The Raid by Lee Lynch. Before Stonewall, having a drink with friends or your girl could mean jail. Would these women and men still have family, a job, a place to live after...The Raid? (978-1-60282-753-0)

Month of Sundays by Yolanda Wallace. Love doesn't always happen overnight; sometimes it takes a month of Sundays. (978-1-60282-739-4)

Jacob's War by C.P. Rowlands. ATF Special Agent Allison Jacob's task force is in the middle of an all-out war, from the streets to the boardrooms of America. Small business owner Katie Blackburn is the latest victim who accidentally breaks it wide open, but she may break AJ's heart at the same time. (978-1-60282-740-0)

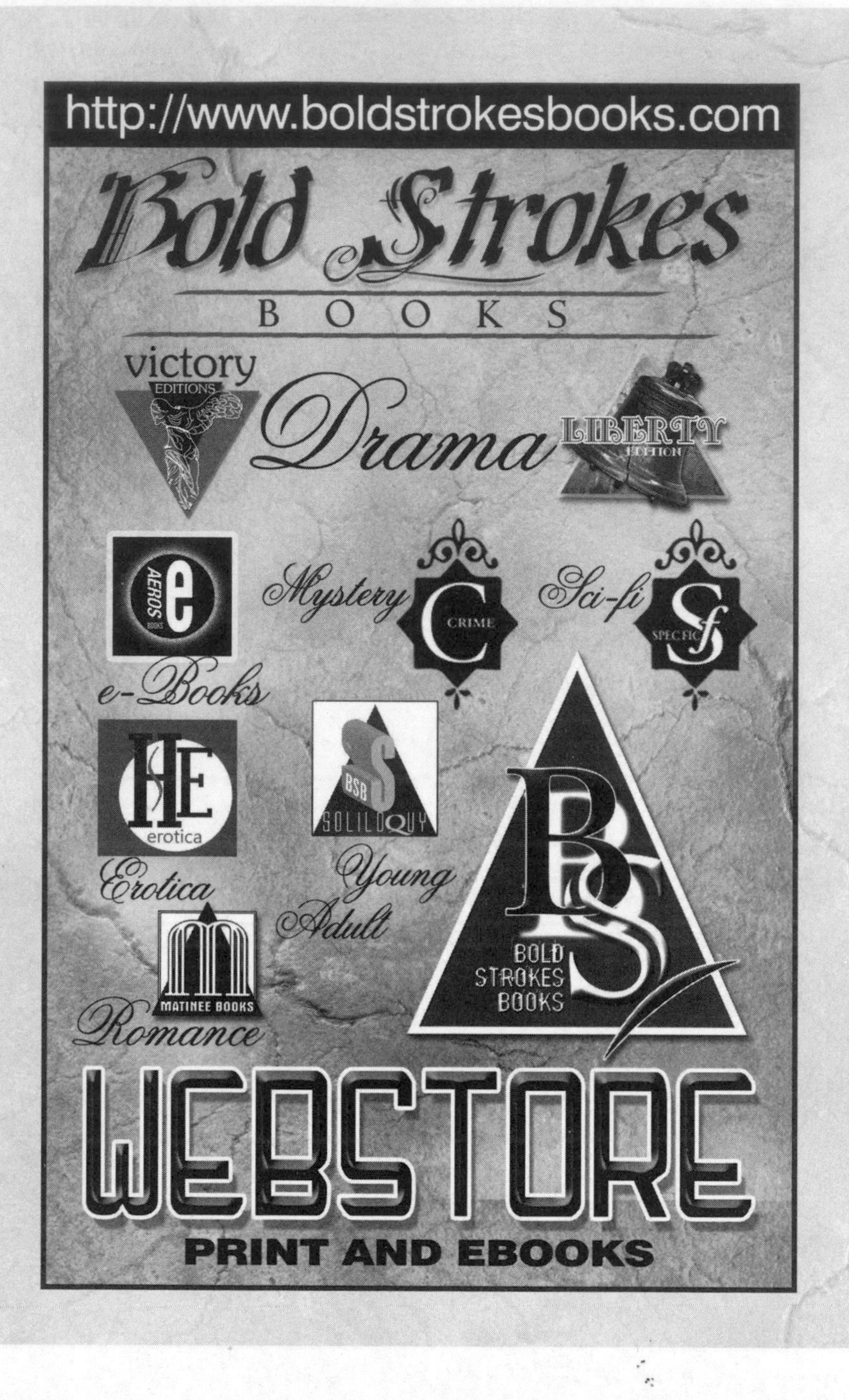

http://www.boldstrokesbooks.com
Bold Strokes
BOOKS
victory
EDITIONS
Drama
LIBERTY
EDITION
AEROS
e
BOOKS
e-Books
Mystery
C
CRIME
Sci-fi
SF
SPECFIC
HE
erotica
Erotica
BSB
SOLILOQUY
Young Adult
MATINEE BOOKS
Romance
BS
BOLD
STROKES
BOOKS
WEBSTORE
PRINT AND EBOOKS